SHADOW WITCH
RISING

COLLEEN VANDERLINDEN

Shadow Witch Rising
Colleen Vanderlinden

Published in the United States
by Building Block Studios LLC

ISBN 0986444510
ISBN-13 978-0-9864445-1-7

http://www.colleenvanderlinden.com
http://www.buildingblockstudios.com

DEDICATION

As always for Roger;
My light in the dark.

CONTENTS

Give light, and the darkness
will disappear of itself.

— Desiderius Erasmus

CHAPTER ONE

Sophie unlocked her front door with a sigh of relief. Long day. A busy day, which was always good, but she was more than ready to take a cup of tea out to her garden and lose track of everything other than the perfume of herbs and the trilling melodies of the songbirds in the woods that bordered her cottage.

As she turned and grabbed her mail out of the box, she noticed a rumbling motorcycle turn into the driveway down the road. The farm had been empty for nearly a year. She grimaced. The idea of hearing a motorcycle all the time wasn't exactly appealing. She shook her head and went into the house.

The second she walked in, everything just felt right. She breathed in the scents of the herbs drying from the beams above, a pungent bouquet of rosemary, lavender, and thyme, mingling with the refreshing aroma of spearmint. Just below that, a subtle, sweet hint of the beeswax she used in her candle making. The soaps she'd made the day before were curing on wooden racks in the next room, and they perfumed the entire house. She flipped on the radio, started bobbing her head immediately as Nirvana wafted from the speakers.

She shrugged out of the crisp maid's uniform she wore for work and pulled on a pair of well-worn jeans and a faded Detroit Red Wings t-shirt.

That done, she headed for the kitchen, passing through the cozy living room, debating over whether she wanted a salad or scrambled eggs for dinner. The tiny cottage she'd slowly but surely made into her home was little more than one large room; a living room with a daybed set into an alcove, which led into a small, serviceable kitchen that was separated from the rest of the house by a small island, its butcher block top gleaming from the oiling she'd recently given it. The kitchen window looked out over the land behind her home, and it was a sight that never failed to make her feel as if she was living in a dream.

She'd just decided on a salad of peppery arugula when there was a knock at the door. She glanced in that direction, then at the clock. She rarely got visitors out here, and never unexpected ones. That was one of the reasons she'd been so thrilled to have inherited the little stone cottage and the surrounding twelve acres a little over a year before. One of many reasons, but a reason just the same.

Sophie waited a moment, thinking that maybe the visitor would just leave. That really was the preferred outcome. Yet, the large, hulking form she could see through the wavy old stained glass in the front door remained. Even after all this time, it irritated her that a knock at the door could knot her stomach and make her palms slick with sweat.

She shook her head, chastised herself for overreacting, and peeked out of the small window beside the front door. The man on her porch was clad in denim and a t-shirt. He faced away from her, looking across the road, and even though he stood still, he looked as if he was capable of pouncing at any moment, coiled energy evident in his posture. His wavy blond hair was in need of a trim, the strands just brushing the tops of what she couldn't help noting were impressively broad shoulders.

Sophie opened the door slightly, bracing it with her leg. "Yes?"

The man turned around, and Sophie's mouth went dry.

His hair was unruly, as if he'd just climbed out of bed, and it contrasted with his short, neat beard. Long black lashes. Dark blue eyes.

Eyes she'd dreamed, eyes she remembered as if they were burned into her very soul. Eyes that accompanied the occasional terrifying dream that spoke of danger and heartbreak, and she'd wake from them confused and in pain. Longing for something she'd lost.

"Hi," he said, and his voice was deep. Low. Almost a growl. "I just moved in across the road. There's a goat in my yard. Wondering if it's yours."

She blushed. "Oh, shit. That would be Merlin. Sorry." Sophie stepped into the sandals she kept by the door and forced herself out onto the porch on legs that seemed to have forgotten how to function. She tried not to stare. Tried to remember how to breathe.

Just breathe.

Beside him, she felt tiny. He was easily over six feet tall, and her five-six put her roughly at chest level.

And what a chest it was, she thought to herself. Holy broad-and-muscled, Batman.

"I'll get him. I'm so sorry about that. I just got off work and haven't even checked on them yet." Stop babbling, she told herself, and clamped her mouth shut.

"It's not a problem."

"It will be if you plan on having livestock. I've been putting off reinforcing the fencing. I'll have to get on that."

"Not planning on any livestock," he said as he followed her across the road.

"No? You've got over sixty acres, right?" she asked.

"Yeah. Mostly, I just wanted somewhere quiet and where I could spread out a little. No neighbors on top of me."

She smiled to herself. He sounded like her. Sounded the same. "And your first day in, you have a neighbor's goat in your yard."

"Well, goats I don't mind so much," he answered, and she could hear the smile in his voice.

They crossed the two-lane road side by side, and it occurred to her that she was walking away from her home, her sanctuary, her safe haven, with a man she didn't really know, because memories and dreams aren't knowing, and she, maybe more than anyone, should have known that.

If she was one of those witches who could summon fire or wind or something, she'd have less to worry about.

She cursed her stupidity, but walked with him nonetheless. It was entirely possible this was not the man from her nightmares. But she knew even as she thought it that even that was a lie. She knew he was, and why, though the dreams were memories. She wasn't prepared for this.

She followed him around the side of the tall, narrow farmhouse, numbly noting that the white paint was flaking off, exposing the gray wood below, and then up a long gravel driveway and around a rusted blue monstrosity of a car. A gleaming black Indian motorcycle was parked behind the house and a few feet away was Merlin, calmly chewing some grass near one of the fence posts.

"Merlin, you devil," Sophie muttered under her breath. She clicked her tongue at him, and he raised his chocolate-brown head and studied her. She walked toward him calmly, nonchalantly, as if she had no intention whatsoever of grabbing the blue nylon collar he was wearing and leading him home. She was aware of tall, muscled, and gorgeous watching her and felt even stupider for the ploy she was making.

Sophie sprung at the goat and he tried to buck away, but she grabbed his collar and held tight when he tried to fight his way away. He pulled, and tried to pivot, and she planted her heels in the soft soil and tried to hold him fast. After a few attempts of breaking free, he just gave her a bored look and bent to chew at the grass near their feet.

That settled, Sophie chanced a glance toward her new neighbor. He was watching her, an unreadable expression in his eyes.

Sophie gathered as much dignity as she could and led Merlin back toward the driveway.

"Sorry about that," she muttered, well aware that her face burned with embarrassment.

"No problem," he answered. "Does he get out a lot?"

She was walking down the driveway, and the fact that he joined her only made her nervous. "Yes. I'll fix the fencing. I just need to get the replacement fence." And the money to pay for it, she thought to herself. "Goats are a major pain. Wish I'd known that before I bought them," she said aloud.

"Why do you have them, then?" he asked, shoving his hands in his jeans pockets as they crossed the street again.

"For their milk. I make soaps," she said, shrugging. "Made more sense to have them around for that. I was stupid to accept a male, though, since I could just borrow a male when I need one for the girls. I felt sorry for him," she finished, feeling like a babbling idiot.

She glanced toward him, caught him studying her before he was able to look away.

"Anyway. It won't happen again," she said, looking with hope toward her door. Something in her told her to run from him, to get away and stay away. She'd be setting wards tonight, she thought. Weak as hers were, they were better than nothing.

"If it does, at least I know who he belongs to," he answered. "I'm Calder, by the way."

"Sophie," she said, glancing toward him again, feeling relief once they stepped into her yard. She could feel the energies of her own magic, that of her ancestors, there. It was the only place she felt safe. "Um. I recognized you, actually. I mean, I remember you. We were in pretty much every class together through middle school. Sophie Turner?"

He was watching her, a blank look on his face.

"We hung out at the falls in the summer with Layla and that whole group, acting like idiots." *You were my first kiss and nothing's lived up to it since. I told you every single secret I had, and you were the one bright spot in my life,* she thought, trying to keep her expression neutral.

He shook his head. "Sorry. I don't remember you. There were a lot of girls around when I was thirteen," he said, a crooked smile on his mouth.

"Right," she said. He wasn't wrong. There were. Not that their town was huge, but there had always been a decent number of girls around Calder and his younger brother Jon.

"Well, Sophie—" Calder began, when a delivery van pulled up and stopped on the shoulder of the road. The driver jumped out, noticed Sophie standing with Calder at the end of her driveway, approached and shoved a clipboard into Sophie's hands. He was holding a manila envelope, waiting for her to sign. She knew what it was already, tried not to show her panic. She signed, and the driver handed her the thin brown envelope and departed with a nod. She looked down at it, hating the way her hands trembled.

She'd failed.

She took a breath. "Sorry again about the goat. Welcome to the neighborhood," she said absentmindedly. "Excuse me." She led Merlin to the yard and put him back in the enclosure with her other three goats. She heard gravel crunching as Calder walked away. Calder was her neighbor, she thought with some disbelief.

Well, not her neighbor for long. She looked down at the envelope again, opened it with trembling hands.

She'd failed.

"We regret to inform you that, due to your inaction in satisfying the lien against your property at 113 Mayfair Road, the property will be put up for auction on September 30th to satisfy the debt owed to the holder of the aforementioned lien. You will have thirty days after the auction date to vacate the premises. If you do not vacate, law enforcement may be summoned to remove you."

It was signed by the lawyer she'd been trying to deal with, unsuccessfully, since learning about the lien in the first place.

Sophie sank down onto the bottom step of the back porch, the stone cool and unforgiving beneath her. She looked around at the animal pens, the vegetable garden overflowing with tomatoes, lettuces, and zucchini; the herb garden buzzing with bees. She looked at the two beehives, the tiny chicken coop and the woods beyond that. She'd tried to save it and had lost it all.

"Damn you, crazy aunt Evie," she muttered, swiping tears away from her eyes in anger. Her aunt Evie had, apparently, taken on a loan from a local handyman at some point to make repairs to the old cottage. Roof replacement, repairs to a crumbling foundation. She'd let the loan slip more and more into default, partially from forgetfulness, Sophie believed. And whether out of pity or something else, the handyman had never called in the lien, and his son had taken over management of the family business.

It was just Sophie's luck, as Evie's only living relative and new owner of the property, that the son decided to call in the lien at the worst possible time. Over twenty thousand dollars owed, with interest, plus court fees. She'd been fighting for the last year to scrape money together, to come to some kind of agreement with the son and his lawyer. It had all come to nothing.

She looked around again. Felt the spirits of her ancestors, witches, every one, mourning with her. They'd lived in this little cottage in Copper Falls, at the very tip of Michigan's upper peninsula, for over two hundred years. Witches, warlocks. Sophie's mother had been the one with the lineage of witches, though she had no actual power herself. Her father had thought it was all nonsense, and when Sophie slipped up, and he caught her doing magic when she was thirteen, he'd moved the family away, seeming to sense that the place and the magic were entwined. Even after they'd moved to Detroit, and she continued to feel the magic within her, he insisted she was imagining it, that she was playing childish games.

Her life away from Copper Falls had been a nightmare pretty much from the moment she'd left. She closed her eyes and remembered more than she wanted to. Fear. Death. Endless threats and her own desperation. That feeling of being trapped, of being helpless, came to be all she knew and she hated it. All of that had changed two years ago when she'd gotten her letter from the attorney, telling her she was the sole beneficiary of Evie's will, and that the property was now Sophie's. The timing couldn't have been better, and she'd felt like the universe was finally giving her a second chance.

She let out a sardonic laugh as she sat there, staring at the letter. So much for that idea.

She forced herself back up and into the house. Well. She might be losing everything, but she had a book club meeting in an hour. She washed up, then started slicing vegetables and setting out the cheese platter. A local wine, some hard cider. She could feel the beginnings of fall in the air. A magical time in this part of the state. And she would miss it.

"Nope. Not thinking about that now," she said aloud. She carried the cheese platter to the living room, set it on the old pine coffee table in front of the overstuffed sofa. She glanced around, made herself stop as another wave of melancholy hit her.

She grabbed a few glasses for the wine and cider and set them on the sideboard in the living room, along with the ice bucket and a large punch bowl of ice cradling the cider. She glanced around. The wood floors gleamed, the cushy sofa beckoned, and candlelight danced over the walls. Candles she'd made, with beeswax from her own hives and essential oils she'd bartered from another witch for a few bars of her handmade soap. The clean white plaster walls made everything feel airy and comfortable. Serene.

Her heart ached. If it hadn't been for the sound of two female voices in her front yard, she would have started crying. Instead, she shook her head, walked to the front door, and threw it open. She watched as her best friend, Layla, and her sister Cara pulled themselves together, adjusting clothing, pulling shoes on. Layla's head was lifted, smelling.

"Hey, girl," she called to Sophie.

"Hey, yourself," Sophie called, stepping off of the porch and toward her friends.

Layla's eyes widened. "Whoa."

"What?"

"You had a bear here. Better keep your trash locked away or you're going to have a mess."

"Oh, great. One more thing to worry about," Sophie grumbled, hugging first Layla, then Cara. She looked at her friends. Both reminded her of Amazon goddesses, Wonder Woman. Tall, trim, and powerful, with flowing dark curls and ice blue eyes. Identical twins who couldn't be more unalike.

Except that, unlike Wonder Woman, they had the ability to become wolves when they wanted to. In her book, that made them just about the most magical things she'd ever seen.

When she'd arrived in town, broke but excited for her new life, Layla had been the first person she'd run into, as if it was fate that the girl who had been her best friend through elementary school was now there to greet her. Layla and Cara had welcomed Sophie into their circle of family and friends immediately, and Layla and Sophie had picked up their friendship as if they'd never been apart. And for the first time since she'd left Copper Falls as a teenager, she hadn't felt alone.

Another thing she'd lose.

No. She wouldn't. She'd find a way to stay in Copper Falls, even when she lost her house. It wasn't like she had anywhere else to go.

"What's wrong?" Cara asked, watching her with concern.

Sophie shrugged. "I got the letter today. It's over." She looked down, told herself she would not cry. The twins came and folded her into a hug, the three of them standing in Sophie's flower-filled front yard. They made Sophie feel safe, loved, and she held both of them tight.

"You can stay with us. You know that," Cara said softly as Sophie forced the tears back. "I know it's not the same. I know this land calls to your blood. But it's something."

"It is something. Thank you," Sophie whispered.

"I could bite someone in the ass for you if you want," Layla said, and the three of them fell apart in a fit of teary giggles. They were just starting to pull themselves together when the rumble of a motorcycle distracted them. All three turned toward the sound, to see Calder rumbling down his driveway, and then turning onto the road, heading in the opposite direction.

Layla glanced at Sophie. "Is that who I think it is?" she asked as she stared after him.

"Maybe. Calder Turcotte?" Sophie asked Layla.

Layla looked after him. "I didn't know he was moving back here. He's still friends with Bryce, but I haven't seen him much at all the past few years."

Cara laughed. "You mean the very same Calder Turcotte you used to drool over in Mrs. Redleaf's class?"

"I didn't drool over him," Sophie said, laughing.

Layla looked down the road, in the direction Calder had headed. "I thought he was living out at his father's place. Imagine that. Sophie and Calder in the same place again, all grown up," she said, giving Sophie a sly look.

"Not for long if I don't figure something out," Sophie said. "Anyway, I believe we have a book club meeting scheduled," she added, steering the twins toward the house.

"Taskmaster," Layla grumbled, and Sophie laughed. The three friends walked into the cozy house. Sophie poured them drinks, and they sat in the living room.

"Wuthering Heights. Have we all read it?" Layla asked, popping an olive into her mouth.

"Yes," Cara and Sophie chimed.

"Thoughts?" Layla asked.

"Heathcliff was a scary asshole," Sophie said.

"Passionate, though," Cara said.

"And Cathy was a jerk," Sophie added.

"Yep."

"I'd do him. All in favor?" Layla said.

"Aye," Sophie and Cara chimed.

"Good. Awesome book club meeting, ladies. Now tell us about Calder," Layla said, tucking her feet under her body.

Sophie rolled her eyes, and as the candlelight danced and the hard cider flowed, she told the tale of her embarrassingly clumsy goat capture, including the fact that Calder didn't remember her. Layla gave her hand a gentle squeeze at that.

"You should bake for him," Cara said. "The man would be putty in your hands." She took a sip of cider. "Um. You did bake something for tonight, didn't you?"

Sophie laughed, and Layla threw a pillow at her sister.

Sophie got up. "Yeah. I made those triple chocolate cookies you like so much." She went into the kitchen, picked up the cookie jar, and carried it back to the living room with her. She plunked it down on the coffee table, and Cara and Layla both attacked it immediately.

"I had no idea wolves were such fans of cookies until I met you two," Sophie said with a smile, settling down in one corner of the sofa again. Layla was snuggled into the other end of the couch, and Cara had claimed the cushy chair Sophie liked to sit and read in sometimes.

"Not just any cookies, though. Wolves are picky that way," Layla said. They were all silent a few minutes as they indulged in chocolatey, gooey goodness.

Layla licked some of the chocolate from her thumb. "So, when's the auction?" she asked quietly.

"Next Saturday," Sophie answered. The room went silent again, for a different reason.

"Are they doing it here?"

Sophie nodded.

"You should come down to the diner," Cara said. "You don't need to see that."

"I want to see it. I guess maybe I'm hoping no one will bid on it."

"You know that's not going to happen," Layla said. "Some hunter will snatch this place up like that," she said, snapping her fingers. "Or someone will buy it for their vacation home. Don't hang around and watch it happen, Soph."

She sighed. "I'm hoping maybe I can convince whoever wins it to let me buy it off of them in payments or something. I know it's a long shot, but I have to try. I mean, in the time I've been here, I managed to save almost ten thousand of what was due. If Danny Franklin wasn't such an all-or-nothing jerk, we wouldn't even be having this conversation. I'd pay more than the place is worth just to keep it." She paused. "Honestly, they'd make money." She didn't know at that point who she was even trying to convince. "I just can't lose this land. It's the one thing that's ever been mine. My magic is finally becoming something, and I know it's thanks to this place and the power here. I feel like I belong here," she finished quietly.

"You do belong here, in Copper Falls, whether it's on this land or not. Right?" Layla asked. Sophie nodded, not trusting her voice.

Cara changed the subject, and they spent the next couple of hours talking and eating, and when Sophie escorted her two friends to the woods not too far from her house, they talked and laughed as the twins removed clothing and shoes, and Sophie watched her two friends change, their skin becoming silvery fur, limbs changing, popping as the shift overtook them. It was a mesmerizing, magical process, and every time Sophie saw it she still couldn't quite believe it. They each picked up their bundle of clothing in their jaws, then bumped her legs with their foreheads and loped off into the night. She felt grateful that, if nothing else, she still had them.

Now she just had to get through the auction and convince whoever won her house to let her have it back.

.

CHAPTER TWO

It never fails, Sophie thought as she pulled herself out of bed the morning of the auction. When you're looking forward to something, it feels like time drags, as if the minutes are hours, and days feel like weeks. Dreading something, you can count on time flying.

She'd spent the last two weeks calling lawyers and begging for more time and trying to make deals... all of which she knew was pointless. The decision had been made, and all her pleading and cajoling had earned her was the knowledge that Danny Franklin, who was calling in his lien, needed the money because he owed a bunch of back payments for child support and was feeling his own kind of heat. It just made her dislike him even more.

She forced herself out of bed and into the shower, feeling like she was dead on her feet. It felt like she'd barely slept at all. She'd woken several times, either worrying about the house or sure she'd heard something outside. After a shower and a strong cup of tea, she felt almost human again.

Sophie pulled on her usual yard work ensemble: torn, worn jeans and a faded t-shirt, slipped her feet into the grungy old sneakers she wore for working outside, and headed out.

Yes, some jerkoffs would be around in a couple of hours to snap up her family's home. Still, there were animals to feed, goats to milk, and vegetables and herbs to harvest.

She set about her work, her mind clouded, almost hyperaware of everything around her. She was a jumble of emotions as she tried to focus on the beauty of the place, to etch it into her memory. Alongside that was a good dose of grim determination. She patted the three female goats' heads, murmured to them softly as she milked them. She'd make another batch of soap today, and finish off the candles she'd planned to make the day before.

Soaps, candles, balms, teas. These were the things that had kept her afloat since hearing about the debts on the property. Her full-time job as a maid at the Falls Resort didn't pay all that well, and her second job as a clerk at one of the many local souvenir shops had just ended, now that tourist season was over. It was her handmade goods, which she sold wholesale to local shops and online, that had been responsible for helping her put a dent in the debts. Or so she'd hoped.

Still, there was only so much soap one woman could make in a year. It hadn't been enough.

Sophie let the rhythm of the daily chores, the sounds in her quiet little corner of the world, soothe her. She harvested herbs to dry for tea blends, and was in the house hanging bunches of them from the rafters in the kitchen when she heard the car doors slamming on the road. She glanced at the clock over the stove.

Eight fifty. She stood still, forced herself to breathe around the way her stomach twisted, the way her heart was breaking. She felt her magic, usually so placid, barely there, really, rising within her. It did that sometimes during moments of stress.

She listened to more car doors slamming. Too many. She'd held a ridiculous hope that no one would show, that she could buy herself more time. She knew better, of course. Nice location, in a beautiful part of the state. The twins had been right. Her little cottage was attractive as a hunting camp or vacation home. She had a feeling none of those interested in buying the property knew what the true value of it was. She was only just beginning to learn that herself.

Her mind flashed back to her former home, and the reason she'd left. She remembered being hopeless, almost completely lost. Terrified. She closed her eyes and her nightmare was there, a pair of inscrutable gray eyes, a cold voice that promised her destruction.

Copper Falls and, even more, her family's land, had been her salvation. She'd given up hope, and then, suddenly, there was a light amid the darkness, purpose in her life.

She couldn't, *wouldn't*, go back to the way things were.

She walked out the back door, and around to the front. There were over a dozen people on the gravel driveway, along with two official-looking men carrying clipboards and wearing badges. She recognized one as the lawyer for the lienholder, gave him a cool nod. She guessed he and the other man were running the auction. She looked around and was shocked to see her two best friends in the crowd. She made her way toward them, resisting the urge to throw an elbow at one prospective buyer who was commenting that all of the "messy" plants had to come out so he could put in a lawn.

She gritted her teeth instead.

"What are you two doing here?" she asked as she walked up to Layla and Cara. They hugged her.

"If you're going to insist on watching this shit, you shouldn't have to do it alone," Layla said. Sophie rested her head on Layla's shoulder.

"Misery loves company, huh?" Sophie asked, trying to make light of it, even as something died inside as she watched the people gather near her porch. She moved closer so she could hear, Layla and Cara still beside her.

"And no matter what happens here today, you won't be alone. Right?" Cara said.

Sophie squeezed her hand and faced the auctioneer, who had taken his place on the crooked front steps.

"Bid starts at twenty-five thousand dollars," he said. "Raise your paddle number to bid." He started, and the bid went from twenty-five thousand to over fifty quickly. It kept rising. Up to fifty-five, then one bidder dropped out. At sixty, the other man dropped out, and it was down to a kindly looking older woman and a thirty-ish looking guy wearing a camouflage jacket. Sophie was setting her hopes on the older lady. Yes, the woman was a stranger, but she'd been remarking to the man next to her that maybe she'd just do some renovations and resell it for more. An investment. Someone like that, she could negotiate with.

The woman beat out her opponent. He gave up with a shake of his head, and Sophie felt a little bit of hope.

"And a new bidder joins in at seventy-five thousand," the auctioneer said. Sophie looked around in confusion.

Behind her, toward the back of the crowd, was the new mystery bidder. Calder. She glared at him, and he didn't seem to notice her. She'd only caught glimpses of him since that first fiasco with Merlin. Other than hearing his motorcycle drive by, and the occasional clanking noise from the garage, he'd been scarce.

She guessed she knew why, now.

He and the woman battled it out, up to ninety. When they hit ninety-five, the woman shook her head in irritated defeat.

"Going once. Going twice. Sold to the gentleman at the back for ninety-five thousand dollars," the auctioneer said. Sophie stood and glared at Calder as he talked to the two men. He paid her absolutely no mind. They exchanged paperwork, then Calder walked back across the road without even a glance in her direction.

"What. An. Asshole," Layla growled.

Sophie watched as he walked around the back of his house. "Maybe I can work something out with him," she said. "He said he didn't want neighbors. I didn't think that included the one house across the road from him."

"Cool off a while before you try talking to him," Cara said softly. "Remember, you have a place to stay. I know this house means a lot to you—"

"It means everything to me," Sophie said. "I'm finally learning about what I am. What I can do. I can feel my ancestors here. It's like I'm finally getting a glimpse of where I belong."

The twins hugged her, and then prepared to leave. The rest of the cars had already driven off, including the auctioneers.

"This place reeks of bear again," Layla said. "Have you heard anything?"

Sophie shook her head. "There's really not much around here for them to eat. They'll move on," she said. After a few moments, she watched her friends climb into their little black convertible and drive away.

She glared across the street at Calder's house. Later. She'd deal with that later. She turned and went into her house, climbed back into bed. Wouldn't be such a bad thing to start the day over again.

CHAPTER THREE

When Sophie opened her eyes, she glanced at the clock and realized she'd been asleep for over three hours. It was past noon. She couldn't remember the last time she'd slept that late.

Well. Yes, she could. But she preferred not to. She grimaced and sat up. She went into the little yellow bathroom and splashed cool water on her face and just generally freshened herself up a bit. Not too much. She wasn't concerned with impressing the asshole, just trying to get him to work with her. She pulled her long mass of brown curls up and secured it loosely with a clip, then she stepped into her sandals and headed out.

She crossed the road, and the first thing she noticed was Calder in his driveway, hunched over the engine of the ugly blue car she'd noticed the other day. It was some kind of classic car; lots of chrome. Calder's back was to her, and she hated herself a little for admiring the view.

Sophie walked up the driveway, scuffling her feet a little in the gravel so she wouldn't startle him. Though why she cared was beyond her. When she was a few feet away from him, Calder stood up straight and slowly turned around, those icy eyes watching her every move as she made her way toward him. He picked up a rag and started wiping grease off of his fingers, gaze still fixed on her.

Sophie stopped a couple of feet in front of him.

"Do you have a minute, Calder?" she asked softly, trying not to sound emotional or put out. Even if she did kind of want to claw his eyes out.

"I was expecting you sooner than this," he said.

"I needed some time to calm down," she answered. "Look, I know you don't want neighbors, but I swear I'm quiet. I'll keep my goats away from you, and you'll never even know I'm here."

He didn't say anything, just watched her with that hard look in his eyes.

"We can work out some kind of payment thing. I mean. You paid a lot for it and it'll take time, but I swear I'll pay it. I'll get another job or..."

He held his hand up. "Stop."

"Please," she said quietly, looking into his eyes.

He looked away, shook his head. "You're the only neighbor I have. I get you out of the way, I've got a hundred solid acres that are all mine."

"Calder. That house has been in my family for over two hundred years. I need it. It's the first place I've ever felt belonged to me. Please," she said again, and hated the desperate note that had crept into her voice.

"It really means a lot to you, huh?"

"It does."

He was looking down, and his eyes started slowly but surely making their way up her body. She forced herself to remain calm, to not run at the way he looked at her. So many memories. Enough to make her want to puke. Enough to make her wish she'd brought her gun. "How much are you willing to do to save it?"

"I'm not a whore, Calder," she said.

"I never said you were." Calder stood there watching her. He hadn't meant to make that implication about her sleeping with him. His senses were out of whack, standing there with her, just as they'd been the day he'd found her goat in his yard. That mass of dark, shining curls, brown eyes. Soft curves everywhere, the kind of body that gave a man plenty to hold on to, soft places to sink into. The smell of her, something clean and wild. Warm.

The memory of her kissing him, what felt like a lifetime ago.

Focus, he reprimanded himself. This was what she was. Letting her bewitch him, throw him off of his goal, would be foolish.

"I knew your property was in trouble before I moved into my place. In fact, it's what prompted me to move back after all this time."

He watched as her expression hardened, as her shoulders went rigid. "Why?" she asked, in a voice that shook just a little. She folded her arms over her chest. It made her look softer, more vulnerable, having the opposite effect of what it was supposed to.

"You're a witch," he said. She opened her mouth to disagree, and he held his hand up. "I can feel your power. Don't deny it." And he remembered. Those first heady signs of magic, her face alight with wonder. He shook it away.

"And you're a shifter. I remember that much."

He gave an irritated growl. "Yeah. I'm a shifter."

"Okay. So?" she asked, still glaring at him. She was still like the girl he'd known in middle school. Quiet, unsure, but prickly. He'd found it cute then and, damn it, he found it even more enticing now.

"There's this curse on my family," he said. "My line was cursed. By a witch."

21

"Oh," she said softly, as if she was understanding something. "I'm not that kind of witch, Calder. I can't lift the curse. The only thing my powers are good for is protective wards and really low-level healing. But curses are something else altogether. And I'm new at this."

He let out a rough laugh. "I think you don't know yourself as well as you should."

She didn't answer.

"It was your line that cursed mine. So somewhere in there, you are capable of it."

She shook her head. "I'm not."

"You are. And if you want your house back, you are going to find a way to fix it."

He watched as she stared at him. "I know nothing about curses, Calder! We could both be dead before I figured it out. I can help you find a witch who does that kind of thing, maybe—"

"No. *You* are going to do it. Your line cursed me, and we've tried everything. The one thing that's supposed to really work is to have the blood that caused the curse, lift it. One of your line can break it. You know that much, at least."

She shook her head. "No. I didn't know that."

"You're really that clueless," he said in disbelief, feeling dread settle into the pit of his stomach.

"I told you. I'm new at this. It came from my mother's side, and she had no magic at all. I never had anyone to teach me anything about it, and my father forbid it, so I learned what little I know on my own. Why the hell didn't you ask my aunt Evie to deal with this when she was alive?" she asked in exasperation.

"Evie was batshit insane," Calder huffed. "We did try. The old woman couldn't even brew tea without screwing it up."

"Maybe our magic has been depleted over the years, then, if she was so messed up. I can't do it, Calder."

He stepped forward, took her arm in his hand, felt her flesh, warm and soft as he pulled her toward him roughly and looked down into her eyes. "You will do this, witch. I don't care what it takes. I don't care what it costs, and I sure as hell don't care if you hate me or not. You will lift this curse from my family."

She tried to pull away, and he held her tighter. "I can't," she whispered, and her fear scented the air, nearly sent his beast into ecstasy.

"Here are the terms, Sophie. Listen carefully, because I'll only say this once. You have until the autumnal equinox to lift the curse. That's sixty days. If you don't, I keep your house and your land. And you'll want to run, because my beast seems to have taken a liking to you."

She stared, shook him off. "I don't think you need the beast as an excuse, Calder. You're a monster without it."

He stepped back. "Just take care of it."

He watched as she left, throwing several worried glances over her shoulder. Once she was out of sight, he took a deep breath. He picked up the huge piece of tree trunk at the side of the driveway and threw it, listened to it crash into the woods, rage and frustration making him just want to destroy.

He'd have to hunt that night. It wouldn't change anything. A momentary distraction, but one he needed before he lost his mind. It wasn't anything even remotely close to what he really wanted to do, he thought as he watched Sophie disappear into her house.

If he was a normal man, he'd be flirting with her. Trying to impress her. Instead, he was threatening her. He turned back toward the car. Self-loathing. That was something he was good at.

Why, of all the witches in the world, did it have to be this one?

At work the next day, Sophie's mind was almost continuously on Calder. When she wasn't remembering the boy who'd once been her closest confidante and first love, she was enraged and nearly in tears over the fact that he was blackmailing her to lift a curse she didn't have a chance in hell of lifting. And she couldn't even find it in herself to focus on the curse at all, because of him. Because the angry, cold man she'd spoken to the day before was nothing like the boy she'd known. The Calder she'd known had always been the first to stand up for her, the first one to sense she needed something. This blackmailing, conniving jerk was not the boy she'd loved so much. She really needed to get that through her head, right away, before it ended up causing her even more pain.

She greeted her coworkers at the resort almost mindlessly, as if she was on automatic. She'd been fortunate to land a rare full-time, year-round job in the small resort town she'd grown up in, thanks to Layla and Cara's mother and her connections. She was grateful for it, especially once she'd found out about Aunt Evie's debts. While her second, part-time, job wouldn't start up again until late spring, she could rely on this one, as a maid at the resort, all through the winter. It wasn't nearly as busy as during summer, of course, but they still got the occasional couple on honeymoon or single guy interested in skiing or hunting in the off-season. Copper Falls was known mostly for its beaches, pure sand on the shore of Lake Superior. Its lush woods and mountain views to the south were just added bonuses. The fishing was good, the hunting not too shabby, and the views, according to just about everyone who called it home, the most beautiful in the world.

So she was able to keep busy, which she was grateful for. As she changed bedding and vacuumed rooms and hallways, she forced her mind away from Calder and instead tried to remember what she knew of her family, since he'd said one of her ancestors had done it.

Honestly, she didn't believe it. Or she didn't want to. She had her suspicions, since Calder had mentioned the curse the night before, that maybe the reason she had so little magic, and her mother and Aunt Evie had had none at all, was because one of their line had cursed someone. That was a big no-no for their kind.

Unfortunately, she knew almost nothing about her family beyond her immediate relatives. Her mom and dad were both only children, and there was no magic in any of her grandparents, either. In fact, she was the only one with any magic at all that any of them knew of. Her father had married her mother, knowing she was from a witch family, despite his own dislike of magic. He'd voiced his opinions of magic and its dangers often, making it clear how grateful he was that her mother didn't have any. Of course, it wasn't until much later in life that Sophie learned he'd had a tiny bit of magic of his own, and it terrified him. She wished she could have talked to him about it. She wished she'd known. When Sophie started showing signs of power, she kept it a secret from her family, because she knew they'd freak out.

The fact was, she'd once had more magic than she presently did. When her powers first manifested, she'd been quite a bit more powerful. Powerful enough that her mother had felt it in her, despite lacking it herself, and it had freaked her father out enough that, when he'd caught her practicing a spell, he'd quickly moved them out of the town of Copper Falls, with its other-powered residents. It quickly became a topic of contention between her parents. Her mother, who was from a long line of witches (even if they were magic-less), believed she should be able to embrace her gifts, while her father refused to even consider encouraging Sophie and her magic. Her mother had started sneaking her books on witchcraft, her ally in trying to figure out who and what she was. She studied, and she learned (thank goodness for the internet as well) many spells, including the fact that there were warding spells you could do to protect yourself and your home.

Those had come in handy a few years later, after her mother had died, after her father had closed in on himself, after she'd begun to feel invisible.

She closed her eyes, forced her mind away from that. "One nightmare at a time, Sophie," she muttered to herself.

She finished up with her assigned rooms, headed into the dining room, on her way to the kitchen. There were always table linens to be pressed and folded. As she walked through, she smiled at a young woman and her two toddlers sitting near the window, overlooking a gorgeous view of Lake Superior. One of the toddlers was standing on the chair, intent on looking out the window. She saw his foot slip, saw him start to go down, and she mouthed a silent spell, warding him from injury. He fell (she couldn't prevent that, unfortunately) and his head hit the edge of the table. He should have had a bloody nose, or a split lip at the very least, as hard as he'd hit; instead, he sat right up again and laughed at his mother, who was jumping up, ready to soothe him.

Sophie hid a smile and headed into the kitchen.

"Linens?" she called, and the head of the waitstaff grinned and gestured to a pile of newly-washed maroon tablecloths.

If it kept her from thinking about curses and childhood loves for a little while, she'd iron until her arm was numb.

CHAPTER FOUR

Sophie drove home from work, singing along to Taylor Swift and, as always, enjoying the scenery on the meandering two-lane highway. Forest on both sides, and the leaves were starting to turn from vibrant green to shades of red and. The sumac at the base of the trees along the roadside were already crimson, like rubies dangling from arching branches.

The sun was just starting to set, washing the landscape in deep orange. She drove with the window down, and let the cool breeze reinvigorate her after eight hours of cleaning up other people's messes. Not that she wasn't grateful for it. She was happy to be back in the place she'd grown up, and happy she could support herself. Not only had it been the place she'd spent the happiest times of her childhood, not only was it the only place she'd ever lived where there was actually a community of "others," including witches and shifters, but it was more friendly and welcoming than anyplace she could imagine. The year-round residents all knew one another. Her first winter, no less than six people she knew from town had driven out to check on her, knowing she was a city girl and, most likely, needed help. She hadn't, but she'd been touched by the gesture, especially after spending most of her teens and twenties utterly alone.

She rounded a curve and noticed a large form lying at the side of the road. As she got closer, she recognized it as a deer. Its legs were moving, but it seemed to be struggling.

Sophie pulled over onto the shoulder and got out of her car, leaving the car running and the headlights on so she could see clearly in the darkening evening. She reached the deer and crouched down near its head. It was a doe, she realized. She caught movement in the brush at the side of the road. When she looked, there were at least two fawns there.

Looking back down at the doe, she noticed that its left shoulder was bloodied. She touched it gingerly, felt bone shift beneath her fingers, and the doe let out a pained call.

"All right now," Sophie murmured, keeping her tone low and soft. She rested both hands over the wound, focused. The doe calmed, stopped flailing, stopped its mournful calling. Sophie closed her eyes, focused what little Light magic she had. From what she'd read, she was basically doing everything wrong. It seemed that many Lightwitches felt and went by instinct more than anything else. Maybe it was because Sophie's power was so meager in the first place, but she didn't rely on feeling and intentions. When she closed her eyes, after a while, she could see, in detail, the way the deer was injured, and she worked her magic in and around it as if binding the broken bones. Her magic wasn't a sensation or a spirit or whatever her fellow Lightwitches called it. Maybe that was the way it was supposed to be. That was entirely possible. But to Sophie, her magic was and always had been more like a tool, something she could focus and use to her own will. There was really nothing ethereal about it, not the way she used it. Maybe if she'd been trained by another witch instead of learning on her own, it would have been different.

It worked, and that was all that mattered to her. Even with the meager amount of Light magic she possessed, Sophie soon felt the doe's shoulder healing, bones knitting back together. Had the break been more substantial, she knew she wouldn't have been able to fix it. Minor wounds, she could heal. Anything beyond that was impossible for her. Her real power seemed to be in protective wards. This was just a side thing she'd figured out as a teenager.

Pulling her hands back, she opened her eyes and looked down at the doe. She was no longer bleeding, and was already trying to stand. Once on her feet, she gave Sophie one final glance, then bounded toward the woods where her fawns were waiting.

Sophie smiled and stood up. The after-effects of using her magic left her warm and peaceful. And, just as the few times she'd managed to heal before, she felt a little more powerful, almost as if Light itself was rewarding her for doing something good with her power.

Sophie got back into her car, took a couple of wipes from the canister she kept in her back seat, and cleaned the drying blood from her fingers. It was dark now, and the woods looked less friendly. Time to get home.

She put the car into drive and maneuvered onto the empty highway. When she pulled into her driveway, she shook her head. The twins' familiar convertible sat in her driveway already, the sisters sitting on her porch waiting.

She got out of her car and slammed the door.

"Finally!" Layla said, and Cara elbowed her.

"You smell like deer," Cara said in greeting.

"Nice to see you, too," Sophie said. "What are you guys doing here?"

"Were you saving wildlife again?" Cara asked with a wry smile.

"Maybe," Sophie said.

"You know we're probably just going to hunt it later, right?"

"Don't. You. Dare," Sophie said, and Layla laughed. "She's a doe, with fawns. Be nice."

"Fine," Cara said.

"Come on. Go wash the deer stink off you... although, maybe not. That might actually work for you," Layla said, and Cara laughed.

"What in the hell are you even talking about?" Sophie asked, unlocking her front door. The twins followed her in.

"We're going to Jack's. And you're coming with us," Layla said.

"Oh, hell, no. I am not. I'm going to take care of my goats, and take a shower, and read..."

Cara let out an exaggerated yawn.

"Babe, you're gorgeous, sweet, and you have the kind of boobs I can only get from a really expensive push-up bra. We need to find you someone to get friendly with."

"I do not need to get 'friendly' with anyone."

"Girl, if that stick gets any further up your butt, I'm gonna start calling you Popsicle," Layla said, and Cara snorted. "You need to let loose a little and get your mind off of all of this crap for a while. Now, let's go."

Sophie rolled her eyes. "What are the chances you're just going to get up and go without me?"

"Right around zero, Popsicle," Cara said, and Layla erupted into a fit of giggles.

"Ugh," Sophie said, though even she had to laugh at the ridiculous nickname. "Fine. Let me go take care of the animals. Are we in a hurry?"

"Not really. We don't work tomorrow. You?"

Sophie nodded. "Later shift, though."

"Good. Go do your thing. We'll be here, rummaging through your cupboards."

Sophie grabbed the bucket off of the back steps, shaking her head to herself. They did this every once in a while, got it into their heads that she needed to be more sociable, that she was sinking into melancholy. And, usually, as with now, they were right. She always felt better after a night out with them, so she didn't put up much of a fight anymore. And they were stubborn as anything. Crazy wolves.

She milked the goats, secured them and the chickens for the night, then carried the milk bucket back inside and put it in the refrigerator.

"It'll be a few minutes," Sophie said.

"Take your time," Layla said, flipping through a magazine from the coffee table.

Sophie headed into her bedroom, grabbed a gray tweed skirt, a form-fitting black sweater she liked, and her pair of knee-high black boots. She showered (pulling her hair up and stuffing it into a shower cap, because it would take forever to dry and even the twins wouldn't be okay with waiting long enough for her to mess with her crazy mop of hair). Makeup, clothes, arranging a few of her curls that kept trying to twist funny, and she left the room.

"Okay?" Sophie asked, holding her arms out.

"You are so gonna get laid," Layla said, and Cara whistled.

"I am not going to get laid," Sophie said. "I'm going out to have fun and relax and stop thinking about the jerk across the road for a while." She grabbed her purse and they headed out, getting into the twins' car.

"Speaking of which. Have you talked to him?" Layla asked as she backed out of the driveway.

On the way to Jack's, which sat near the interstate beyond the edge of town, Sophie told the twins about her talk with Calder, about the curse he mentioned, and how if she broke it, he'd give her her house back, free and clear.

"Whoa," Cara said after a few moments of silence. "What does the curse do?"

"I don't know. I didn't have it together enough to ask him," Sophie said in irritation as she looked out the window. When she looked back toward the front seat, she saw Cara giving her an understanding look. "What?"

"You've still got it for him," she said softly.

"I do not."

"You totally do," Layla said.

"Shut up," Sophie said.

"Why are you embarrassed? It's sweet. First loves and all that," Cara said.

"It would be more sweet if he wasn't blackmailing me."

"Yeah, there is that little detail," Layla said. "I don't like this. Be careful, girl."

"I intend to be."

"Calder wouldn't hurt her," Cara said. "You know that."

"I never would have seen him blackmailing her, either. And he's become practically a hermit the past few years. And then all of a sudden he's moving back near town, all to blackmail her? It's creepy and I don't like it. This doesn't sound like the boy we knew."

"Lay, he goes hunting with Bryce every month. If there was something wrong with him, Bryce would know," Cara pressed.

"Men are clueless. Calder could have a raging case of the crazies and Bryce wouldn't even notice, especially in the thrill of the hunt. As long as they get to kill stuff, they're happy."

"How is Bryce, anyway?" Sophie cut in, not really wanting to talk about Calder anymore. As could be expected, Layla shut up, and she and Cara exchanged an amused glance. "I haven't seen him in a while."

"Well, the studio keeps him busy during tourist season, but now that it's settled down, he's around more. He's supposed to meet us there tonight, actually," Layla said.

"Oh. That explains the skirt, then," Sophie said, and Cara laughed. Layla was the least girly-girl they knew, happiest in jeans and running the hunt. "Just ask him out."

"I'm not asking him out," Layla said.

"Why not?"

"Because my ego is fragile and I'm not ready for rejection just yet. At least this way, I can keep pretending it's a possibility," she said.

"He would have to be completely stupid to say no," Sophie said.

"Well, since he hasn't done anything about it yet, I'm going to have to assume he's not interested."

"Or he's just sure you'd say no," Sophie said, and Cara nodded. It was clear to everyone but the two of them that Bryce and Layla were crazy about one another. But getting the town's sexy yoga instructor shifter and their resident tough girl together was like pulling teeth.

"It's like the worst soap opera ever, watching you two," Cara said, and now it was Sophie's turn to nod in agreement.

"Can we stop talking about it now?" Layla grumbled. Cara and Sophie exchanged a small smile, and they drove for a while in silence.

"Who's designated driver?" Cara asked.

"Me," Sophie said. "The last thing I need is to do something stupid tonight."

They didn't argue, and when they pulled into an empty spot in the gravel parking lot outside of Jack's, Layla pulled the keys out of the ignition and passed them over her shoulder to Sophie, who stuffed them into her purse.

Jack's was a mostly nondescript building. Low, brick, with a few small windows and a blinking red neon sign over the door that said "Jack's." A wooden sign on the door said, "No bullshit past this point. Don't make us call our wolves."

It wasn't an idle threat. The non-supernatural types just thought it was a clever joke, but everyone else knew better. Jack's was probably the most well-known shifter bar in the state, partially because it was surrounded by some of the best hunting grounds anywhere, but also because the owner was one of the most respected alpha wolves in the state. He was the alpha of the pack that Layla and Cara, and every other wolf in the area, belonged to.

"Jack would totally do you," Layla said as they walked in and the alpha's gaze settled on Sophie.

"Not interested. Boobs are his only prerequisite as far as that goes."

"Picky, picky," Cara said, and Sophie rolled her eyes. Her gaze landed on the table in the corner, where Bryce was standing to greet them, waving them over. The three of them exchanged hugs with him, then sat (Cara and Sophie making sure to put Layla beside Bryce). They ordered, then sat back and relaxed, chatting, watching a few of the patrons playing darts, listening to the music the DJ, which was a Friday night thing, was playing.

"So if you're not going to get laid, are you at least going to dance?" Cara asked Sophie.

"Who's getting laid?" Bryce asked, tearing his eyes away from Layla.

"Not me," Sophie said.

"Oh, good. Because if some asshole starts coming on to any of you in here, I'm going to kick some ass. These guys are shit."

"You hang out here with Calder and Jon a couple of times a month," Layla pointed out with a laugh.

"Yeah, so I know better," Bryce said. "And you stay away from Jack and his grabby hands," he said to Sophie. "I see the way he looks at you when you come in here, and he's always grabbing the waitresses and some of the more receptive female customers. I really don't want to have to kick my alpha's ass."

"You wouldn't get into a fight over that," Sophie said, laughing.

"The hell I wouldn't," Bryce said. "The guy has no respect. Typical alpha shit, thinks he can do whatever he wants."

"It wouldn't be worth fighting over," Sophie said, at which all three of the shifters at the table stared at her incredulously.

"Aren't Lightwitches all about protecting and shit like that?" Bryce asked.

"Well, yeah. But you're not a Lightwitch, and your alpha could make life really, really miserable for you if you pissed him off."

"I'm not a Lightwitch but I'm a shifter. I come from a long line of shifters who took no shit. And we used to play in the sandbox in my backyard together, along with those two," he said gesturing at Layla and Cara, "so if he touches you, I'm gonna break his face."

Sophie shook her head and smiled, stupidly touched by the words.

"Still feels like an outsider," Cara said, and Layla nodded.

"Because I am. You all got to grow up here together. I wasn't here," Sophie said.

"But you're one of us. All those summers, all that time we spent in school reminding one another not to let on what we actually were to the dumbass normal kids. All those hot days at the falls. You're one of us," Layla said. "And no one messes with one of our own."

"Speaking of which.... Did you know your buddy Calder is blackmailing Sophie?" Cara said to Bryce, and Sophie groaned.

Bryce looked uncomfortable. "I know."

"What?" Layla exploded, and Bryce actually winced.

"He told me. And he told me why, and I hate it, but I know how desperate he is," Bryce said.

Layla and Cara stared at him, and Layla turned away from him in disgust, crossing her arms over her chest.

"He didn't know who the witch would be, okay? Evie didn't even share her last name! He needed a witch from that line, and he saw an opportunity and took it." Sensing that he was only digging himself in deeper, he took a deep breath and looked pleadingly at Sophie, then at Layla. "She's gotta break it. And if she can't, we'll find her another place in town. I know it's not the same," he cut in quickly, interrupting what Layla had been about to say. "I know. I know you need that land to heal, I know you need it to learn more about yourself and what you can do. I know the magic of your ancestors imbues the place, and you need it. I know. Okay? But this shit with Calder... something has to be done and we'll do our best to take care of you if it all goes wrong."

"What does it do?" Sophie asked him.

He shook his head. "That's his story to tell. All I know is, I hope you can end it, Soph."

"Speak of the goddamn devil," Layla muttered. Sophie followed her gaze, to where Calder was walking through the front door of Jack's, along with another man who looked like a slimmer, shorter version of himself. That would be Jon, Sophie remembered.

Calder's gaze landed on Sophie. His eyes met hers across the crowded bar, and she found it almost impossible to look away. She finally tore her gaze away from his, looked down at her drink.

"It would be shitty of me not to invite him over," Bryce said in a low voice. "Bar's packed, we have plenty of room, and we're all old friends. You okay with that?" he asked Sophie. She nodded, barely. "Be nice," he said to Layla, and she ignored him.

Bryce stood up and called Calder and Jon over, and they slid into the booth, Calder beside Sophie, Jon beside Layla.

"Thanks," Jon said. "Hey, Sophie," he said, his gaze flicking away from hers almost immediately.

"Hey," she said. The six of them sat, mostly trying to avoid looking at one another, it seemed. Layla tapped listlessly on the side of her glass, Bryce seemed to have found something really fascinating about the wall behind Sophie, and Jon pretty much just stared down at his hands on the tabletop. Sophie shared a quick glance with Bryce, who saved the situation by talking about the car he'd just bought that he was going to have Calder restore.

"What kind of car?" Sophie asked, relieved there was finally talking happening, happy for anything that would distract her from Calder's huge, warm body beside hers, his knee pressing against hers in the crowded booth. He sat silently beside her.

"It's a sixty-eight Mustang. Mostly in good shape, but it's not running and some of the details are missing."

"I didn't know you fixed cars," Sophie said to Calder, determined to act somewhat normal despite everything.

"That's what I do for a living. I work out of my garage, no co-workers. I specialize in vintage cars. Restoration, mostly," he said, and when she looked up at him, he was watching her. "It's something I kind of fell into."

"He's good at it too," Jon said. "Gets calls from people all over the country."

Calder didn't say anything.

"That's great," Sophie said. "I noticed a car in your driveway. Is that it?"

Calder nodded.

"Don't judge on first impressions. It's going to be killer once he's done with it," Bryce said.

"It has no wheels and it's the most ugly shade of sky blue I've ever seen," Sophie said. Layla and Cara laughed.

"I know. I was with him when he bought it and I tried to talk him out of it. I didn't know you were taking it to Calder, though," Layla said.

"Who else would I take it to?" Bryce asked.

"I don't know. Maybe someone who isn't blackmailing one of your oldest friends?" Layla said.

"Drop it," Sophie muttered. Calder had gone rigid beside her, and when she glanced over at him, she saw that his jaw was clenched, a muscle jumping there. He didn't seem angry. Uncomfortable and irritated, maybe. "That's my problem. Not yours," Sophie said. Layla tried to argue, and Sophie cut her off. "I'm a big girl. I don't need anyone to save me." Layla looked at her in disbelief, and Sophie shook her head. She couldn't even explain it. As pissed off as she was at Calder, as hurt as she was that he didn't remember her, she wasn't about to let anyone else lay into him.

"I should go, probably," Calder said.

"No. You shouldn't," Sophie said. "Stay."

He stayed, and several times during the evening, Sophie almost wished she'd agreed and told him to go. It wasn't that he was rude or anything like that. He was polite toward her, even laughing with her a time or two over some story she'd told. It was other things. The smell of him, the feel of his body so close to hers. It threw her off, exhausted her. They spent a lot of the time almost trying to pretend the other wasn't there, and then they'd forget and actually talk or joke, and it would be nice, and then get awkward again.

"You seriously don't remember her?" Layla demanded, and Sophie regretted telling her that part of their conversation.

Calder shook his head, and even Jon threw him a disbelieving look.

"Dude, you gave her tongue on that rock down by the falls. You're seriously telling me you don't remember that? You had a goofy smile on your face for days afterward," Bryce said, and Layla laughed and clapped her hands. "And not just that, but you were obsessed with trying to figure out how to get her to kiss you again. I'm pretty sure 'I'm gonna fucking die if she doesn't kiss me again soon' were your exact words."

Calder shrugged and Sophie looked away from him, mortified at the way her face was burning. "You all have better memories than I do, maybe," Calder said, and Jon gave him another look. "What was I? Thirteen? Fourteen? What guy at that age isn't a raging hormone? I don't remember stuff from that long ago."

"Can we stop talking about it?" Sophie said. "This is just a little bit awkward."

Even though she put a light tone and a little laugh to her words, it was clear he'd hurt her feelings. Calder wanted to kick his own ass for doing that. For pretending he didn't remember, when she'd been his first kiss, his first crush, his first love. His first heartbreak. He couldn't afford to remember that now, because if he did, he'd lose sight of what mattered. But, damn, did he want to tell her. He wanted to tell her how he'd spent night after night lying awake, even years after her family moved away, craving her. How, soon, it turned into a sad longing, the realization that he'd never have that sweetness in his life again. The universe was an enormous asshole for finally allowing her back into his life, but under these circumstances.

He just couldn't seem to act right around her, even beyond the whole curse mess. The few times they forgot to keep their guard up, it was almost too easy to lose himself in her soft voice, the way her eyes lit up when she smiled. Amid the typical dank smell of the bar and the scents of so many other shifters around, the only scent that mattered was hers. So he sat next to her, and listened, and occasionally talked to her and tried not to be a complete asshole. He sent warning glares toward any men he noticed looking at her (and there were way too many for his liking), and as a result, they all stayed the hell away. Which was lucky, since he was on edge and would have been more than welcoming of a fight.

He even held it together when, after dancing with Layla, and then Cara, Bryce pulled a laughing, protesting Sophie out onto the dance floor. Layla and Cara had headed to the ladies' room, leaving him and Jon sitting at the table. He burned as he watched Sophie in Bryce's arms, really trying hard to remember that he probably shouldn't rip his best friend's head off his shoulders.

"Oh, yeah. It's obvious that you don't remember her," Jon remarked with a smirk. "Stop growling."

"I'm not," Calder said, a growl still remaining in his voice. He cleared his throat in irritation. "It doesn't matter if I remember her or not. This needs to get done. There's no reason to complicate things."

"It looks pretty complicated already, man."

"Don't worry. I'll take care of it," Calder said, balling his hands into fists as Sophie threw her head back and laughed at something Bryce had said, those waves of lush brown curls flowing down her back, over his arm around her waist.

"Do not kill Bryce," Jon said.

"I'm not. I don't even care."

"Obviously," Jon said, taking a swig of his beer.

Calder's gaze went back to Sophie. The way her top flowed over her hips, the small, teasing sight of her legs between the bottom of her skirt and the tops of her boots. For some reason, that little peek of flesh made him feel warmer than he should.

What he did know was that he really, really hated seeing her touching Bryce, even knowing that Bryce was stupid in love with Layla.

"Okay, well, then stop staring at her. Because you're right. This shit has to get done, and she's our last hope. So pull it together, man."

"I'm fine." Another guy approached them, asked Sophie if he could cut in, and Calder was on his feet before he even realized.

"Next dance was mine," he said, pulling Sophie into his arms as Bryce stepped back with a smirk.

It only took the other shifter looking at Calder's face to know this wasn't a battle he wanted. He watched his opponent (since that's immediately how he'd begun to see him) slink away with some satisfaction, then looked down at Sophie, who was looking up at him questioningly.

"I didn't say I wanted to dance with you, either," she said, pulling away from him.

He stepped back, dropping his hands to his sides. "Right. I just... I figured you might not want a stranger cutting in. He is a stranger, right?" he asked, irritated at the growl that had entered his voice again.

She raised an eyebrow. "That's none of your business."

She turned and headed toward their table, and he stood watching her, mesmerized by the sway of her hips, the swing of her hair, irritated as hell that she was walking away from him. After a moment he followed her, growling at a wolf shifter who was staring after her. The wolf submitted immediately, lowering his head in apology.

Calder slid into the booth beside her, scented the air, very aware that Sophie's luscious body seemed even warmer beside his, that she was flushed and that she smelled even more delectable than before.

Across the table, Jon cleared his throat. "I think it's time for us to go," he said, tapping inconspicuously at his own mouth, their signal that Calder was getting fangy. Calder nodded, now even more pissed off that he was having to leave her. It was just starting to be fun, and her scent was intoxicating.

"Make sure she gets home all right," he snarled at Bryce before stalking away.

"He's very concerned about the curse," he heard Jon explaining as he stalked outside, leaving everything, leaving *her*, behind. Before Jon was even out, Calder was heading toward the woods, shucking his clothes once he was away from the parking lot.

"I'll meet you at your house," Jon said, picking up the discarded clothing. "Get your head on straight, man."

Calder growled at him as he bounded away, into the woods. He knew one thing for sure, even in his wild, somewhat crazed state. He needed to stay the hell away from her. As far away as he could.

CHAPTER FIVE

Sophie woke up too late the following morning, not because they'd stayed out insanely late, but because, even after she was in bed, she couldn't sleep. Damn Calder. Damn his eyes and his muscular thighs and his arms and the way he'd growled at the shifter who'd tried to dance with her. Damn the way she reacted to him.

She'd tossed and turned, and ended up taking a long, cold shower, and then tried to sleep.

Her sleep, when she found it, was full of nightmares. Nightmares in which she ran, and matter how hard she pushed herself, it wasn't fast enough. Each step seemed slower, and she could hear the warlock behind her, each moment bringing him closer to her until she could practically hear his breath in her ear, his whispered promises that she couldn't fight him off forever.

They were getting worse, she thought as she woke up the third time. They'd nearly stopped, once she was free of him. Once she'd gotten used to not having her steps haunted by the warlock who'd been stalking her since she was fifteen.

Marshall. Even the name was enough, now, to make her blood run cold.

"Nightmares aren't real," she whispered to herself, trying to settle down again.

But she knew better. The nightmares had first started just before she'd seen him the first time, as if warning her. Her mother, in those rare moments they'd stolen to talk about her magic, had wondered if Sophie had some power of foresight. She remembered times when she was very young, when she'd told her parents about things that hadn't happened yet.

Sophie didn't know about her powers of foresight. If she had that, one would think she would have been able to sidestep a few of the disasters life had thrown her along the way. But she knew well enough that her nightmares about Marshall were a warning.

Or maybe the Calder situation had her so messed up, she was having old nightmares again. Of the two possibilities, that was actually the preferable one.

She dozed off, waking with the sun shining brightly onto her face and the goats bleating outside, waiting to be milked and fed.

"All right, all right," she muttered, swinging her legs out of bed. She tossed on jeans and a long-sleeved top, pulled her mass of frizz up into a clip, and clomped outside. She let the chickens out of their henhouse, threw down some scratch for them, then went and let the goats out, milked the females as they ate. She swore they looked at her with disappointment.

Merlin kept trying to work his way under the fence in the new pen she'd moved him to, and she cussed him out and he bleated at her in response, then went back to what he'd been doing. She grabbed a few of the metal stakes she'd picked up in town, used them to reinforce the old chain link fence around the pen he was in. He admonished her with a few bad-natured bleats, pissing on her boot to ensure she understood his displeasure.

"Keep it up and I'm gonna let Layla and Cara hunt your ornery ass," Sophie warned him. He just stood there chewing.

Animals cared for, Sophie gathered eggs and picked the few meager tomatoes left. They'd be getting a frost soon, and then she could kiss her garden goodbye. Maybe permanently, if she didn't break Calder's stupid curse. She harvested some of the remaining sage, rosemary, and lavender, breathing in the pungent aroma as it hung in the air around her. She'd bundle and hang them to dry, and then she'd use some of it in her soaps, some in teas.

She took everything inside, put it away, then fired up the wood stove on the back porch. She thanked, again, whichever of her ancestors had had the idea to put a second stove there. She didn't know what they'd used it for, but it was the perfect place for her to make her soaps, out in the fresh air. She got the stove warmed up, then hauled her big soap pot, lye, fats, oils, herbs, and goat's milk, and went to work.

She let herself get lost in the familiar, comforting routine of soap-making. It was always one of her more enjoyable tasks, especially that moment when the soap came together in a perfect luxurious swirl of fragrant creaminess.

Of course, her soaps and lotions always had a little extra something to them. It was the reason she'd managed to establish a fairly profitable business as quickly as she had. While there were many good soaps out there, as a Lightwitch, she was able to put a little something extra into her products, and each bar of soap, each tub of lotion she sent out, had a little bit of actual magic to it. So while she had scents called "Vibrance," "Good Fortune," and, her best seller, "Amorous," the names had as much to do with the spells she worked as she made her products as they had to do with the scents themselves. As she stirred, she closed her eyes, focusing on drawing her magic. She pictured the magic winding its way into the fragrant liquid, imbuing it with the properties she intended as she chanted, murmuring soft words she didn't even have to think of anymore. They came automatically, out of habit, and she could see, the way she could see the landscape around her home, the strands of magic twisting, turning, working their way into the soap itself. It took some work, some strong focus to make it all work, and it was very easy to lose a spell like this, to have it all unravel before the last bit of it wound its way into the soap. She could see it in her mind, feel it all through her body, the instant the spell had been completed successfully, and she smiled. The spells broke on her less now than they used to. She finished, whispering gratitude to her ancestors for their assistance, knowing, just as she knew anything, that her magic was augmented by the space she inhabited. When she used her magic, as she just had, she could feel, very clearly, her ancestors' magic, still strong after all of these years, around her. One didn't live in a place so long without leaving a mark on it. She only hoped that she'd live there long enough to leave remnants of her own magic behind.

Of course, she knew well enough that her way of dealing with magic was unconventional. She made do with the little amount she had by forcing it to work with her. It probably wasn't the best attitude for a Lightwitch to have toward her magic, but it worked, and the magic hadn't left her when she'd started using it that way, so she let that be enough.

She finished stirring, the soap having come together as it should, and went to work pouring the smooth, fragrant liquid into wooden molds. She would let them sit and harden for a few days, then slice them into bars and let them cure before packaging them.

She cleaned up, threw together a quick salad, then headed into town to do a short shift at the resort. It passed quickly, mostly because her mind kept flashing, stupidly, back to the night before. Calder.

Part of what had gotten under her skin was the way he had warned others away from her. And she knew. She knew that there was a way to do that that was disrespectful and controlling. And while he'd certainly been doing it for himself, she was grateful for it. She had been uncomfortable when the strange shifter had cut in with Bryce. Whether he'd picked up on that or he'd just been doing the typical possessive shifter thing, she was just glad she hadn't had to deal with it.

It just felt weird to have someone looking out for her instead of her constantly being on guard for herself all the time. And as nice as it had been, to her surprise... it still wasn't something she should let herself get used to. Because when she wasn't being a daydreaming idiot over Calder, she knew damn well that he had huge ulterior motives where she was concerned. Warning other men off of her was likely his way of making sure no more of her time was taken up with anything other than figuring out his curse. He didn't remember her. He had no emotional attachment to her, not the way she did with him. She had to remember that. They were coming from two completely different places, and if she didn't get herself together regarding him, it would be a mess. And she'd had enough of those to last a lifetime.

She drove back home, and every stupid song on the radio made her think of him.

Calder's hand slipped on the wrench, and he banged his knuckles against the engine. "Fuck," he cursed, shaking his hand, inspecting his knuckles, all split and bleeding. Again. He sucked on the worst one, then lowered his hand and shook it again in irritation. Bryce's ugly car would keep him busy for a while, and he knew what Bryce was up to. Yeah, sure, Bryce wanted the car. He also wanted to keep Calder busy. Bastard wasn't nearly as sly as he thought he was, but Calder appreciated it nonetheless.

Her. She was driving him nuts. He glanced across the road, even though he knew she wasn't there. Which was a good thing. He was finding it really hard to stay on his own side of the road when he knew she was there, when he'd catch the occasional glimpse of her walking from her house to her car or from her house to her mailbox. And she didn't even know she was doing it. She didn't even know how crazy it had made him to sit beside her the night before, to smell her, to feel her softness against him, to look in her eyes and be taken back almost twenty years, to long days and even longer nights, sitting on the porch swing behind her house talking about nothing and everything.

When she'd been everything, and he still had a stupid, misguided hope that he'd be normal, despite what he'd already seen his father going through.

He shook his head, picked up the wrench again.

He raised his head as a white truck drove down the road, slowing in front of Sophie's house. He leaned forward on his forearms on the hood, watching. The truck had pretty much stopped at her driveway, and Calder could make out the profile of a man in the driver's seat. As he watched, the guy sat there, looking at Sophie's house, and just the fact that he was there made Calder want to pull him out of his shiny city-boy truck and ask him what he thought he was doing. His house and Sophie's were the only ones around, surrounded by acres of forest.

He didn't look like he was supposed to be there. And if he was supposed to be there, if this was someone Sophie knew... how stupid was it that he already considered the guy an adversary?

He shook his head, went back to work, and he heard the truck drive away a few seconds later. None of his business. She was none of his business. He didn't remember her, and she wasn't his first love. That was the story he'd told her, and he would stick to it. This was complicated enough already.

He kept working. His stomach rumbled, his mouth was dry. He was on edge, barely able to stay still, feeling his curse eating at him, feeling it wearing him down. Every day was harder, every day a new lesson in hunger. And the curvy, drop-dead gorgeous dream girl from his past was the key to saving himself and his family. His having a severe case of blue balls now that she was back in his life was a small price to pay.

It wasn't like he was unfamiliar with ceaseless hunger. This was just one more thing.

Sophie pulled into her driveway after her shift at the resort, climbed out of her car, and, even though she told herself not to, glanced across the road toward Calder's house. He was in his usual place, bent over the engine of Bryce's ugly car. Before she looked away, he stood up straight, and his gaze found her.

It was disconcerting, to say the least, the way he seemed to home in on her like that. It had always been that way. And she was pathetic and she hated herself, but she could barely even breathe when he looked at her.

He started walking across the road, and she took a step closer to her house. Something crossed his features; irritation, maybe. He slowed to a halt a few feet away from her.

"I'm working on it," she said, forestalling anything he might say.

His expression hardened a little. "Good."

"Okay. So you can leave now," she said, taking another step toward her house.

"I'm not going to hurt you," he said, and she let a sardonic laugh escape her mouth.

"No. You're just going to threaten me and take everything I own if I don't fix someone else's mess. You'll just have to excuse me if I don't have the world's highest opinion of you, Calder. I've seen your type before, and all you are is bad news." She almost felt guilty for her tone. Almost, except that she'd barely had him in her life for a week now, and he'd already sent her into a tailspin.

"My type?" he asked, his voice a low grumble. He studied her in a way that had her stomach twisting. "And what type is that?"

"The type who doesn't know the meaning of the word no, who takes what they want no matter whose life they trample all over," she said, and it was as if she'd slapped him. He went completely still. "Now if you'll excuse me, I have work to do if I have any hope at all of not having my life torn to pieces by you." She turned and went into the house without another word, locking the door behind her.

For extra peace of mind, she murmured a few soft words, ran her hands along the sides of the front door. Her power flowed through her, barely there, but warm and comforting nonetheless. When she'd finished setting the additional protective wards, she glanced out the front window to see Calder stalking back across the road.

"Good. Stay over there," she muttered, shaking her head.

She grabbed an apple and ate it as she checked on the garden, tossed the core to Merlin, then did the evening milking. Once everyone was settled for the night, she went back inside. Her plan was to go through more of the old books that had stocked Aunt Evie's shelves. She'd been thrilled to find two shelves of the old built-in bookcases in the living room had been packed with old spell books and books about witching history. She loved those books. It felt like every page she read was a clue, a piece of the puzzle to figuring out what it was her power could do, exactly.

She pulled a black leather-bound book out and, as she did, another smaller book which had been perched on top of it fell onto the floor. She set the larger volume down and bent to pick up the fallen book. It had a floppy leather cover, and the pages were yellowed with age. She flipped through it gently, noting the dates, from the 1970s. Evie's journal, she guessed. She sat on the floor near the bookcase, started reading. Mostly, it was recipes for pies and preserves. Hardly a mention of magic at all. An occasional note about the gentleman from town that she was seeing. Sophie smiled, reading her fond recollections of him.

Though fun, the book was pretty much useless. She held it in her hands, fluttered through the pages with her thumb. Then she stilled, and looked up.

The attic.

When she'd moved in, she'd gone up there precisely once, and, overwhelmed by the sheer amount of stuff packed into the space, she'd come right back down and closed the door.

But if an ancestor of hers had caused Calder's curse, and she knew that generations of her ancestors had lived on this very land, wasn't it possible there was something up there — a letter, a journal... something — that would have some answers for her? It was unlikely. But it was better than sitting there mooning over the blackmailing jerk.

She headed up into the musty attic, pulling the chain on the light fixture at the top of the stairs, then sweeping her flashlight beam across the room. There was another light fixture further into the attic, and she made her way to that, turned it on as well.

She looked around helplessly. Where the hell was she even supposed to start?

She shrugged and opened the closest box. She'd planned to clean it all out anyway, because it would make the perfect place to hang herbs for drying if it wasn't packed floor to ceiling with decades worth of stuff. Of course, she might not have the house for next year's herb harvest, but she definitely wouldn't if she didn't at least try to figure it all out.

After a few hours of sorting through dusty, grimy boxes, mostly filled with old clothes and other useless crap, Sophie was ready to head back downstairs and declare defeat. Why did people hold on to stuff like this? What good was an entire box of plastic dishes, or boxes and boxes of paperbacks, which had been chewed mercilessly by mice? Books should be read, should adorn a room so you could look at them and remember the amazing places they took you. They shouldn't be boxed up and stuffed in an attic.

She had to grin as she looked though them. Someone, in the seventies and eighties, had been a big paperback romance reader. The covers, complete with bodice-ripping heroes holding their prizes, made her roll her eyes. Not in a bad way, though. She remembered pilfering the same types of books from her mother's bedside table.

She set the books down. She was too old for fairy tales.

She got back to work. If there were answers to be found about Calder and his curse, she'd find them. She had to.

After another few hours, she had about half of the attic sorted through. She had a few boxes of things she could use, mostly kitchen and gardening equipment, along with some decorative things that had caught her eye. She had a pile of clothing to donate, several boxes of paperbacks (that hadn't yet been chewed by mice) and other miscellaneous stuff to donate. She'd already tossed several garbage bags outside. She'd have to drive them to the dump later.

As Sophie carried the "donate" boxes out to the front porch and stacked them along one side, she reminded herself to call Purple Heart to come and pick them up. She went out back and did the evening chores in the dark, feeding and watering the animals, giving the goats their second milking of the day.

As she did, she thought. A name. A date. Something. She didn't know anything about her family besides Evie and her family's almost non-existent magic. If Calder had been looking into the curse enough to know (supposedly) that it was her ancestor, then he must have names or dates or something to base that on.

CHAPTER SIX

Sophie finished up, washed up a little, then headed out the front door and across the street. Calder was pretty much where he'd been earlier that day, hunched over the car.

She walked up to him and leaned against the side of the car, watched him for a few minutes. He didn't acknowledge her, and she tried not to let that irritate her.

"Can you tell me anything about the curse? What does it do, exactly? Which of my ancestors did it? Anything you know would be helpful, since I know absolutely nothing," she said softly.

Calder kept his eyes on the engine. After a few more minutes of tightening things and fiddling around, he stood up and started wiping his hands. "What have you been doing all evening? I knocked on your door twice trying to talk to you."

"I was in the attic. There's so much stuff up there, going back who knows how long. I'm hoping I can find something, anything, up there that will help me figure this out. But I figured if I can find out what you know, that will give me a head start. And maybe I'll know what I'm looking for when I find it. I should have tried to find out before. This is all so insane."

He nodded in agreement and headed toward his front porch. He settled his huge frame on one of the steps, and she sat beside him.

"It happened about two hundred years ago," he began. "My ancestor, Luc, was involved with your ancestor, Migisi."

She watched him. "What kind of name is that?"

"Ojibwa, we think," he said.

Sophie pulled the small notebook out of her jeans pocket, wrote the names down. "I was always told there was some Native American in my line, but no one knew much," she said as she wrote. "Did she live in my house?"

"She at least lived on the land. We're not sure if she was the one who first lived in the house or whether it was family members from later."

"Okay."

"So they were involved, and from what I hear, she was completely in love with him. But Luc had a wandering eye, and she caught him with another woman. She was heartbroken. And pissed off."

"Rightfully so," Sophie said, raising her eyebrow.

"You'll get no argument from me on that."

Sophie laughed a little.

"Anyway. The story goes that when he went to her to apologize, she had a curse waiting, and she did the spell, and that was that. She moved on. Married another man and had children. Luc spent the rest of his life cursed, mated, and the next generation was born. Cursed, just as he had been."

"Can you tell me more about the curse?"

Sophie watched as he looked down at his hands. "Our line are shifters. You already know that."

"What do you shift into?" He'd always, back then, been tight-lipped about his animal, and Jon had been the same way. She'd known early on that Layla, Cara, and Bryce were all wolves, but he'd never gotten into it, and it was clear Bryce knew but never even considered telling them.

"Bear."

"A bear?" she asked, surprised.

He nodded.

"Are you the bear Layla and Cara keep smelling around my house?"

"Yeah."

"So you were spying on me?"

"I was making it clear that's my territory."

"Why?"

"To keep others away," he said.

"Is there something I need to be worried about?"

He looked up, met her eyes. Her heart stopped at the intensity in his gaze. "No. Nothing's going to happen to you."

"Except for you taking everything I own if I can't figure this out."

He blew out an irritated breath. "I'm desperate, Sophie. It's getting worse, and it's only the last few generations that stopped being stupid about the curse and actually started researching how to break it. Started tracing her line. And what we kept finding was that for the most part, you're all powerless. Until you. I was prepared to make the move down to Detroit, but this is so much better. You came here for a reason, and it's clear you need this place."

"Lucky you," Sophie muttered.

"For what it's worth, I don't make a habit of bullying women."

"Congratulations," she said icily.

He took a breath, and she shook her head in irritation. One bright spot in the situation was that she had a couple more months in her house. Of course, that would probably be it, because her chances of breaking a curse as obviously powerful as this one were probably less than zero. "The shifter part isn't the curse, though," she finally said, determined to at least try to figure it out.

He shook his head. "We were born shifters. And until we hit puberty, we can shift into our animal without any problems. After that point, shifting becomes a punishment of its own. When we take our animal form, we start to become more beast than man. You have friends who shift. You've been around them when they're in their animal form. You know that even though they have the senses, reflexes, and instincts of their animals, their thought processes remain human."

Sophie nodded, watching him. Why did he have to be so good-looking? It was hard to hate him when he looked at her with that intense, serious gaze, or, worse, that tiny lift of the corner of his mouth when he was amused. How could she hate him when she could still see the boy she'd been so enamored with?

"Okay. Well, with the men in my family, we start losing that humanity. At first, it's just..." He paused, shook his head.

"Calder. I need to understand. Okay?"

"At first, it's like your beast starts taking control when you're in that form. It does things you'd never do, out of its mind, and all you can do is watch. You're still in there, but you're powerless to do anything other than wait it out. At first, it's really only a problem on full moon nights. The rest of the time, we hold it together, and it's almost normal. Full moons are a nightmare." He paused. "And it's not that our beast is evil. It's just desperate. The real thing with the curse is that it makes you just endlessly dissatisfied. There is no such thing as enough food, enough water, enough violence, enough..." He trailed off, and she caught his eyes sweeping over her body before he looked away. She felt a blush rise to her face. "Never enough," he continued. "We want it all, all the time, and getting it never satisfies. It's like having an itch that never stops, and slowly but surely, it drives you mad. And the more insane you get, the less of your humanity you can remember, until, even in your human form, when you can remember to take it, you're like an animal."

She kept her eyes on his and listened, and the concern, the empathy in her eyes made it hard for him to breathe. Her scent surrounded him, and the warmth radiating from her body made him want to touch her so badly he burned with it. He forced his mind back.

"My father hasn't shifted back to his human form in over six months. He is likely lost to us. The best any of us can do is keep him contained, so he doesn't hurt anyone. Jon cares for him, but it's not easy on him. We agreed that I would be the one to... convince you to help us. And I can feel the curse strengthening in me as well."

"And Jon?" she asked him.

He shook his head. "It only affects the oldest male in each family. And we've tried ending it that way. Tried not getting anyone pregnant, or killing off the eldest son before the curse begins. It either jumps to a younger sibling or to a male cousin. She wasn't messing around when she made that curse."

She was quiet for several moments. "Your dad and brother. Do they live around here?" she asked, and the tremor of fear in her voice grated at him.

"No. They live in the middle of one of the larger state forests. Very isolated."

She nodded, and he watched her. She seemed to be thinking.

"So, the hunger. That's the real part of the curse. Right?"

He nodded. "That seems to be it. That we would never be satisfied. That the constant dissatisfaction eventually drives us mad."

She was watching him. Jesus, she smelled good. His bear, his beast, practically rumbled in ecstasy at her scent, just as it had a few nights before at Jack's. So close beside him, her curvy body warming his, her thigh almost touching his.

It was hard to breathe.

"And you say you're starting to feel the effects of the curse?" she asked softly.

He nodded. "I still mostly have control of my beast."

"Mostly," she repeated, and her fear scented the air, made his beast raise its head in interest.

"It's bad around the full moon," he said. And he knew, already, that this next full moon would be absolute torture. There was something he suddenly wanted more than just about anything else, and it would make his beast even crazier. "The equinoxes are hell. That's why I put that deadline in there. This is the first year I've started losing control, and I know from watching my dad that the equinox is a nightmare. Fall and spring," he added.

"Why?" she asked.

He shrugged. "I think it has to do with the bear part of what we are. Fall, a bear would be preparing to hibernate. He'd be stuffing himself with food and getting sleepier. And spring..." He forced his thoughts away from that.

"What's with spring?"

"That's mating season," he answered, trying to keep his voice flat.

"Oh," she said. She looked way from him, tapped her pen against the small notebook she'd been jotting things down in.

"So, Migisi. Do you know anything else about her?"

He shook his head. "The only reason we know her name at all is because there's this story that Luc ended his life in front of his own son, and he screamed, 'Is this what you wanted, Migisi?' right before he jumped off one of the outcroppings on Brock mountain."

"Is that how it usually ends?" she asked quietly, and the compassion in her eyes made him hate himself even more.

"Sometimes," he answered. "And sometimes, we go beyond the point where we even have enough sense to know we should end it. My father is there now. Even if he wanted to end his life, he's too out of control to even attempt it. It's like he's hardly in there at all anymore."

"It seems like she went kind of overboard on the curse thing," she said. "Is it possible there's more to it than that?"

He shrugged. "I don't know. It's possible. All I know is what's been passed down over the years. We lost track of her line for a while. Your place sat empty for decades in the early 1900s, I guess. And then we found Evie, which led us to you. Evie didn't know anything about anything. She knew you all have some magic, but she also knew that it was pretty much nonexistent in her."

"My mom had no magic at all," Sophie said. "I knew there were stories, that there was some magic on my mother's side, but it wasn't something we were really allowed to talk about. And then my dad found out I had some power and he freaked out. And then we moved away from here. I think he thought that would end it."

He watched her, felt the almost irresistible urge to try to comfort her. It wasn't the words, so much. It was something behind them, some sense that she'd been through more than her share of bad.

He couldn't afford to worry about her feelings now.

He looked across the road, at her little cottage. "Have you found anything up there?" he asked, gesturing toward the small window in the attic.

She shook her head. "Not yet. But at least maybe I'll know it when I see it. If there's something up there that can help, I'll find it. And now I have names to work with. What was Luc's last name?"

"Same as mine. Turcotte," he answered, watched her write it down. "Sophie," he said, unable to take his eyes off of her and hating himself all over again.

"What?" She raised her gaze to his, and heat shot through him at just the meeting of their eyes.

He almost said it. Almost apologized for the mess he'd made of her life, for the way he'd strong-armed her into helping him.

"If you find anything out, let me know," he said, aware of the short, gruff tone of his voice.

He watched as she withdrew into herself again. There was still that compassion in her eyes, but it was like watching a door close, watching her pull away from him.

What did he expect?

"I will. And I should get back to work," she said, standing up.

He stood up, too, walked with her down his driveway.

"You don't have to come with me. It's not like I'm going to get lost or anything."

He smiled a little. "I know. "

"Having the names has to help, right?" Sophie murmured as they strolled across the road together. He got the sense she was trying to make herself feel better. Or trying to make him feel better, which just made him feel like even more of a bastard. They reached the shoulder of the road on her side, started walking toward her driveway. "Having Migisi's name especially. Because then if I run across—"

Her voice stopped on a strangled sound. Her heart pounded, and her adrenaline flooded the air. He shot a glance toward her. She stared at her driveway, and he followed her gaze.

A single yellow long-stemmed rose lay at the end of the gravel driveway.

And the look on her face, the defeat he saw there, made him want to hit someone.

"Sophie," he said quietly, trying to shake her out of the panic he could see quickly overtaking her.

She was breathing hard, as if she was on the verge of hyperventilating. Her hands were shaking.

"Sophie," he repeated, and she shook her head.

"No. Not again. Not already," she said.

He reached out for her, took her shoulders in his hands and turned her toward him, away from the rose, which she couldn't seem to stop staring at.

"Sophie," he repeated. "What the hell is going on?"

She shook her head, hard, her eyes unfocused, her breathing coming in soft pants now.

He leaned down so she had no choice but to look in his eyes. "Tell me. What the hell is this?"

"I need to go in. I need to re-set my wards."

She was fucking terrified. "Who did this?" he asked. "What's going on?"

"I ran here to get away from him," she whispered. "Please, let me go now."

He wanted to do the complete opposite. He wanted to press her for more information, keep her with him. Disembowel whoever had upset her this badly, this "him" she'd referred to. But the way she'd asked, as if she almost didn't expect to have her wishes honored, the way she seemed to expect to have to fight for herself... he hated it. So he let her go, and the relief on her face when he did told him he'd done the right thing.

"If you need me, call." He pulled one of his business cards out of his pocket. "Okay?"

She gave a tiny nod, walked up her driveway, giving the rose a wide berth, as if the damn thing was going to leap up and bite her. Calder watched her unlock her door, then go in. He could see her moving past windows. He waited a few minutes, her panic clearly having infected him as well. He was waiting for a scream, a shout. Something. After a while, there was no sound, and the lights in her house were still on. He looked down at the rose again, bent and picked it up. He took it back across the road with him, tore the bloom off and threw it in the ditch, followed by the stem.

He'd let his beast run that night, see if he could catch a scent. And maybe patrol around her property.

All in the interest of protecting the one person who could actually break his curse. At least, that was what he was telling himself.

Sophie locked the door behind her, including the shiny new deadbolt she'd added as soon as she'd moved into the house. She did the same at the back door, double and triple-checked every window. She lit three of her ritual candles, then grabbed one of the smudge sticks she'd made with herbs from her garden a few weeks ago. Herbs for protection and cleansing.

She absolutely and completely needed both.

She let the herbs ignite, and held a small stone bowl underneath them to catch any embers. She slowly walked through the house, letting the smoke waft through the rooms. As she did, she murmured the same spells she'd been repeating since she was sixteen years old, since the summer she'd learned what fear really was.

As she walked, and chanted, she tried not to think about those years. All of those years, fearful of the time she'd inevitably slip up. All those years of dark eyes following her every move.

Years of yellow roses left in places he'd known she'd find them. Not endearments.

Warnings.

Every one, a warning. Eventually, she'd forget to watch her back. She'd do something careless, forget to lock the door, get caught in a place where she couldn't protect herself.

And when it happened, the things he'd written to her would come to pass. Every violation, every bit of degradation.

At sixteen, she didn't even know what some of the things he'd threatened meant. She came to learn. And so much more.

At eighteen, she'd lost her family. At twenty-four, she'd lost the man she had hoped would protect her and give her something to hold on to, and, at twenty-eight, when she finally had a chance, she'd run.

Her mind went back to the yellow rose. Her hopes of living in peace for a few years more had been stupid. She knew better. She always had.

Her home as protected as she could make it, she grabbed the small pistol she usually kept somewhere on her body and sat on her sofa, gun lying on her thigh, in her hand.

She knew better. He couldn't get through her wards. He'd try. His magic was more powerful than hers, and she'd spent years wondering when her wards would finally break under his assault. It hadn't happened yet.

So she sat, and she listened, and she hoped. And she tried not to think about how fast everything had fallen apart.

CHAPTER SEVEN

April 10, 1852

Migisi watched in amusement as the trapper bent and inspected his cages, low, muttering sounds meeting her ears from her perch on the rocky outcropping above. She watched as he baited the trap again, small pieces of meat. He re-set the latch, and moved on, still looking irritated.

He'd find every single trap the same way. The small cage traps he set for the minks, the larger ones he set for the beavers. Even the deadly-looking jaw traps he set for bears. Migisi grinned to herself and trailed him from her path along the hill. Each empty trap resulted in a new bout of grumbles, many of them curse words she'd heard often around the white men, the French voyageurs, as they called themselves. The missionaries never said words like those.

Migisi couldn't say why she found so much enjoyment in thwarting and observing the brawny Frenchman. If she was trying to be pious, she would say that she was saving the animals, doing her duty to her forest by protecting sacred beings from this man and his endless supply of traps.

And surely, that was why she'd started her campaign to see him fail. It had angered her the first day she'd seen him in her forest, forest in which she was the one and only human being for miles around. And he came stomping in with his big furry boots and acted as if he had every right to be there.

But part of it, too, was that the Frenchman intrigued her. She'd seen more than a few like him in her visits to the village of her family. The French were ever-present, trying to convert her people to the ways of the Church. For the most part, the people of her clan had gently, and with a good amount of amusement, rebuffed their attempts. Few had decided to at least hear of this God the white men spoke of. Migisi had used the opportunity to pick up the French language, which the missionaries were more than happy to teach her, believing, as they did, that teaching her a "proper" language would bring her around. She'd smiled, and learned, and let them think what they wanted. Besides the French, there had been Brits, and she found that language fairly easy to pick up as well. She found the Europeans amusing. They made everything so difficult for themselves all the time.

So it wasn't because he was intriguing in that way. She'd been around plenty of his kind. There was more. She found his form pleasing to her eye; he was tall, easily towering over her compact frame, she figured. His dark brown hair curled at the ends under the fur hat he wore, and his clear blue eyes, the way he inspected things so carefully, spoke of a certain intelligence, she supposed.

But it was those moments in which he'd discovered her tampering, those moments when he cursed, and, if the mood was right, laughed in consternation, that she saw more. The way his face lit up, the way the hard planes of his jaw softened, and those eyes held a warmth she found intriguing.

So her game continued, because it pleased her. And he knew, by now, with so many moons having passed, that it was much more than animals thwarting his enterprise. Sometimes, when he talked, when he cursed, he addressed "the ghost" and leveled promises as to what he'd do if he ever found his nemesis.

And all she could do was smile. Because she was power, and Light, and these woods belonged to her.

Here, she had nothing to fear. Especially not from him.

She crouched on the rocks above, her pliant leathers keeping her both warm and camouflaged in the spring forest. Her boots, made by her own mother, barely made a sound as she trailed her prey. He was bent over yet another empty trap, and he held it to his nose, as if he was scenting it. Migisi watched, tilting her head, trying to get a better look at his baffling actions.

The shrubbery off to her left rustled, and she was distracted by it for a moment, watched. Some small animal, most likely. She turned her attention back to the trapper.

He was definitely sniffing the trap.

It went on for several moments, and when he finally re-set the trap and moved along Migisi was sure he was possibly insane.

Perhaps her games had gone on too long.

And then she smiled to herself and turned toward the simple camp she called home. They hadn't gone on long enough, apparently. He was, after all, still in her woods.

Luc set the last of his useless traps, irritated the entire time that he continued to waste his time in a place where he'd had nothing but failure. The fact of the matter was that his enemy, his *fantôme*, had continued to confound him at every turn. He'd set the traps in new locations, tried camouflaging them better, even tried spying to discover his adversary, all to no avail.

Today, though... today, he'd managed something he hadn't before. He'd detected a scent, barely there, as if his enemy was so much a part of this very forest that its scent was indiscernible from his own. It was hard to describe; the same as the fresh scent of the forest, but, more. A warm undertone of something he couldn't quite identify. Luc trudged back toward the camp he shared with two of the other *voyageurs*. He'd come out later that evening and do more investigating.

As he entered the camp, he was met with the two Robillard brothers arguing, as always. Robert, the elder, was ready to move on to more fertile ground. Aaron, the younger, was determined to stay, as they'd managed to keep their location secret from the other trappers, and despite their bad luck, knew well that the area was full of mink and raccoon.

"Put it to a vote, then," Robert said, spying Luc as he neared the fire. "Stay, or go?"

Luc studied the two brothers. "I am staying. I can understand, however, if you choose to move on. We are losing money as we sit here."

"And should we work it out, we stand to be rich," Aaron said, looking pleadingly at his brother. "You know this, man."

"We've not trapped a single thing while we've been here," Robert said with a sigh. "Meanwhile, others are settling into areas probably nearly as good as this one, but without the unfortunate interference we seem to be facing. I still vote to move on."

Luc clasped his hands. Honestly, he would be thrilled to get rid of the argumentative brothers. "Here is a thought. What about the area we passed through on the way here?"

"Where the river divides?" Robert asked, and Luc nodded.

"That area was full of raccoon. And we were successful trapping there."

"Excellent. We move tomorrow," Robert said, clapping once for emphasis.

Luc shook his head. "I have a better idea. You two settle there, and begin trapping. Meanwhile, I will continue to work here, keeping our claim on this area. I can work at discovering the cause of our misfortune. And, if and when it is eliminated, you can come back and we'll get to work. And if not, then you've already established our presence to the west of here, and we can make our fortunes there."

"It's dangerous to be out here alone," Aaron began. Luc gave him a look of disbelief, and he shook his head. "I forget who I'm speaking to. Never mind," he added, and Luc let out a short laugh. The brothers eventually agreed to go and give it a try, and Luc barely repressed his sigh of relief. He'd met the brothers on his way north from Detroit, and, having learned they were all from the same area, the men struck up a quick, relaxed friendship that had eventually developed into a business relationship.

Luc grimaced. That would teach him to enter into agreements during alcohol-filled meetings.

Arguing aside, the brothers were actually very good trappers and decent businessmen. It would have been a fine arrangement if Luc ever felt the need for companionship for long stretches of time. But he didn't, and their constant presence grated on him.

After sitting with the brothers into the night, he excused himself.

He needed this.

He strolled into the woods, in the direction of his traps. Specifically, the one that had had that scent on it. Before he reached it, he began shucking his clothing: heavy hide pants and boots, a warm cotton shirt, heavy leather coat and hat. As soon as he was free of his clothing, he focused, and he felt the quick yet always-painful sensation that came with turning. Fur sprouted, and his already bulky body grew until he stood well over eight feet tall. Claws sprouted, bones popped, grew, re-formed. It left him breathless every single time, yet grateful.

He never felt so alive as he did when he took his animal form. Like his father and grandfather before him, he shifted into a bear, but one unlike any he'd seen in the wild. He had the size of the polar bears he'd observed on his seal hunting trips to the north, the deadly claws and long fur of a grizzly, and the pure, black coat of a native black bear.

In full bear form, he approached the trap, sniffed at it, focusing on the scent that had no business being there. A few moments later, the scent firmly in focus, he began following it; along the stream, through the woods, and finally, to a small clearing. He sat on his haunches, lifted his nose into the air. His trap vandal was here, for sure. A smallish structure, built with wood and covered in animal skins, sat in the center of the clearing, a wisp of smoke coming out through a hole in the top of the tent. As he watched, he could see the flap of the tent open. A small figure came through; thin, petite, dressed in warm-looking leathers, a long wool cloak thrown over the shoulders. Long black braid, and a voice murmuring words he did not understand.

A female voice.

He tilted his head in surprise, then ventured closer. She stilled, zeroing in on him. This woman was much more attentive to her surroundings than many people he was used to. They stared one another down. He nearly forgot his irritation over her continual sabotage of his traps. She was stunning, in every way. Long raven hair that shone in the moonlight, warm brown eyes, a narrow nose, and full lips. And her scent... no wonder he'd picked up on it so quickly earlier. She smelled better than anything he'd ever experienced: wild, warm, clean. An herbal scent clung to her like a veil, and he lifted his nose and sniffed at the air, breathing it, breathing *her*, in.

She was watching him.

She spoke words in a language he didn't understand, and he tilted his head.

She smiled, showing a flash of straight white teeth. She said more words in a language he did not understand, though this sounded, perhaps, like English. He tilted his head again.

She shook her head, and spoke a third time. "*Je ne ai jamais vu un ours aux yeux bleus.*" And, finally, he understood the words. She'd never seen a blue-eyed bear before.

Luc raised his head and sniffed again.

She continued in French. "I have been harvesting herbs. Is that what you're sniffing?" She smiled. "You. You are not all you seem to be, are you? I have never seen a bear as magnificent as yourself in my woods. And a bear that seems to understand French, no less."

He tilted his head at her in acknowledgment, sauntered closer to her small dwelling. She sat on a nearby rock and studied him.

"You are magical," she said breathlessly, admiring him, and it took everything in him not to puff out his chest in pride. "Stunning."

They sat in silence for several long moments, bear and woman taking one another's measure. "Shapeshifter?" she asked. "I have heard of your kind." Then she laughed, and the sound of it lifted his spirits. "I wonder if the man is anywhere near as magnificent as the bear."

He huffed out a breath, and she laughed again. And then, she stilled. He tilted his head at her again.

"Those eyes. Are you my adversary from the stream, perhaps? Have you come to exact your revenge on me?"

He knew then, that moment, that even if he had intended to hurt her, there wasn't a chance in all of Creation that he could now. He stepped behind some native holly bushes, wishing he'd thought to bring his clothing along. Taking a breath, he shifted back. He was impressed by how still she sat, though her eyes widened when he started shifting.

Once he was back in his human form, he and the woman studied each other in the cool night air.

"I am Migisi," she said, perfect French flowing from her lips. "And I think the man does the bear justice."

Luc smiled and bowed his head. "I am Luc, and I am freezing my testicles off."

She laughed, loud, clear, and full of such joy that he found himself laughing too. She went inside, then came out with a thick blanket, which she tossed toward the bush where he was sheltered. He wrapped up then stepped toward her.

"It is a pleasure to meet you, even if you have destroyed my business for the past several weeks," Luc said, and Migisi smiled.

"Well, don't try to trap in my woods, and we won't have a problem." She gestured toward the fire, and he nodded, seating himself on the ground nearby. He watched her, and knew, the way he seemed to know where the best places were to trap or when the weather was about to go bad, that this woman would change his life forever.

"Remind me why we're doing this again?" Sophie asked as she, Layla, and Cara rolled out their yoga mats on the wooden floor of the sunlit studio.

"Tourist season is over. This is how we help keep our friends in business until the next tourist season," Cara said simply.

"Yeah, but shifters don't need yoga," Sophie said, tugging at the elastic waist of her black yoga pants.

"We don't, but you like it and you need some relaxation in your life. And then Bryce gets to keep working until the summer people flood in again," Layla said, throwing a glance toward the front of the room, where Bryce was unrolling his own mat. He caught Layla's glance, threw her a smile. Cara and Sophie looked at one another and rolled their eyes.

As they did, they could hear two of the local non-magical women tittering, admiring Bryce. There was a reason the town's only yoga studio was so popular among the female residents of Copper Falls, and it had just about everything to do with the prime specimen of manly goodness standing at the front of the room. Sophie hid a smile when something sounding like an irritated growl came from Layla's direction.

The girl had it bad.

"Did you talk to Calder more about the curse yet?" Layla asked, changing the subject.

"Yeah. If I talk about it right now, yoga isn't going to do a damn bit of good for my mood."

"All right. Later," Cara said in her "don't even argue with me" voice.

Sophie gave a small nod. She'd slept like crap the night before, trying to work out Calder and his curse and panicking over what would happen if she lost everything. She had some savings, but they wouldn't get her far. She hated that she'd come to depend on the house she'd inherited from her crazy aunt Evie to be her lifeline. She'd never expected to actually feel safe there, or to feel her power steady, just a little, on land that generations of her family's witches had inhabited. She'd never expected to rediscover old friends or find creative, soothing work she was actually good at.

She cursed Aunt Evie again for letting the taxes pile up. And then she cursed Calder (though apparently not in the same way her ancestor had) for taking advantage of it all.

But at the same time, more than her own situation, she worried about Calder. From what he'd said, the curse was essentially torture. And as angry as she was with him for putting her in what was pretty much an impossible situation, she felt sorry for him.

Not to mention the fact that she'd dreamt about him every single night since he'd shown up on her porch, and she'd dreamed various degrees of things she shouldn't even be thinking about doing with Calder. She couldn't even think of the man without wanting to scream or cry.

Stupid hormones. Stupid stress. Stupid ancestors and their stupid curses.

She let out a breath and did as Bryce instructed the class: she tried to clear her mind, get rid of negativity on her exhales, take in positivity with her inhalations. Within a few minutes, she was still doing her best just to keep her shoulders away from her ears and unclench her jaw.

"Stiffer than a board, Soph," Bryce murmured when he walked past. "Relax."

"Trying," Sophie muttered, giving him a glare as she settled into a downward dog.

"Yes, I can tell," he said with a grin. She heard Layla laugh a little off to her side and rolled her eyes. She heard the tiny bell on the front door to the studio tinkle, and then she heard what sounded like a strangled growl behind her. She craned her neck to the side, still in her downward dog, and saw Calder there.

And his eyes were on her.

She stood up straight, glancing at him once more before turning toward the front, where Bryce was instructing them to raise their arms. As she did, he walked toward Calder. Sophie tried to focus on what she was doing, almost hyper-aware of Calder and the feel of his gaze on her.

"Hey, man," she heard Bryce greet him.

"Hey," Calder said, his voice a low growl. "I was around and just wanted to let you know those parts came in." Sophie heard the jangle of keys.

"Oh, thanks. I'll get the money—"

"I'll pick it up another time. I know you're good for it," she heard him say. And then the bell on the door tinkled again, and he was gone.

And it felt like she could breathe again.

She glanced to her left to see Layla studying her. She gave a tiny shake of her head, then faced the front again as Bryce started the next sequence.

Any relaxation she'd been heading toward was gone. She went through the motions, but the appearance of Calder, that growl, that expression on his face — there was no way to feel settled after that. That look had called to her in a way she couldn't have imagined, and she knew she was past the point where she could set aside any feelings she might have once had for Calder, because after just a few days, she'd developed new, stronger, less rational ones. She loved her memories of the boy he'd been. But the man he'd grown into was something else entirely, and he both thrilled and frightened her. And she had no idea what to do about that.

They finished, and then the twins dragged Sophie down the street to the diner their family owned. The Mine was a homey little place, decorated with mid-century Formica tables and chrome and vinyl chairs, a cheery combination of buttery yellow and vibrant red. A long red counter ran the length of it, with chrome stools arranged along it. The big front windows looked out onto Falls Street, which was pretty much where everything happened in town. The twins' mother, Joyce, hugged Sophie hard and told her they were there if she needed anything, and then she prepared some of her heavenly chocolate-banana smoothies and Sophie and her friends settled into a corner booth with them.

"Okay. Spill it," Layla said, stirring her smoothie with her straw.

Sophie took a breath, and she told them everything. Calder's ancestors, her ancestor, what the curse did (which immediately put both of the twins in defense mode, not liking the idea that Sophie lived so close to him in that condition). She left out her dreams about him, and the way he'd looked at her at the yoga studio. Layla hadn't missed it, though.

"I think you need to watch yourself," she said, choosing her words. "He wasn't looking at you like a man in a business negotiation, which is really what this is supposed to be. And he wasn't acting like an indifferent party at the bar the other night, either."

"I know."

"He wants you."

Sophie shook her head, waving it off. "I can't think about that now. I can't lose the house. And on top of that, I feel guilty by association. No matter how much I agree that his ancestor was a jerk, it seems a bit much for Migisi to have cursed him so completely that his family is still paying." She paused. "I mean, really... I get being hurt, but that seems like an amazing over-reaction."

Layla smiled. "Well. Maybe she had a gigantic ego and couldn't take the fact that he even dared to look at someone else. Or maybe theirs was such a passionate, intense relationship that it was destined to end the same way."

Sophie screwed up her face. "You read too many romance novels. Really, how intense could it have been? They didn't even speak the same language, most likely."

"I don't think the words said are what makes an affair passionate, if you know what I mean," Layla said with a wink.

"Back to the actual problem, though," Cara said, taking her usual role of bringing them back into focus. "You need to learn about the curse. The sooner you get this done, the better."

"If I can even do it at all," Sophie said. "So far, what we know is that she was Ojibwa. Maybe if I can learn something about her, it'll lead me to the curse, or to learning more about her powers, or something like that. I don't know where else to start."

Layla nodded.

"I'll check the library for any books, but I know that won't likely help with this," Sophie said, thinking. Then a thought struck her. "Do you guys remember Mrs. Redleaf?"

"From sixth grade?" Cara asked.

Sophie nodded, feeling more excited. "Remember her? She was Ojibwa, and she was a total history buff. Remember how she used to tell us those stories from her tribe, or how she'd piss off all the little white kids and their parents by pointing out all of the ways white people messed with her people?"

Layla laughed. "I remember that!"

"She lived on the reservation back then," Sophie said. "She can't be that old. She could still be around, right?"

Cara nodded.

"It's a start. I'll head out there and ask around. Even if she's not there anymore, maybe there's someone they can point me to who knows the history of the local Ojibwa. I'm half expecting to find out that Calder was full of crap and she wasn't involved, somehow."

"You're hoping, you mean," Layla said.

"Yeah, I'm hoping," Sophie admitted, taking a sip of her smoothie. "One of my people wouldn't have done this crap. It goes against every single thing we believe in. Lightwitches don't curse people. I think he's wrong."

"Well, girl, for your sake, I hope you're right," Cara said. They finished up, and Sophie made her way to her car, thoughts on when she'd find time to get out to the reservation. Better that it was sooner rather than later.

Calder ran, letting his bear, his beast, run off some of the excess energy and tension he was dealing with. He'd stuffed himself, buying and then devouring three sausage pizzas, following it up with a two-liter of Coke. It wasn't enough. It never was.

And none of it was what he wanted.

So he ran.

Sophie. Her name filled his mind, just as her scent seemed to be everywhere. The sight of her, bent over, her round ass presented perfectly for him, had nearly been his undoing at Bryce's studio. The way she'd turned at the sound he'd made, not even realizing he'd made it, the look of awareness in her eyes, the way she'd flushed a gorgeous shade of pink at the meeting of their eyes... shit.

So he'd left as quickly as he could, because the temptation to drag her away with him and make her beg, make her scream his name, was almost impossible to resist. And now, all he could do was run, let his beast run free, let it experience freedom. He, *it*, raced through the forest, powerful legs launching him through the dense trees, out of breath, heart pounding, muscles tiring, but unable to stop, because if he stopped, he'd have to feel it again. Exhaustion was his only savior, his only distraction from the never-ending hunger that was his life.

As he ran, he focused on not thinking. Not about her and her perfect ass. Not about his father and his insanity. Not about his brother and the way he'd been saddled with a life that left no room for actually living. And sure the hell not about himself and the way he could feel the curse strengthening every single day.

If he thought about that, he'd want to hurt somebody. And that would not go well for anyone.

CHAPTER EIGHT

Sophie decided not to waste any time. If she was going to figure this out, or prove to Calder that he was completely and totally wrong, she had to get going. She worked a short shift at the resort, then double-checked her map on her phone and headed down the highway, toward the Ojibwa reservation outside of town.

Finding the reservation wasn't hard. She'd passed it several times during the drives she sometimes took when she needed to clear her head. She drove the winding road through the woods, and when it wound its way along the coast of Lake Superior, she snuck several glances out at the sparkling water. The sun was shining, early autumn's low-slanting rays giving the canopy of leaves along the side of the road an almost stained glass effect. She drove with the windows open, the radio off. She watched the rearview mirror as well, years of habit ensuring it was something she never forgot to do.

Every time her thoughts went to Calder, she forced them aside. It was unnatural, really, how drawn she was to him. Maybe it was part of the curse? She dismissed the thought almost as soon as she'd had it. She knew better. There was nothing magical about the way she felt toward Calder. He was everything she'd ever imagined she'd want the man in her life to be: strong, handsome, with a sense of humor and a strong protective streak. The boy she'd known had grown into the single most mouthwatering specimen of manliness she'd ever seen.

Of course, he was also a monster. Which was pretty much her luck, so at least her life was consistent.

And he was determined to stay away from her. She had to admit that between the two of them, he was the only one acting with any kind of sense at all. He stayed on his side of the road, avoided her completely, and the whole time, she had to find ways to stay busy so she didn't wander across the road. To do what, she didn't know. Stare at him? Drool over the sight of his shoulders and forearms? It was stupid. And the even dumber thing was that even though he scared the living hell out of her, she kept remembering that night at Jack's, when she'd felt, of all things, safe. She'd felt safe. And if that wasn't insane, especially given what he'd told her about his curse, then she didn't know what was. The only thing she knew was that, when she really thought about it, he was the first and only thing she'd ever wanted, just for her. He wasn't something she needed. He wasn't something forced on her. He wasn't something she was forced to settle on because it kept her safe. In fact, he was pretty much the opposite of that in every way.

She just knew that when she looked at him, hard as she tried to fight it, the first word that came to mind was "mine."

And that was wrong, but it felt so damn right.

She shook her head as she maneuvered her car onto the dirt road that led into the reservation. A wooden sign at the side of the road welcomed friends and visitors to the home of the Keweenaw Community.

The reservation looked mostly like a small subdivision of modern houses. There was a long, low building near the center of the reservation, with a simple sign reading "meeting hall" near the front walk. Sophie brought the truck to a stop, parked it in front of the building. There were a few other cars around, and in the nearby playground, she could hear children calling to each other. She put the handles of her bag over her shoulder and headed up the walk, then the low concrete steps that led into the meeting hall.

When she opened the door, a small bell dinged. She looked around. There ware chairs, upholstered in a cheery orange fabric. Many houseplants. There was a counter in front of her, and to the left she could see a hallway that led to other parts of the building. She approached the counter, looking around. A few moments later, she heard someone call, "be there in a second," from one of what she guessed were offices behind the counter. Within a few seconds, she spied a woman making her way toward the counter. She was short, compact. Her long white hair was braided in a long rope over her shoulder, and she wore jeans and a warm-looking gray wool sweater. She greeted Sophie with a smile, and Sophie recognized her.

"Can I help you?" she asked, and her warm tone put Sophie immediately at ease.

"Hi. I'm Sophie. I have what might be an odd request," she said.

The woman smiled again. "It wouldn't be the first. What do you need, Sophie?"

"I don't know if you remember me or not. You were my teacher in fifth and sixth grade."

Mrs. Redleaf studied her, then smiled. "Sophie Turner?"

Sophie grinned, and the woman came around the counter with a smile, folded her into a warm hug.

"Look at you, home again! You and the Marlier twins were so much trouble sometimes," she said with a laugh.

"We still are!" Sophie said, and Mrs. Redleaf laughed again.

"Wow. It is wonderful to see you again. You've grown into a beautiful woman," Mrs. Redleaf said, and Sophie blushed a little, nodded her thanks. "What can I do for you?"

"Well, Mrs. Redleaf—"

"Thea, kiddo. You can call me Thea."

"Thea, then," Sophie said with a smile. "There's this story I heard about a woman who was supposed to be an ancestor of mine, and I know you were always a history buff, especially of tribal history."

Thea nodded. "Yes, indeed. Was she from around here?"

"Supposedly," Sophie said with a shrug. "I hadn't heard about her until a few days ago, and I don't quite even believe the person who told me the story was right."

"Well, we'll find out. This will be fun! Who was your ancestor? To be honest, you look like you may have some of the first people in you. I thought so when you were a little girl, too," Thea said, studying Sophie closely.

"My ancestor was named Migisi, according to what I've heard."

A look of shock spread over Thea's face, and she quickly schooled it into a neutral expression, but not before Sophie noticed it. "Migisi?"

"Yes. My aunt Evie lived at my cottage before me, and generations of my family before her, and supposedly, Migisi was the first one who lived there."

Thea shook her head. "I've never heard of Evie. I don't get into town much, though." She paused, looked unsure. "Migisi, you say?"

"You know her name?"

She smiled. "We all do, kiddo."

"How?"

"She has long been known among our people as *Nimaamaa*, or the mother. She was our tribe's first and greatest medicine woman. She healed. She healed," she repeated, closing her eyes. "Migisi's own."

"At least, I think I am. My understanding of our family isn't great. I inherited the cottage and land from Evie, and she said that land has been in our family since the early 1800s."

Thea nodded slowly. "That would have been when Migisi lived there." A look crossed her face, and she looked uncertain.

"What is it?" Sophie asked.

"My dear, are you sure you want to start digging?"

A cold prickle went down Sophie's spine. "I kind of have to," she said softly. "Why?"

"Migisi was known as *Nimaamaa*. That is how we choose to remember her, because she deserves to be honored that way. But it is not all she is remembered as."

I don't want to know, Sophie thought to herself. "What else?" she forced herself to ask.

"She was also known as *Ninishkaadiz*."

"What does that mean?"

"More commonly, 'the Mad,' she answered, looking away from Sophie. "We try not to call her that. But if you start digging into this, it will come up."

Sophie stared at the woman. "That's not entirely unsurprising. I've heard things that would indicate that she wasn't right." That would be putting it mildly, she thought to herself, thinking of Calder. "I need to know. It's important. I know this is a weird request, but would you help me? Would you tell me what you can about her? Or could you point me to someone else who can?"

Thea studied her. "I will help you. I need you to answer a question for me."

Sophie stilled, watched her. "Yes?"

"Do you take after her?"

Sophie stayed silent. "I'm sure I don't know what you mean," she said softly.

"I think you do. Do you take after the mother or the mad one?"

"What do you know of it?"

"I know enough to know life is more than those things we can see, more than those things that can easily be explained away. If we are going to begin digging, I need you to trust me. And I need you to be honest with me."

Sophie stayed silent for several long moments, then took a breath. "I am not mad," she finally said.

Thea took her hand. "Neither was she. That is not who she was, or what she was. Whatever happened later, it wasn't her."

Sophie squeezed her hand in thanks, for some reason, more touched by the woman's words than she could understand. "Could she speak French, do you think?" she asked, remembering the conversation she'd had with the twins, and the language barrier.

"She spoke it well, by all accounts," Thea said. "English as well, in addition to our own language." Then she smiled. "Knowing that *Nimaamaa* spoke French was the reason I learned it in the first place. I chose it as my required language in college, though I don't remember much." Her face softened. "Know that no matter what else she was, she is one of our most beloved ancestors. Whatever happened to her later... it doesn't undo the amazing things she did for us."

Sophie took a deep breath, nodded. "Is there anything I can do to repay you? I don't know how much time this is going to take, or—" she began.

Thea waved it off. "It is my pleasure to help you. We will look through our archives. I know there are articles and other items of interest about her."

"That would be a huge help. Thank you so much."

"And if you can shed any light on what I know, or you find out anything in your research, I can add it to our archives," Thea said.

Sophie smiled. "I think that's a great idea. We can do that."

Thea held out her hand, and they shook on it.

"When can we start?" Sophie asked.

Thea glanced at the clock behind the counter. "I have a youth meeting I need to attend in a few minutes. It won't take more than a half hour or so for my part. If you wouldn't mind sticking around, we can get to work right after. Most of those old files are in storage in one of the back offices here, and you can help me dig them out."

"Thanks so much. That sounds great," Sophie said. She watched as Thea shut down computers, turned off lights, and checked windows. Then she followed her former teacher out of the building, and toward another building. "This is the youth center. Mostly, it's a large gymnasium where they can play basketball and run off some of their energy when it's cold out," Thea explained. "There are a couple of small meeting rooms here for study groups and our youth group."

"What does the youth group do?" Sophie asked.

"Mainly, they talk," Thea said, shrugging a little. "They meet weekly, and they talk to each other about school or their families. It's part friendly gathering, part support group, I guess. This group has been meeting like this since they were very young. I'm going today because sometimes they have speakers come in, and they want me to tell them what I know about getting into college. I've been helping our young people with the admissions and financial aid process for years," she added.

Sophie smiled. "Would have been nice to have had someone like you around when I was a teenager," she said.

"Where did you end up moving to?"

"Just outside of Detroit. I lived there until nearly two years ago."

Thea nodded. "It must have been an adjustment."

"It was. I was homesick for this place for years. So when I had a chance to move back, I grabbed it."

"And was that difficult after so long away?" Thea asked, glancing at her, maybe picking up something in her tone.

"Actually, it was exactly what I needed. I feel like I belong here."

They entered a small room, and for the next forty-five minutes she listened to Thea field questions about applying for college and getting financial aid. She had a genuine rapport with the teenagers, and Sophie thought, again, how great it would have been to have had someone like that around at that age.

When her part of the meeting was done, the teens thanked Thea, and the two of them left, the sounds of the group discussing the next item on the agenda behind them.

"Such good kids," Thea said. "Really, most of them could go to their parents and ask the same questions. This group, though," she said with a smile. "They believe in making things happen for themselves. They want to learn something, they bring someone in. It makes it fair, so that those who don't have a family member they can go to have the opportunity as well. The kids in that room are going to make all of us proud. I can tell," she finished, and Sophie smiled.

"They're much more driven than I was at that age," Sophie said, and Thea laughed.

"Kiddo, they're more driven than most adults I know, period," she said, and Sophie nodded. "We can go back to the meeting house. I have a frozen pizza there we can heat up so we can eat first."

"Oh! I didn't even think — we can do this another time, really."

Thea waved it off. "Not a chance. I am dying to dive into the archives and see what we can find for you."

Thea let them into the meeting house, and through the offices toward the rear of the building, where there was a small kitchen. "We use this for some of our community dinners. Also when someone's sick, usually a group will get together here and cook a few meals for them."

"It sounds nice," Sophie said, sitting at the long table in the center of the room. She watched as Thea set the oven and pulled a disk out of the freezer. She'd expected to see a boxed frozen pizza like you get at the grocery store, but this was obviously something homemade. It was wrapped in cling wrap, with parchment paper beneath it.

"You clearly know how to do frozen pizza better than I do," Sophie commented, and Thea grinned.

"Pizza is a gift. It should be treated as such. And homemade is the best," Thea said, and Sophie nodded in agreement. While the pizza baked, the two women sat at the table.

Thea pulled a piece of white paper out of the printer nearby, drew a symbol on it. "I'm wondering if you've seen this before," she said, sliding the paper over to Sophie.

Sophie inspected it. It looked something like an arrow, but where the feather fletchings would have been on the end it looked almost like birds in flight, wings curving gracefully. To either side, of the arrow shape, were smaller, simple shapes that looked like crescent moons.

Sophie shook her head. "What is it?"

"That is Migisi's rune. I have the feeling that, were you to look around your land, you'd likely see it carved into tree trunks. There were stories that the runes helped protect her land."

"How do you know that?" Sophie asked, still looking at the paper.

"We have journals, articles in the archives from her day. Before things went bad, as I mentioned before, she was a renowned healer. She wrote to members of the tribe. She always signed her letters with her name and this rune. Most healers have one." She pulled her eyes away from the paper, looked at Sophie. "I feel like there are things you're not telling me, kiddo."

"There are. They're not my story to tell. Not entirely. If we come across references to them, I'll explain what I know. I'm hoping we do."

Thea nodded thoughtfully. The oven timer started beeping, and for a while they sat in companionable silence, eating their pizza. Once they'd finished and cleaned up, Thea led Sophie back to another room, this one full of long black metal filing cabinets and rows and rows of bookcases, almost like a miniature library. "Our community here, thanks to one of our predecessors, has always been devoted to recording our history, including personal stories, spoken histories that we transcribed and stored. We know, all too well, how easy it is for people to get written out of history, so we make sure we write and remember our own."

Sophie nodded. This sounded exactly like the Mrs. Redleaf she'd known so many years ago. "I think it's sad that more communities don't do this," she said. "Imagine all of the stories that get lost over time."

"It is a shame," Thea agreed. They maneuvered their way down a narrow pathway between two rows of bookcases, Thea scanning the shelves as they passed.

"Here we go," she said, stopping before a section of black-spined books that looked, to Sophie, just like all of the other books they'd passed. "So, what do you want to hear about first? We have a bound book of newspaper articles written about Migisi and her work with the community. We have collected correspondence. And we have stories people she knew shared about her."

"Can we start with the stories first?"

Thea nodded, pulled one of the books, this one fairly thick, from the shelf. They headed back to the room with the long table, and Sophie pulled a notebook and pen from her bag.

They began reading, heads bowed over the book. It was written in Ojibwa, so Thea read aloud while Sophie took notes. Most of it, while interesting, was useless as far as Sophie was concerned. Story after story about Migisi, as a young woman, healing this child or that elder, or helping crops that were failing, or speaking words to bless a hunt and men returning with record-sized deer or bear. Over the next couple of hours, two things became evident: Migisi had been the ultimate do-gooder, and it sounded, to Sophie at least, as if she had never denied a request for help, no matter how insignificant. There was a story from a woman who remembered asking Migisi to heal an ailing sparrow that the woman, who was quite lonely after the death of her husband, had become attached to, and Migisi had done it, and the sparrow lived for another five years, and by the time it died, the woman was no longer lonely, having found love again.

"This explains how she was so powerful later on," she murmured, noting that the dates of the recollections were from when Migisi would have been a teenager.

"What do you mean?" Thea asked.

"A Lightwitch's magic becomes more powerful with each good, kind deed they use their magic for. She did all of this in the span of a couple of years."

"And these are likely just a fraction of her deeds. These are just the ones we managed to record," Thea added.

Sophie nodded. "Right. And what I've heard, from two people now, is that she was ridiculously powerful at her peak. This is how she got that way."

"Has this answered any of the questions you have, though?" Thea asked.

Sophie blew out a breath, shook her head, trying not to be irritated.

"It's a thick book, kiddo. We have a lot of reading ahead of us," Thea said, patting her hand.

Sophie nodded. "Thank you for your time. I wish it had been more interesting."

Thea gaped at her. "Are you kidding? I loved every moment of this. And we learned that she was good, and we have recollections of some of her recipes, which you wrote down, I noticed. Her thoughts on popular books of the time, which she discussed, apparently, with those she was helping. She was very well-educated."

"Does that fit with what you already knew of her?"

"Everything I know from the stories told of Migisi is that she had an insatiable mind. She spoke our language, French, and English, as I mentioned before, simply because she wanted to."

Sophie helped Thea clean up, replacing the book in its original place, then they headed out, and Thea locked up. "Have you heard any stories about a Frenchman and Migisi? Like a romantic relationship?"

Thea looked uncomfortable, and that was the instant Sophie knew that there was something to Calder's story.

"What?" Sophie asked.

"She was rumored to have had a French lover. A fur trapper."

Sophie watched her, trying to keep herself calm. "Do we know anything else about this trapper?"

Thea's phone started ringing. She glanced at it. "My grandkids have arrived," she said.

"Oh. I should go. Thanks so much again for your help."

"When will you come back?" Thea asked. "I want to read more!" she said with a smile.

"When will it work for you? I work most weekdays."

"Same time on Friday?" Thea asked, and Sophie nodded. Thea walked her out, locking the front doors behind them when they stepped out onto the front walk. It was getting dark, and Sophie cursed herself for losing track of time. Especially since it had been pretty much a waste. Now she'd have to do her evening chores in the dark. She hated having to juggle the flashlight along with everything else. And now, with Marshall around, she was even less happy about being out in the dark.

They walked toward Sophie's car. "You asked about the trapper," Thea reminded her.

Sophie nodded.

"The stories we have... Migisi the Mad. That all starts with him. The stories go that he was the first victim of her madness. I don't know all of the details. There was supposedly a curse."

"Was she 'the Mad' before the curse?" Sophie asked.

Thea shook her head. "After. Whatever it was, whether it was regret or guilt or something else, the stories say that she slipped into madness afterward."

"Wouldn't you have to be kind of nuts to curse someone in the first place?" Sophie asked, unlocking her car door and setting her bag on the passenger seat.

"It depends. I can see the value of cursing someone who deserves it. Don't you? Haven't you ever heard of someone, or known someone, who just deserved to have bad things happen to them?"

A face flashed to her mind immediately.

"It still seems a little extreme. Especially if it made her go mad afterward."

Thea shrugged. "Maybe we'll learn the whole story. I'll see you Friday."

Sophie thanked her again, got into her car, and watched as Thea climbed into a shiny silver pickup truck. She gave Sophie a wave as she drove past, and then Sophie put the car into drive.

On her way down the highway toward her house, she tried not to be too frustrated and irritated over what little they'd accomplished. She had learned a few things. Useless as far as Calder's curse was concerned, unfortunately.

She did have one key piece of information, though. There had been a French lover, and the story that he'd been cursed was known to more than just Calder and his family. So it was something, at least. She wasn't sure if that made her feel better or worse. She had kind of been hoping she'd be able to tell Calder he had the wrong witchy family.

As she neared her property, her headlights swept across the driveway, illuminating a yellow rose near the road. She took more than a little pleasure in running over it.

It was pathetic. Maybe it was something with being there in Copper Falls. Maybe it was feeling like she had some control over her life for maybe the first time, ever. Maybe it was age and maturity, or maybe she'd just reached the point where her anger was stronger than her fear. Whatever it was, she was more angry at Marshall and his games than anything else. Where he'd terrorized her before, he enraged her now. Without a doubt, he still freaked her out. Memories, too many memories, of his threats, written in his hand, whispered in her ear... too many.

Maybe she was angry now, finally, because she realized how she'd lost part of herself trying to get free from him. That was power she'd had to work very hard to get back. Once you profaned your power, as a Lightwitch, it wasn't easy to make amends.

Which brought her thoughts back to Migisi. The Mad. It had obviously made Thea uncomfortable to have to break that to her. And though she hadn't pressed, Thea hadn't seemed all that ready to share exactly what her "madness" entailed.

If the rumors were true, if what Calder knew was true, it had all started with Luc.

She got out of the car, taking her bag with her. She also flipped the top on the canister of pepper spray on her keychain, just in case Marshall managed to get by her wards and surprise her. He always did like the sneak attack.

She knew that, tired as she was, she wouldn't sleep, expecting every single sound to be him.

CHAPTER NINE

The next morning, Sophie showered, dressed, and put on some makeup, mostly to hide the dark circles under her eyes. Another night of nightmares, of jumping at every sound.

She hated it. And she was torn between wanting to hide in her house forever and wanting to go back to the way things had been before Calder, and then Marshall, had thrown her life into chaos.

Concrete plans, she told herself. Lists, action steps. Focus on things she could actually do, because focusing on anything else would drive her insane. She wanted to stop by the tiny library in town to see if they had any books about local Ojibwa. It was a small step, but at least it was something.

She did her morning chores, then got in her car, eyes darting around her, expecting to see a face, dark hair, dark eyes. But she knew better. He'd made his presence known, knowing it would mess her up. He'd bide his time now, letting her wonder and jump at every sound, until he left her any other "gifts."

She drove into town, keeping her eyes on her rearview. She made a quick stop at the hardware store, then into the library, where they had two pretty old books about local Ojibwa. She checked both of them out, then walked a couple of blocks down to The Mine to have some of their double chocolate cake and a cup or five of tea. She brought her books with her, figuring she could start poring over them while she ate. She also had her pen and notebook. She could use something else to focus her mind on for a while.

She walked into the diner, placed a quick order when the waitress, who was one of Layla and Cara's younger cousins, greeted her. She settled into one of the booths in the back where she could see the front entrance easily.

Old habits never really died, she realized. It felt like the past two years hadn't even happened. Different place, same nightmare.

The waitress brought her cake and tea, and she dug in, started flipping through the pages of the first book. It was a compilation of journals and letters written by an Ojibwa chief in the early 1900s. After Migisi's time, but maybe there would be a hint of her descendants or something.

She kept glancing at the door every time the bell tinkled. So when Calder walked in, she saw him right away. And, as seemed to be the case with him, he noticed her right away as well.

He walked toward her booth. Lumbered, really, was a better word for it, his huge frame seeming to fill the tiny diner.

He stopped at the side of her table, studied her for a moment or two before opening his mouth.

"Hi," he said, and Sophie nodded in response. "Can I sit here?"

"Can anything I say I stop you?" she asked, raising an eyebrow in irritation.

He watched her wordlessly, seeming to try to decide what to say. "If you tell me to go, I'll go," he finally said. "But I hope you don't, because I have something I want to talk to you about."

Sophie nodded after a moment, and he slid into the booth. The waitress came over and he ordered coffee, black. They sat, awkward, trying not to look at one another until the waitress brought his coffee. She caught Sophie's gaze over Calder's head and gave her a thumbs-up. Sophie did her best not to grimace.

Calder was looking at the books she had on the table. "Any luck so far?" he asked after gulping down some of his coffee.

She shook her head. "Not yet, but I really just started reading. I don't expect to find much, but you never know."

He nodded. When she finally raised her eyes to his, he held her gaze for a few long seconds and then she forced herself to look away. When she looked back up at him, he was rubbing a hand over his face, agitated.

"Are you going to tell me what the deal was with that rose the other day?" he asked her. She looked away again. "You looked like you wanted to cry. You were shaking. And you look like you haven't been sleeping. You keep looking at that door like you're expecting the devil himself to come through."

"What does it matter?" she asked, meeting his gaze.

"You can't focus on my problem if you're distracted," he said.

Sophie looked up at the ceiling, let out a bitter laugh. "Right."

"And if you want me to be honest, I had this vision of you as being this cool, collected person. Even when I won your house, you didn't bat an eye. I think I was used to seeing you holding it together, and you were about to fall apart the other night. So I'm guessing that whatever that rose meant, it wasn't anything good." He paused. "And I'm not that far gone yet. It pissed me off to see something scare you that bad."

"Because you need me focusing on your issues, not mine."

"And because you actually seem to care about my problem, despite the fact that I've been an asshole about it."

Sophie didn't answer. He drank more coffee, and she stirred her tea listlessly.

"I did some sniffing around that night. There was someone new at your house. But you already knew that," he said.

She met his eyes. "That's not at all intrusive," she murmured.

"I was waiting to hear a scream or something, the way you looked. So I passed some time sniffing around in my bear form," he said, irritation lacing his tone. "A trace of power, too. Warlock?"

She gave a short nod.

"He was gone by the time we got to your house. There was just a faint trace of him leading through the woods to the west of your cottage. It ended at that road over by the falls."

She sat in silence. "It didn't circle in toward the house at all?"

He shook his head. "Straight line, pretty much, from your driveway, to the western edge of your property, then to that road."

"Thanks," she said. "I think that's good news. The wards protecting the property seem to be working, for now, at least."

"Who is he, Sophie?" he asked quietly. "Let me know who I need to hurt."

She shook her head. "You're not going to hurt anybody."

"Whoever he is, he deserves it, I think," he answered. "I have no problem putting on a little punishment. Really, it would probably make me feel better."

"He deserves it. But I won't stand for you causing any pain on my behalf," she said.

"Why?" He seemed genuinely curious. "You're terrified. Clearly." His gaze dropped to her hands, which were wrapped around her teacup, for warmth. He gently took one wrist in his enormous hand, and a shiver, though not an unpleasant one, went up her spine at the touch. He turned her wrist so that it was facing up. She didn't have a chance to pull away before he noted the series of pale scars across it. She pulled both hands away, onto her lap. "Sophie. Tell me," he said quietly.

The intensity in his gaze made it hard to concentrate. "You have to promise me not to hurt him."

"Why?" he asked, irritated again.

"Do you know about the different types of witches?" she asked.

"What? What does that even have to do with this?"

"Do you?" she pressed.

"No. I didn't even know there were different kinds," he said. "Does it matter?"

She stared at him incredulously, and he held his hands up. "Okay. Apparently it matters. Explain, please."

"The witches people tell stories about, the ones who have demonic familiars and cast spells that cause plagues or fires or whatever, those are known as dark witches. Shadow witches."

"Okay," he said.

"They're rare, but they're a lot more famous than the other type. The others are your do-gooder witches. The ones who were their village's medicine women. They heal, and help things grow, and try to help others. They work in the Light, so they're generally known as Lightwitches."

He was watching her.

"My understanding of it is that Shadow witches can do pretty much whatever they want with impunity. Their souls aren't really their own, so any damage they do, doesn't really affect them all that much, though after they're dead, they supposedly become slaves to demons. I'm not sure about that, but that's the word. But the others—"

"You're a Lightwitch," he said, and, after a moment, she nodded.

"So was Migisi," she added quietly.

"I would have thought she was the other kind."

"What you told me the other day about the curse and what I already knew about my family's magic... it proves something I'd kind of already suspected, but wasn't entirely sure about."

"What?"

"The idea is that as long as a Lightwitch uses her magic for good, she will continue to be powerful. That, in fact, if she does enough good, she can become one of the most powerful beings in existence. Doing evil goes against everything we are. And when we abuse our power, when we cause pain or let pain be caused in our name... we are punished."

"Punished, how?" Calder asked.

"Our power twists, turns. Dissipates. I guess that explains why my line is so weak in magic now. The curse Migisi put on your line was a terrible thing. It goes against everything we're supposed to stand for, and, even in my limited knowledge, I know that doing something like that has a cost. Any evil we cause, as Lightwitches, comes back to us. So when she did that, she cursed her own line as well by default," she finished.

"What does this have to do with the warlock and the rose?" Calder asked.

"If you hurt him, I would rejoice in it. I would cheer you on, Calder. I would stand there and watch him bleed and be happy about it. And my magic would suffer. I don't have much as it is, and you expect me to break this curse.

And I need to break it so I can have my house back." She grimaced. If she could even live there in peace, now. Something to deal with later. "If you want this curse lifted, you need to stay out of it."

"What if I took care of things in secret?" he asked, stubborn.

"I'd know, Calder. It would affect me. Promise," she said.

"Who is he?" Calder growled, enraged that she was asking, no, demanding, that he not punish someone who'd obviously hurt her. He may not have held the blade, but Calder was positive whoever had been at Sophie's house that night was responsible for the pale scars on her wrists.

She was watching him, those warm brown eyes seeming to see into the deepest reaches of him, the parts he tried to avoid thinking about. "He stalked me for over eight years."

Calder just watched her. "What else, Sophie?"

"It started when I was fifteen," she began, and he heard a snarl trying to rise deep in his chest. He forced it down, determined to hear it all. "He followed me everywhere. And I did a good job of keeping myself safe, first with locks and just being careful and, later, after he became more determined, with wards." He watched as her fingers toyed with the edges of the white napkin under her tea cup. Her fingernails were short, her hands delicate-looking. "At first, it was just creepy watching. Showing up places he knew I'd be. And then phone calls started, after a couple of years. He just got more aggressive as time went on, until it got to the point where I was completely alone, just waiting for the day I slipped up." She took a breath. "I called the police, finally. The officer in charge of my case disappeared before it went anywhere, and he had no problem admitting to me that he'd taken care of it, that whoever else I went to, including my dad or whoever, would disappear as well. So I kept it to myself, because I knew he would do it."

She looked up at him again, a small, sad smile on her face. "It got worse. My mom died suddenly the next year, and we never were able to figure out the cause of death. And then my father had his accident when I was eighteen, and I had nothing. So I hid, and I went to work. I married a sweet man who loved me."

That made Calder want to rip someone apart.

"And he killed him," she finished quietly, and all of the rage went out of Calder. "I don't even believe I'm telling you all this. I guess I still think of you the way you used to be. We used to do this kind of thing a lot," she finished with a small laugh, a roll of her eyes.

He wanted to tell her. Wanted to tell her that sitting and listening to her had been his salvation when his dad had first started showing signs of the curse, that she had been his rock when he'd felt the first signs of the curse in himself. He watched her, and wanted to tell her every bit of it, and realized it would only make things worse. He'd crossed a line the moment he'd decided to blackmail her, and he had no business, no right, to be in her life now. He'd tell himself that, yet here he was. "You're not telling me everything," he said.

"It's enough."

"Enough to make me want to rip his throat out, yes," Calder answered, and she shook her head. "I won't, at least not right now, because you asked me not to. But I want to."

She smiled again, and this was a more genuine smile. It actually reached her eyes, and he remembered how much he really loved the way her eyes warmed when she smiled like that. She didn't seem to do it all that often anymore.

Or, maybe she just didn't do it around him.

"And then I was nosing around your property, marking it as my territory... that must have brought back some negative shit for you," he said after a moment, the realization hitting him.

"Well. It's not the first negative thought I've had toward you," she said, and he had to laugh at the matter-of-fact way she said it. "I'm not kidding though, Calder. Stay out of it."

"What about if I just wander your woods sometimes, and, if I happen to come across him, I scare the hell out of him? Can I do that much? Give me something here."

She laughed again, and it nearly took his breath away. That was still the same. When Sophie felt something, she didn't hide it. Joy radiated from her when she laughed, and when she was angry, she wore it like a cloak. He had the feeling she did everything in her life thoroughly. He realized, sitting there with her, that she was, always had been, the most alive person he'd ever known.

He glanced back down at her wrists, at the scars she'd now hidden beneath the sleeves of her gray sweater. The most alive person he'd ever known. And someone had hurt her, scared her so badly, that she'd wanted, maybe, to give up on her life.

"You can scare him," she said, watching him. "Chances are, you won't be lucky enough to even get to do that much, because he's very good at disguising his presence. But if you do manage it, I want you to be careful. He's powerful, and evil..."

"Are warlocks the same as witches? So would he be a Shadow warlock?"

She nodded. "So you see what I'm saying. He has no issues with using his powers for evil and he is a hell of a lot more powerful than me. Okay?"

"Give me some credit," he said, and she rolled her eyes.

"Can I ask you something that's been bothering me?"

"Sure," he said, watching the way she leaned forward, the way she focused on his face, as if she could read the answer to her questions there. Maybe she could.

"Why didn't you and Jon ever tell the rest of us you were bears?"

"We told Cara and Layla and Bryce once we all got older," he said. "It must have been after you moved." He knew damn well it had been. He hated lying to her, but he pushed it away. "We're in a town of wolves. They're not especially fond of bears. It just made more sense to keep it to ourselves. I mean, they knew, if they sniffed around enough. Layla and Bryce figured it out without us telling them." He shrugged. "Considering everything else my family has going on, having the local wolf pack on our asses because we were going around yapping about being bears seemed to be the last thing we needed. We kept to ourselves."

She was watching him, and it made him want to tell her anything she wanted to know.

This entire situation is nuts, he thought to himself.

"Was there any weirdness with Layla and the rest of them over the bear thing?" she finally asked.

He shook his head. "Nah. By the time they realized it, we had all been friends for a long time."

"I think Layla might have suspected it was you on my property."

"That does not surprise me."

She laughed a little, and damn, did he want to make her laugh some more.

"I should get going. I have reading to do," she said, starting to rise.

He choked back the protest that immediately rose to his lips, the urge to ask her to stay. Knew, now more than ever, that it wouldn't be welcome. "At least tell me you can protect yourself if your wards fail or something," he said, standing up with her.

She flashed him a smile, and his gut twisted. "Calder, I can probably shoot better than most of the loud-mouthed hunters around here. I trust in my wards and what little magic I have. If the day ever comes where my magic isn't worth fighting for, know that I can pull a trigger just fine."

And for some reason, that really, really did something for him.

As if every word out of her mouth, every single gesture she made, didn't already do something for him. She drove him insane, and he wanted more.

"I will keep that in mind," he said.

"Good." And with that, and a small smile that made his entire body warm, she turned and walked out of the diner, calling a "bye" to the waitress as she left.

He sat back down, wiped a hand over his face, thanked the waitress when she topped up his coffee. His mind ran through his conversation with Sophie.

He'd keep an eye on her property. He'd try to stay away from her, he promised himself. That wasn't a complication he needed just then, anyway. Even as he made the promise, he knew better. He knew he was hers, absolutely drawn to her, and that staying away was nearly impossible.

After sitting for a while, downing a couple more cups of coffee and trying to figure out his Sophie problem, Calder took a deep breath and headed out. As much as he could have easily spent the entire day brooding over Sophie, the reality was that he had the fallout of the curse her ancestor had set to deal with.

He got on his bike and drove out to the two-lane highway that led out of town. He went in the opposite direction of the way he usually went to get home. Instead, he went inland, away from the coast, deeper into the woods. The longer he drove, the signs started showing up, signs for the state forest in which his father and brother lived.

He loved driving through the woodsy areas of the state. The trees almost made the highway feel like a tunnel, the foliage just starting to show the first tinges of fall color. The air smelled clean, and he could drive miles, sometimes, without coming across another car or bike.

As he neared the land his father had owned for the last thirty years, he steeled himself for what he'd see. He turned left, drove up the long, winding driveway that led deeper into the forest, into the thirty acres his parents had bought, knowing they'd be raising shifter kids, wanting to allow plenty of space for Calder and his younger brother to run.

It had been great until the summer Calder had turned thirteen, which was the same summer his father started showing the first signs of the curse that would eventually destroy him.

His parents had put off having kids, his father dead set against passing his curse onto anyone else. Even knowing it would just jump bloodlines and infect a cousin or whatever... he didn't want to do it. And his mother had been on board with that. So when they found out, just before Robert, Calder's father, was about to turn thirty-five, that she was pregnant, it had thrown both of them for a loop.

They'd come to embrace it, and Calder grew up hearing about how they'd comforted themselves with the fact that, when Robert's curse finally hit, at least she wouldn't have to deal with it alone. She'd have a child, and, they both knew, a son, by her side. And, hopefully, she wouldn't live long enough to see that son taken by the curse as well.

It had all sounded great until that summer. Calder's dad had been in his late forties by then. And on the full moon that July, he'd seemed to have lost his mind. Calder still remembered that night, his mother sitting with the shotgun in her lap in the rusty old pickup truck, driving with it across her thighs, just trying to stay away from Calder's father. Jon was only ten at the time, and was asleep between Calder and his mom on the truck's bench seat.

When the sun rose the next morning, and they knew Robert would be asleep, his mother had dropped the boys off at the cabin, hastily packed a few things, and was gone.

They'd never seen her again. And, to be fair, they really didn't bother looking.

And then he'd lost Sophie, his one light in what was quickly starting to be a nightmare, when her dad suddenly moved the whole family down to Detroit. And he'd never told her about what was happening, because he'd been ashamed to admit what he was.

Calder shook off the memories as he brought his bike to a halt near the side of the log cabin his father had built. It wasn't a big house, but it had always been comfortable, and for a long time, he'd felt safe and happy there.

He didn't bother going inside.

Instead, he went around to the rear of the house, down a well-worn path that led to a thicker part of the woods behind their house. At the end of the trail was the twelve-foot tall iron fence that surrounded the small cabin his father lived in, when he could think to go inside.

But a giant bear had no need for a house, and one that was out of its mind had even less use for one.

Today, like most times Calder came to visit, he found his father pacing back and forth across one end of his prison. In bear form, of course. His thick black fur was matted and filthy, and Calder wished, stupidly, that he'd at least pull it together enough to groom himself again. His gaze was flat, his teeth yellow, and yet still so long, so sharp, it took almost no effort at all to destroy.

Which was why the fence was necessary now. And, even more, why it was, these past few months, also electrified. And Calder knew that, unless Sophie could break this curse, he'd find himself inhabiting the same prison someday.

He smelled his brother nearby. Within a few moments, Jon was standing beside him, arms crossed. They watched their father pace back and forth, occasionally growling or howling in his insanity.

Neither brother spoke for a long time. Jon finally broke the silence. Jon always did.

"So Sophie's our witch, huh?" he finally asked, and Calder nodded, eyes still following his father. "I didn't want to believe it at first. I know it's hard on you. Can she break it?"

Calder forced himself to look away. "She has almost no magic at all. She thinks, and it makes sense, I guess, that the curse that got us came back to bite her line as well. We get this," he said, glancing at his father, "and her family gets a little less powerful with each generation that passes."

"Fuck," Jon groaned. "I guess that explains why Evie was so useless."

Calder kept watching their father. "She's going to try. We kind of have her at our mercy. She needs that house more than I realized." He hated himself for saying it, hated that it was true. But seeing his father again, feeling the curse working its way, more rapidly with each passing day into his own life, only reaffirmed that they'd done the only thing they could.

"And if she can't, we probably have no chance at all of ending this. If the magic only gets less powerful..." Jon said.

"I know," Calder said.

"You have to make her break it. Do whatever you have to. We can't live like this anymore. And I'll tell you right the fuck now that I can't stand by and watch you like that, after going through it with him. I fucking can't, man."

Calder watched his brother.

"I'm sorry," Jon said, trying to collect himself.

"You don't have any reason to be. I'm sorry. You're stuck with this and at least I get a break from it."

"Yeah, but you're also stuck with the curse, so I still think I got the better deal. I'm sorry for laying that on you. Last night was rough. I swear he sounded like he was getting murdered out here."

Calder nodded. "Almost full moon," he said, and Jon nodded.

They stood together in silence for a while. "What were the odds that it would be her?" Jon finally asked.

Calder didn't answer.

"I know this isn't easy on you. You didn't like the idea in the first place. And then for it to be her... Someone out there has a fucking sense of humor. I remember how you were about her."

"We were kids," Calder said, trying to keep any emotion out of his voice.

"But you loved her. And I know you. The way you were acting the other night, it's clear that's not over. I'm sorry. It's shitty. Does it change things? Because I need to know." Jon watched him, waiting.

"It makes it more complicated. She's still the same. Sweet. She's not evil. It would be better if she was, maybe."

Jon was quiet again, seemed uncomfortable.

"What?" Calder asked.

"She wasn't exactly unresponsive to you the other night, either. Surely you could smell it." Jon paused, gauging his reaction. "That's maybe something you can use, if you have to."

Calder blew out a breath. That was the last thing he wanted to think about. "He looks like shit."

Jon took the hint. "I don't know how much longer we can let him go on like this. He took Grandpa out before he got this bad."

"I know," Calder said. "And there is no 'we' in this. When the time comes, it's my problem. You've had to deal with this all this time." They stood in silence for a while. "We'll give him as long as we're giving Sophie. If she can't break it by the solstice, we won't let him suffer anymore after that." He transferred his gaze to his brother. "Okay?"

Jon nodded, his shoulders bunched with tension. They both knew it would be their job to put their father out of his misery someday. It should have been done before now, if Calder was being honest with himself. As soon as it became clear that his father was unable to take his human form, they should have ended it. A shot to the head, maybe two, if his bear was as tough as he looked.

But Calder had banked on this, on finding the witch from Migisi's line and breaking the curse.

It had to work.

"How are you holding up?" Jon asked, breaking him out of his thoughts.

"I can feel it. This full moon is going to be a bitch," he said, and his mind went, first and foremost, to Sophie. He really would have to talk to her. Give her one more reason to dislike and distrust him. "I'm not too far gone yet, though."

"You want me to come and look out for you? We know he's not going anywhere," he said, nodding to his father, still pacing in his prison.

Calder shook his head. "You're just as much a bear as I am. You need to get out and run. Maybe even more than I do. Take care of yourself. All right?"

Relief flooded Jon's expression, and Calder realized how much he'd been looking forward to running as his bear during the full moon. It had that way of making a shifter feel alive again, and, Calder guessed, he needed that pretty badly, considering what he saw every day.

Calder clapped Jon on the shoulder, gave his dad another glance, then the brothers walked around the house. Before he drove off, Calder promised to keep his brother updated about any headway Sophie made with the curse.

CHAPTER TEN

Sophie finished scrubbing out the toilet, humming a little to herself as her mind raced, trying to think about any spells she might have heard mentioned that had anything at all to do with breaking curses. Between that and running through what she'd learned from Thea about Migisi, it felt like her mind just kept spinning. And, really, it was best that way, because when she let her mind wander, it seemed to wander in the one direction she most definitely didn't want it to go.

So much better to think about life-destroying curses than to start dwelling on the man who'd been cursed. That was a road she could not travel, for about a million different reasons.

So, curses.

The thing was, Lightwitches didn't usually deal with curses. At all. As she wiped down the countertop, then the large mirror, Sophie turned over the tiny bits of knowledge she'd gleaned from the few books and websites dedicated to Lightwitch knowledge and history she'd managed to get her hands on. For the most part, the information about curses amounted to: just don't. Don't do it, because that profanes the magic the Light has given to us. Don't do it, because curses go against every single thing a Lightwitch stands for. They stand for everything a Lightwitch was created to fight against. There is no such thing as a benevolent curse.

Sophie finished up, gave the hotel room a final glance, then carried her cleaning supplies with her, set them on top of the cart in the hallway. She wheeled the cart down to the next room, knocked softly. "Housekeeping," she called, and, after a few moments and no response, she opened the door with her master key. She got to work, stripping the bed, opening the drapes. She headed into the bathroom, mind still on Migisi and Luc. She flipped the light on, and screamed in surprise.

She clamped one hand over her mouth and stared at the man standing before her. She reached behind her to the small pistol in a holster at her back, pulled it out, keeping her eyes on the man.

Him. It was him, and he was here, and she was not in a warded place. His dark eyes watched her every movement, dark, wavy hair, tanned skin, perfectly pressed suit giving him the appearance of authority and affluence. He stood watching her, hands clasped comfortably behind his back, as if he was merely waiting for her to compose herself.

"Sophie. Little girl, how I've missed you," he said, a voice so deep, so warm, like dark melted chocolate. Alluring in every way. Shadow doesn't work through fear and horror. No. Shadow comes looking like a dream, sounding like salvation. And she knew this mask almost better than she knew her own face.

"Marshall," she said, focusing on magic, on keeping her personal wards, those that would at least prevent him from touching her, intact.

"Miss me?" he asked.

She started backing out of the bathroom, not wanting to be in such an enclosed space with him. An almost lazy flick of his fingers, and the bathroom door slammed shut before she could go through it.

"You disappoint me, Sophie," he said, voice still smooth, still almost tender. "You ran from me. Leaving like a criminal in the dark of night. You hid your tracks well, little witch. It seems you learned a thing or two along the way."

She held the gun tighter, prepared, if she had to, to use it.

"You are not going to use that against me. We both know it."

She trembled, tried to force herself to stay calm. It wasn't just that he was physically imposing, though he was, towering a foot taller than she was and at least three times as broad. It wasn't that he even acted all that threatening, because all he did, really, was stand there. That was as it always had been.

It was in knowing that he was stronger than she was, and it irked him that he couldn't break her wards. He tried, even now, standing before her, looking for all the world as relaxed and casual as it was possible for a man to look, to break her. She could feel his magic, dark, slithering, oily feeling, testing her wards, resorting to brute force only after finesse didn't work.

He grinned, sharp white teeth glinting under the fluorescent light over the sinks. "You've gotten stronger, my little witch."

"What are you doing here, Marshall?" she asked, forcing her voice to stay calm.

He ran his hand over the marble countertop. "Did you really think you could hide from me forever?"

She didn't answer.

"Well. At least I know you won't be running from this place. That land, huh? I wondered when you'd finally make your way back here. Safe haven and all that." He smiled again, a smile that, for those who couldn't feel what he was, could have made them do anything he wanted. Even knowing what he was, it was hard not to react to it. She never denied that the Shadow was powerful. She just relied on her faith being stronger.

"Of course, it's more than the land. Curses, old loves. History. History is a beautiful thing, especially when I already know how this chapter will end."

She felt her magic holding strong, though he'd begun, yet again, to test her. She wanted to bolt, but she knew he'd just chase her, or, worse, reappear where she was trying to run to. She knew, after all these years, that he'd test her, that he'd taunt and threaten her, that he'd try to get her to lose her focus, and then, growing bored of the game, he'd leave until next time.

"Yeah? Well, I know that this particular chapter will end with you failing to break my wards, just like every time before."

That wiped the smug smile off of his face.

"Don't get smart, little girl," he said, voice still smooth. "It's not about wards anymore. I have you right where I want you. All I have to do now is wait and let the pieces fall into place." He smiled again. "Of course, that doesn't mean I'll stop trying to break your wards. I have to admit, the last couple of years have done good things for you. It'll be even more rewarding to make you kneel."

"I just threw up in my mouth a little," Sophie said, forcing herself to sound calm. "If that's all, I have work to do."

He laughed. "Sure thing, witch. Go back to scrubbing your toilets. It's all you're any good for until the day I break your wards, anyway." He made a lewd gesture with his hand, and then, as if he'd never been there, he was gone.

Sophie wasted no time in opening the bathroom door and stumbling out into the main part of the room. She kept the gun in her hand, leaned back against one of the walls, taking deep breaths and trying to calm down. This was his thing. This was exactly why, when she'd tried to report him for stalking and threatening her, no one had believed her. He was so smooth, good-looking, confident. He never let anyone overhear the things he said to her. And, of course, no one other than the two of them knew that when they faced off like that, a battle was being waged. She was exhausted from trying to keep her wards intact, exhausted from holding strong against the merciless assault he exacted upon her.

She was fighting, yet again, for her body and her soul, her sanity, her free will. Because if he broke through, he could overpower her so easily. And if that happened, she wouldn't want to live to remember the things he'd make her do. This, she knew for sure.

She pulled herself together, holstered her gun, and finished up the room, forced herself to move on to the next room rather than run screaming for home.

There were stories. Well-documented stories in the books she owned about Lightwitch history and practices, about Lightwitches who'd been defeated by Shadow. How they'd been degraded, humiliated, forced to use their Light-given magic in ways it was never meant to be used, until one day it just faded away completely. After that, they were often murdered.

Burning at the stake was a popular method. The 1600s had been a dark time for Lightwitches, and a period of victory for Shadow, who used their powers to stir hapless humans into violent mobs.

Of course, there were other stories as well. Stories about Lightwitches who turned their back on the Light willingly, seduced by Shadow. Those, every book agreed, were lower than low. Those beings, the books proclaimed, had never been deserving of the magic they'd been given in the first place.

Was Migisi one of them? It certainly looked like it. And it both shamed and worried Sophie that she had that in her history, in her bloodline. She'd rather die than betray the magic she'd been given, especially after working so hard to build it, to learn about it, to make it work.

CHAPTER ELEVEN

Sophie had Layla and Cara helping her go through the rest of the attic. At the pace she'd been going, the chances of getting through it all alone in time to make any difference to Calder and his curse were slim. As they sorted, they talked and joked and sang along with the radio Sophie had propped up on one of the boxes.

They were on hour two, and had about three-quarters of the attic sorted. Sophie listened to Cara teasing Layla about Bryce, and she smiled to herself, pushed yet another crumbling cardboard box out of the way. She knew she didn't have to do it all that day, but she didn't have to work and all of her orders were filled for her soap business, and the twins were available. And it helped to stay busy.

It was better than letting her mind wander. When that happened, she started feeling panic settle in over Marshall's appearance in her life again. Or, Calder's face, those ice blue eyes, and, more specifically, the way he'd looked at her at Bryce's studio. She really didn't want to think about either man, but, just then Calder felt like the more dangerous. She knew what she faced with Marshall. She knew damn well he was dangerous, devious. Obsessed, and more than a little psychotic. All of that, she knew for a fact.

But Calder was something else. Drop-dead gorgeous, protective, gruff and wild. The boy she'd once loved, and a man worth daydreaming about, all in one package. It was a combination that made her heart pound, made her want things she knew better than to want. She wanted to trust him. She wanted to accept the protection she knew she'd find in his arms.

She'd been down this road before. She'd believed, stupidly, that she could have a life, a marriage, someone to protect her from the cold, dark nights. For six months, she'd lived in wedded bliss with a man she'd met at work. They'd dated, and he'd asked her within a year to marry him. As ashamed as she was of not loving him the way he deserved, she'd said yes anyway, because everything seemed a little less terrifying with someone warming the bed beside her at night.

Six months later, out of nowhere, he was dead. She came home from shopping one day to find him in the bathtub, wrists slit. Marshall had laughed through her grief, proudly taking credit for driving him to it. There was no way to convince the police otherwise, and they'd deemed it an open-and-shut suicide.

"Let this be a lesson, little witch. You belong to me, whether you believe that or not."

She would rather die than let anyone be hurt like that again. So she'd take the long, cold nights, and she'd take the loneliness, because losing him that way, no matter how weird things were between them now, would destroy her completely.

"Hey," Layla said, and Sophie jerked her mind to the present, focused on her friend.

"What?"

"What's wrong?"

Sophie shook her head. "Just thinking."

"You look like you just lost your best friend or something," Layla said.

"Guys," Sophie said, knowing they needed to be warned. "Marshall found me."

She was immediately overrun by a barrage of questions, promises of threats to his nether regions if he hurt her, and promises of protection. She held up her hands.

"I need you to listen," she said, and her friends both sobered. "You're both a couple of badasses and I love you. I know your first instinct is to stand around here guarding me now. I need you to not do that. I need you to go on with your lives, and if you see him around at all, especially if I'm not there, I need you to run."

"But—"

"He uses people I care about to get to me. To try to break me. I need you to do this."

Both of the twins watched her silently. She could read easily in their faces how much they wanted to argue, how much they both wanted to run out in wolf form that instant and track him down. They'd drawn the story out of her, bit by bit, in her first few months back. They knew what he'd done.

"Maybe we could get the jump on him," Cara said, and Sophie shook her head.

"I didn't even want to tell you, because I know you want to hurt him. I also know that, strong as you are, he would end you. Or worse. Please don't make me deal with another David."

They both pulled her into their arms at the mention of her dead young husband's name. "Promise me," she said, voice muffled against Cara's shoulder.

"Okay. Okay. We promise," Layla said.

"Watch yourselves. Run if you have to."

They nodded, promised again.

"I'm so sorry, sweetie," Cara said, squeezing her again before releasing her. She studied Sophie's face. "I hate to even say this, but do you think maybe you should just leave? This thing with Calder, and now Marshall showing up... Maybe it's time for you to disappear again."

Sophie shook her head. "I need this land. Now more than ever. This is my best chance of protecting myself and anyone I care about from him. My magic is getting stronger. I need it. And I'm not leaving Calder to deal with this curse alone. If I can break it, I will. I need to find a way."

Layla hugged her again, looking both relieved and annoyed at the same time that Sophie wouldn't be running.

That settled, they each retreated to the corners of the attic they'd been working on, and work continued in silence, the mood definitely darker than it had been before.

Sophie sorted through three more boxes, carried down another box of stuff for the dump, lined it up in the kitchen with the others. She trudged back up the stairs. She was really getting kind of sick of the attic, but there was no doubt that it was looking better. She shoved another box of what looked like threadbare fabric out of the way, and behind it, sitting in one of the corners of the attic, was a black steamer trunk, its sides battered, scuffed.

And it was warded.

She smiled to herself. "Please be what I'm looking for," she whispered as she crouched in front of it. She ran her hands over the trunk, sensing for the wards. They weren't complex, but she could feel familiar power in them.

She opened her eyes and looked at the trunk. The wards had been set by one of her ancestors. And one with, from the feel of it, at least a decent amount of magic.

"What's that?" Layla asked. The twins had come over at her muttering to herself.

"This trunk is warded," Sophie said with excitement.

"It could just be some ancestor's collection of witch porn or something," Layla warned, trying not to let Sophie get her hopes up.

"Witch porn? Really?" Sophie asked, laughing.

"Oh, come off it. I have no doubt that witch porn is a thing," Layla said.

"I wouldn't know," Sophie said, rolling her eyes. "I need some stuff so I can open this." She stood up and left the twins in the attic, heading back downstairs.

She went back and forth across the cozy living room, gathering herbs, candles, matches, a few stones she used often.

Many wards, the maker would work into it that they could be opened if the right person came across them. This was like that, but with an added twist, from what Sophie had seen in the few moments she'd focused on the ward. The person had to have enough skill or magic, or probably both, to be able to counter-ward it.

It was one of the frustrating things about her magic, Sophie thought as she rooted through the kitchen drawer, looking for her spare needle. She understood magic just fine. She could see how even the most complex of spells worked. It wasn't a mystery to her. Which made it even more maddening that her meager amount of power prevented her from actually doing so many of the spells she saw.

She found the needle and put it in the pile of other things. She was just about ready to go upstairs again when there was a knock at her door.

She took a deep breath to fight back the panic that immediately rose, hating it. She knew damn well it wasn't Marshall. Her wards, the wards set on this property by her ancestors, kept him away, and she appreciated that.

Why it let Calder through, who was very likely the one standing on the porch by the sound of the heavy knock, was impossible to say.

Sophie peeked out the peephole and saw that, yes, it was him. She shook her head, forced her impassive face on, hating the way her heart sped up at the sight of him. She unlocked the three locks she'd installed, then pulled the door open, bracing it with her foot.

He was standing there, and it was like every cell in her body screamed for him.

She wondered if maybe her ancestor hadn't cursed them all. The way she wanted him, even though it was the last thing in the world she should want, was terrifying.

"What?" she asked as she opened the door, and it sounded even bitchier than she'd meant it to.

"I need to talk to you a second."

Sophie shook her head. "I'm a little busy trying to break curses and things like that. Can it wait?"

"Not really," he said, watching her. "It won't take long. Look. The full moon is tomorrow night."

"It is," Sophie said, watching him. He blew out a breath, and she watched him roll his shoulders. He was so tense, so angry. "Can we get to the point, Calder?" she asked.

His eyes narrowed in irritation. "Fine. I'll get to the point. Tomorrow night is the full moon, and, as I might have mentioned, I have less control during the full moon now that the curse is taking over. And for some stupid reason, my beast seems to really, really be interested in you, Sophie."

It was impossible to breathe.

"So do us both a favor, all right? Either go away for the night or lock yourself in and stay there until sunrise. I'm strong and I will do everything in my power to stay away, but it's..." He broke off, shaking his head. "I don't want to scare you. I definitely don't want to hurt you. Can you go away for the night? Please?"

"Nope," she said.

"Why not?" he asked in disbelief, crossing his arms over his chest.

"Because this is the safest place right now with that psycho around again."

"Did you miss the part where I turn into a bear that's out of its mind because of a curse? And that it's unsatisfied and endlessly hungry and that, oh, right, it's taken more than a bit of an interest in you? What part about that says 'safe'? I can promise you, kitten, that I'm a hell of a lot more of a danger to you than some piece of shit warlock will ever be."

She shifted, pressing her thighs together. What the hell was it with this man? Why was it that when he said things like that, things that should terrify her, her body was ready to see if he was up to it? And that "kitten" was something that should have pissed her off completely.

"First off, I am not a cat, Calder, and you haven't earned the right to call me any pet names at all. Second, if I had to choose between insane bear you and perfectly sane him, I'd take my chances with the bear. I'm not running. I will stay in my house if that'll make it easier on you. All right?"

"Are you always this stubborn?" he asked, shaking his head.

"Always. Bye now," she said, closing the door in his face. She heard him grumble something as she re-locked everything, and then his heavy footsteps on the stairs as he lumbered away. She shook herself out of her Calder-induced lust haze and gathered her materials.

"Calder?" Layla asked as she walked back into the attic.

"Calder," Sophie said in irritation.

"You poor horny thing," Layla said.

"Shut up," she answered with a roll of her eyes.

"We can take you to Jack's again. Scratch that itch with a hot shifter, you'll be good as new," Cara said. Sophie shook her head.

"It's not the itch that's bothering me. It's him," Sophie said. "Now be quiet so I can do this."

"We should actually get going. I have the feeling this might be personal. I know you like your privacy," Layla said, serious now.

"Thanks," Sophie said with a smile. "You two are amazing."

"We know," Cara said. The twins hugged Sophie and left, promising they'd be careful and also that they'd lock the door behind them. Once they were gone, she looked at the chest again.

She knelt by the trunk, arranged the candles around her, lit them with her matches. She arranged her herbs, stones nearby. They might not be totally necessary, but she'd found that her magic was more focused if she had them nearby. She ran her hands over the lid of the trunk, murmuring a spell of entrance, one she'd only ever read in books, mostly because her focus had always been on keeping people out, not on getting in anywhere.

She felt her meager power rising, felt her own magic doing what it was supposed to do, tangling, weaving itself into the magic in the wards. It went on for a while, and with each time she repeated the spell, her power became more enmeshed with that of the warding spell, until it felt, to her, like they were one. She used the needle to prick her index finger, barely feeling the pain of it, feeling apart from herself in her connection to the magic. As her blood dripped onto the trunk, the magic peaked, and the wards fell.

Sophie took a deep breath of relief, in disbelief that she'd actually managed it. She sucked on her finger and looked at the trunk. There was a latch on the front, and, when she touched that, it sprang open easily, as if all it had been waiting for was her touch.

She leaned forward and lifted the lid of the trunk. There wasn't much in it. A few linens, not in the greatest of shape, but it seemed as though their real purpose had been cushioning the simple pine box in the middle of the trunk. Sophie lifted that out. The lid opened on creaky iron hinges, and, inside, there was a stack of old books. Journals, she figured, based on the glimpses of handwriting she saw as she quickly flipped them open. Three of those, then, on the bottom of the pile, there was another volume, wrapped carefully in layers of linen.

Sophie gently set the other journals aside. Those, she felt, were meant for her, too. But she had to hope that this one, this book that had been wrapped and protected so carefully, was what she was looking for. She sat cross-legged on the dusty attic floor and started unwrapping the linen, first one layer, then another.

Once the final layer of linen wrapping was removed, a thin volume with a dark brown leather cover was all that remained. On the cover were markings she didn't recognize, carved into the leather itself.

She opened it gently, carefully, after wiping her hands as well as she could on her jeans. The first page was blank, and she turned it. It was remarkably well preserved, and she sent a thank you to whichever of her ancestors had so carefully stored it. On the second page of the journal were lines and lines of what she soon realized were words written in French in a neat, exacting hand. The script was small and neat as if the writer had taken just as much care in forming his or her letters as they did in deciding what to say.

She turned several more pages, finding, to her dismay, that they were all in French or what she guessed was Ojibwa, the words similar to those she'd seen on signs near the reservation. There were spells that would give a witch power to read any language and understand it. Without that, many spells would have been lost after their original casters had died. Most witches, it seemed, kept some kind of journal to pass on what they'd learned.

One more thing to add to the list of things she needed to learn, like, yesterday. She needed to find that translation spell.

Sophie scanned the pages, looking, hoping, for some hint that she'd found what she was looking for. Interspersed with the pages full of neat handwriting were several drawings, watercolor paintings. The first one she flipped to, she recognized. Copper Falls. The falls themselves, after which the town was named. She'd spent nearly every summer day as a child there with her friends. She'd kissed Calder there. She'd gone there and cried after her father had told her they were moving away.

She hadn't yet made time to visit them since she'd been back even though the falls were the thing about the town, besides her friends and land, of course, that she loved most. She looked at it for a while longer, then started flipping through pages again.

And then, about halfway through the journal, there it was:

Migisi, And, later, Luc.

Maybe this was Migisi's herself, or maybe someone who knew her or had studied the curse....

Or maybe it was just one of those records of ancestry, saying who gave birth to whom.

But. Luc's name indicated that maybe that wasn't it, because from what Calder had said, Migisi's children had not been from Luc.

And that would be really weird if they had been, considering how hot she was for Calder. She grimaced and stood up, gently cradling the book against her chest. She set it on top of the other journals, then blew out her candles and collected everything. She carried her spell tools and the books downstairs and fell into bed just as the sky was starting to lighten in the east. She had to work in a few hours, after all, and she'd learned over the years that dealing with Marshall was more difficult when she was tired.

Too many things to worry about, and not enough power to fix them with. It was the story of her life.

Sophie pored over the journals as she drank her tea the next morning after she'd finished up with the animals. She had a short shift at the resort later that afternoon, but until then, she'd see if she could make any progress on the curse.

Of course, there was also the advantage that by working in her house all day, she wouldn't risk coming across Marshall again. She'd been awake most of the previous night, despite her intentions to rest. She'd lain in the small bed in the living room, the one set into a nook surrounded by bookshelves, under a quilt someone had made a long time ago. It should have comforted her. It usually did. Instead, she'd lain awake remembering a dead husband and the warlock who'd murdered him. And when she wasn't remembering that, she was thinking about Calder. About Layla and Cara. About how much she risked all of them just by being in their town, but how she also knew she was the closest thing they had to protection if Marshall decided to try to use them against her.

She'd been young, and stupid, and careless, or she could have protected David, too.

Thinking about her young husband raised so many feelings in her, none of them things she actually wanted to be feeling. She was sad, guilty. Mostly guilty. She hadn't been in love with him, not the way he'd been in love with her. She'd cared for him, of course, and they'd been good to one another. There had been a sweetness there that she never would have expected, not for her. But he'd ended up dying because of her, and she wasn't even good or loyal enough to have loved him. She'd been a liar, and he'd paid the price.

And Calder... Calder had been her everything for years. The situation they were in now didn't change that, didn't change the fact that when he looked at her, when he was near her, all she wanted was him. That was something she'd have to keep to herself, because if Marshall realized, there was no way it would end well.

Sometimes, she wished she had it in herself to put a bullet in his head and end it all. She envied Migisi's ability to curse someone so completely, and then felt immediately ashamed for the thought.

This wasn't the time to lose faith or get careless. She was a Lightwitch, she'd had to remind herself over and over again. She'd find a way to handle it that didn't profane everything she believed in.

So she'd woken, feeling raw, as if even the slightest push, the smallest thing, would make her fall apart. It wasn't a good place to be, and she knew the only way to feel better was to sit with it, to go through it. Doing it in the sanctity of her little cabin, on her land infused with the magic of her ancestors, was like a balm. It soothed. And, the longer she sat with it, the more determined she was to do right by herself, and by Calder. She would fix it. She would be the kind of woman, the kind of witch, she'd always worked toward being. And no filthy, conniving, Shadow-sworn warlock would take that from her.

One of the books seemed to be a sketchbook, a few small paintings amid the black and white drawings. She barely spared a glance at that, leafing through the written journals instead. That's where her answer would be. After looking through them for a while, hoping to recognize words that would tell her she really was on the right track, Sophie got up and started flipping through some of the old leather-bound volumes about witchcraft she'd collected over the years. Secondhand shops, used book stores, and garage sales had been great for finding them. Of course, to a non-witch, they often just looked like those old Readers Digest Condensed Books every thrift store in the universe seemed to be overstocked with. A witch could tell, though, could see through the wards that disguised it to non-witches. It was handy to be able to hide things in plain sight, sometimes.

Sophie finally found the translation spell after going through four other books. She sat down on the daybed with the thick book and started reading, slowly and carefully, the section that talked about language spells. When she got to the translation spell itself, she grabbed her notebook and pen off of the nearby table and started jotting the steps down in simple English. Older witchcraft books, especially, tended to be long-winded and full of description. And while that was lovely to read, the way Sophie used her magic, she really just needed a straightforward recipe or instructions to make it work. It was never pretty or flowery, and it often felt like surgery instead of magic, but given enough time and focus, she could usually make most spells work, at least a little bit.

This one actually didn't look too complicated, and Sophie double-checked the materials she'd need, as well as the spell she'd need to recite.

She heard a clattering, clanging sound outside, and she got up and went to the front window. When she glanced toward Calder's house, she saw the source of the noise. She could see him, just inside his garage. It seemed like he was looking for something, since every few seconds, something, usually something large, metallic, and therefore noisy when it landed, would get chucked down his driveway.

Her windows were open to let in the cool air, and she could clearly hear more than a few curse words coming from across the road in a loud, growling voice.

She glanced at the kitchen, where there was a large apple pie the twins' mother had sent over with them the day before. She hadn't yet had any of it, not really feeling all that much like eating. She stood up, stepped into her shoes, and grabbed the pie.

Always hungry, she thought to herself. She knew he was likely feeling the effects of the full moon coming on (something she was really trying not to think about too much) and that a piece of pie wasn't likely to help all that much, but it never did hurt, either.

She crossed the road, watching what looked like the front grille for some old car come flying out of the garage, followed by a bellowed "fuck" as a crashing noise came from inside the garage.

"Cease fire," she called as she started walking up his driveway. He came stalking out of the garage. His gaze was on her immediately, his entire body practically bristling in his current state.

"What are you doing here?" he snarled at her.

"Good morning to you, too, crab ass," she said, keeping her voice light.

He glared at her, and she shoved the pie into his hands, trying not to see the way his muscles bulged under his t-shirt, the way he looked like he was about to devour her, that intense look in his eyes.

"Pie?" he asked, his voice low and hoarse. He hadn't yet taken his eyes off of her.

"Yes. It's perfect and it's guaranteed to put you in a better mood. Taste it."

"Rather taste something else," he growled, and she stared at him in disbelief. He clapped a hand over his mouth, eyes widening, seeming equally shocked by what he'd just said. "Shit," he said behind his hand.

She couldn't help it. The sight of big angry Calder standing there with his hand clamped over his mouth as if he was a little boy caught cursing by his mother or something was too much. She started laughing, and soon, she was covering her own mouth, trying to stop and finding it impossible.

"I don't think it's funny. That was mortifying. Can't you make the earth swallow me up or something?"

She forced herself to stop laughing. Really, it was better than paying attention to what his words had done to her body. Unfortunately, he hadn't missed it. She noticed him scenting the air, and his gaze refocused on her.

"You can stop that, Calder," she snapped at him.

He shook his head. "Really though? Pie?"

"Yes, pie. Eat something. I know you're hungry, right?"

"Pie is not gonna do it, Sophie," he said.

She crossed her arms and glared at him until he released a low growl, opened the bakery box, and used the fork she'd shoved inside to start shoveling flaky apple pie into his mouth.

"Want some?" he asked between mouthfuls.

"I think you'd rip my arm off if I dared reach for any," she said in a wry voice, watching him eat. It was as if he couldn't get the mouthfuls to his lips quickly enough. It wasn't disgusting, though. Every movement was controlled, and she realized then, watching him, how much effort he put into keeping hold of himself. She knew, from the half-crazed look in his eyes, that he was feeling anything but controlled.

"Smart woman," he said. She shook her head. "You should leave though before I finish this. Your scent is driving me fucking nuts right now."

"I don't know whether to be insulted or not," she said, walking down the driveway, irritated at the way her heart was pounding.

"This pie smells good. You smell like heaven. Stay on your side of the road," he said.

"You're welcome," she shouted at him from across the road. "Stop beating up on your car parts now."

She thought she heard a low chuckle from his direction, and she shook her head, went back inside and started getting ready for work.

CHAPTER TWELVE

Sophie was in the laundry room at the resort, pressing and folding white towels to restock the housekeeping carts with. She had her earbuds in, feeling safe enough to do so in the cozy room, facing the door, back to the industrial-size dryers. She was bobbing her head to the White Stripes, trying to keep her mind blank, because she was tired of thinking, and if she let herself think about Calder's warning for that night, the full moon, she'd start panicking.

When Layla came through the door, Sophie smiled in surprise, plucked the earbuds from her ears. "Hey! What are you doing here?" she asked her friend as they hugged.

"Wanted to check on you. How are you holding up?"

Sophie shrugged, grabbed another towel to fold. "I'm all right."

"Have you seen Calder yet today?"

Sophie blushed. That growl, his words.

"Yeah, I guess you have. Bryce said it's probably not going to be pretty. Are you sure you don't want to stay away from your house tonight? We can go out to eat, and you can spend the night at my place. We'll binge-watch something on Netflix and eat too much. Sounds great, doesn't it?"

Sophie smiled at Layla. "I love you. You're the best," she said.

"But you're not going for it," Layla said.

"Even if it is as bad as everyone seems to think—"

"It's bad. Bryce said he went to check on Calder during the full moon a few months ago. He said it was terrifying. And he's going to be going nuts, because he wants you." She waved off the protest Sophie had been about to make. "Don't deny it. That look at Bryce's place the other day. That night at Jack's. And I don't even know what happens when the two of you aren't out in public. He wants you. I'm telling you, as a totally sane shifter, that that's a hard thing to go through, to want someone, to crave them, to be able to smell them and not have them. And he's not in the right mental state." She shook her head. "I'm scared for you, sweetie. Okay?"

"Have a little faith," Sophie said with a smile, taking her friend's hand.

"That's your department. You really believe your Light magic is going to keep you safe from this?"

Sophie gave Layla's hand a squeeze. "I have good wards. I'm on protective land. I have guns," she said, which made Layla laugh a little, which had been her intention. "I'll be fine."

Layla sighed. "I know you, Soph. You're going to hear him, you're going to see him, and you're going to want to try to help. You can't help him. If you try... I mean, he pretty much said it would be bad, right?"

Sophie nodded. "I'm staying in my house, behind all of my wards. I'll add wards. It'll be fine. Believe me, running is tempting. It is. But I feel like, my ancestor did this. I need to at least see what it does. I owe him that much," she finished more quietly.

"I can come stay with you," Layla said.

Sophie shook her head.

"You want to be alone."

"I love you, but yeah. Whatever happens tonight, I'd rather go through it on my own. It's what I'm used to."

"I wish you'd get over that. You're not alone anymore. Learn to lean on others, at least sometimes."

Sophie squeezed Layla'a hand again, then released it. She didn't voice the main thing that kept her so separate. Those she depended on almost always ended up hurting. She wouldn't let it happen to Layla.

They sat for a while, talking about nothing, and Sophie filled her in on what Thea had told her about Migisi. Once they neared the end of Sophie's shift, Layla gave her a hug and got up to leave.

"Be careful, all right?" she said in Sophie's ear. Sophie hugged her harder.

"I'll be fine."

Sophie kept one eye on the western horizon as she fed and milked the goats, not even bothering to change out of her work clothes first. Once finished, she locked them securely in their small barn, carried the pail of milk into the house, then headed back out and secured the chicken coop door. She quickly picked some salad greens, then headed into the house, bolting the back door behind her.

She washed the greens, turned on the kitchen radio, then turned it back off. She didn't want to be distracted. She forced the salad down her throat without really tasting it, then went into the living room, lit a fire in the wood stove, then went to the large gun cabinet in the corner of the room. It had been Ava's, though Sophie had stocked it with a newer shotgun. She loaded it, locked the cabinet. That done, she glanced out the window again.

The sun was just setting.

Sophie lit a couple of her white candles, for protection. Added a couple of stones to the floor in front of both doors, ran her hands over the locks, the doors themselves, as she chanted her favorite protective spell. She was relieved to feel her magic twining with the wards that already existed. In her current nervousness, it would have been all too easy to lose focus.

"My bear is interested in you." Calder's words echoed, his warning from the other day.

Once the wards were as strong as she could make them, she sat on the floor in front of the heavy oak door, leaning her back against it, her shotgun across her lap.

Now all that was left to do was wait. And hope for Calder that maybe he'd been wrong. Maybe his curse wouldn't be too bad. Maybe he had more time than he thought.

That hope was immediately dashed the moment her living room was mostly blanketed in darkness, the flickering of candles, the flames in the stove the only light, augmented by the shining moonlight coming in the windows. A pained roar echoed through the woods, sending chills up her spine.

"Please hold, please hold, please hold," she begged her wards, then began chanting her protective spells.

The next time she heard the roar, the agonized, rage-filled, confused sound filling her ears, it was closer.

And then he roared again. She knew it was no normal black bear. Not sounding like that, so full of anguish, as if he was in actual pain. Tears sprang to her eyes.

He roared again.

Again.

The walls of her tiny cottage seemed to tremble with it. Her ears ached. Her chest hurt, and she whimpered, resting her face against her knees as she kept up the chant. She could feel her wards being tested.

He was close, but not too close. Apparently, her wards had deemed him too unsafe to let him on the property. She sent a silent thank you to her ancestors, hoping with all her heart that they heard it, that they felt her gratitude.

Another anguished roar, full of frustration. Another.

She chanced a peek out the side window, toward the woods in the direction of his house. What she saw nearly took her breath away.

He was enormous. Much larger than any bear she'd ever seen. Midnight black fur against the bright moonlight. And he stood at the boundary of her property, roaring in rage and agony, his muzzle raised to the sky, powerful haunches struggling, trying with all his might to crash his way through the invisible barrier keeping him away from her.

"Oh, Calder," she whispered. He was terrifying. She could see his huge teeth the next time he opened his mouth to roar, foam dripping from the corners of his mouth. He grunted and growled and pushed like a mindless monster against the wards.

She couldn't look anymore.

Sophie sat back down, back against the door. She considered turning the stereo on as loud as she could, but it seemed unfair. Her ancestor had caused this. If he had to go through this agony, this madness, the least she could do (aside from breaking his curse) was listen to it.

He sounded like he was in pain.

She closed her eyes and held her shotgun on her lap, and chanted and listened, bearing witness to his agony.

It went on all night.

His growls, his angry howls never ceased, only growing more enraged, more agonizing as the night went on. Sophie sat, motionless, and listened to his anguish, his desperation. Once she realized that her wards would hold, fear was replaced by pity, but, more, by anger. How could Migisi do this? What could possibly drive anyone to curse anyone in this way? The longer she sat, the more she hated Migisi and her vile curse. Her eyes kept darting to the journal, the one with Migisi's name in it. She'd find the spell to break it. It had to be in there somewhere. If not, she'd find it some other way. She'd track down information about Migisi. If there was an answer to be found, she would find it.

And she'd work on herself, too. See if she could get back some of the magic she'd lost. There had to be a way to make herself stronger. Better.

She couldn't let him go on like this. And his father had been going through it for years, from what Calder had said.

He roared again.

"I'll fix it, Calder," Sophie whispered. "I promise."

It went on until the sky started to lighten in the east, turning the living room a dusky pink tone.

The roaring ceased, and Sophie looked out the front window again, wincing at the way her hips had stiffened from sitting so long in one position. The bear was lumbering across the road, toward Calder's.

As he got near the porch, she watched as everything shifted, bear turning into bulky, muscled human flesh, and then Calder, in his human form, stumbled into his house.

She didn't think. She didn't give herself a chance to second-guess what she was doing.

She set the gun down, stepped into her sneakers, and jogged across the road.

His front door hung open, and she crept in quietly, thinking that she was an absolute idiot. She had to know if he was okay.

She walked quietly through the house, hoping, praying his bear wouldn't make a reappearance just now. She took the stairs to the second floor, noting that Calder's house was clean, sparse. At the top of the stairs, she headed toward an open door at the end of the hallway.

Sophie peered in and found Calder, nude, sprawled across a twin-size bed on his stomach. Sweat gleamed over his back and shoulders, and he was breathing raggedly between snores.

Sophie bit her lip, glanced down the hallway. She could leave without him knowing.

She wanted him to know. She wanted him to know she wasn't turning her back on him, not now. Not after hearing what he'd been through the night before. She walked into his room.

It smelled like him. Clean, woodsy. Wild. Comforting, when it definitely shouldn't have made her feel that way. Especially not after seeing what he was.

And it struck her, the irony that she'd spent years running and hiding from one monster, only to walk into this particular monster's bedroom willingly.

She crept over to his bed, intending to pull the blankets up over him. He trembled, groaned a little, and she guessed it was the after-effects of the night before. She tried not to stare at him, but she couldn't resist letting her eyes travel the sculpted muscles of his shoulders and back.

She rested the sheet over him, and froze when he opened his eyes.

They were too bright. They looked the way someone's eyes looked when they were very sick, feverish. And when he reached out and snagged her wrist with his hand, she could feel how warm he was, as if he was running a high-grade fever.

"Sophie," he said hoarsely, looking at her, but still looking unfocused. "Stay."

"I shouldn't," she whispered, fighting tears back.

"Please, stay," he said again, the anguish in his voice undoing her. She let herself, against every sane thought screeching in her mind, be pulled into bed beside him, lay there as he wrapped her in his arms and buried his face against her neck, breathing her in, a deep rumble that felt almost like a purr vibrating his body. After some hesitation, she put her arm lightly around his waist, and he held her closer.

"Stay," he rumbled.

"Okay," she whispered. Scared to death, cursing herself for her stupidity. What kind of moron gets into bed with a monster who spent the last twelve hours raging that he couldn't get to her?

And, idiot that she was, her heart broke for him. His breathing eased, the tremors stopped, and his arm soon became heavy on her waist. Light snores filled the room, and, against her better judgment, she closed her eyes. If he was going to kill her, there wasn't a whole lot she could do just then.

For some reason, she didn't believe he would. She felt stupidly safe. She just hoped she'd live to regret getting into bed with him.

She couldn't have said how long she slept. She slept the sleep of the dead, more soundly than she'd slept in years.

"What the hell are you doing here?"

Her eyes shot open to see Calder looming over her, still lying with her in his bed. His icy blue eyes were narrowed in irritation or confusion, she couldn't tell which.

She couldn't answer. Too aware of his naked, muscled body beside her, above her. His warmth.

"Sophie," he demanded.

"I came to check on you," she finally said. "Once I saw you turn back."

He shook his head, got out of bed, and she forced her gaze away from him. He pulled on a discarded pair of jeans near the bed.

"I'm surprised you didn't put a bullet in my head while I was sleeping," he said.

"Well, I forgot my gun," she said, sitting up, chancing another look at him now that he was at least partially clothed.

His jaw was clenched, eyes blazing. "And how did you know I wouldn't hurt you?"

"I didn't," she said.

He let out a frustrated breath, seemed at a loss for words. Sophie climbed out of bed, stepped back into her sneakers, which she'd kicked off right before falling asleep.

"You were in so much pain last night," she said softly. "I could hear it."

"So, what? You feel sorry for me?" he asked, jaw still clenched, not looking at her.

"Do you want me to?" she asked.

He looked at her then, giving her a glare. "No. I would have preferred you not see me like that at all. Or see me afterward," he said, looking away again.

"My wards held," she said.

"Yeah."

"They didn't let you near the house. I had wondered, since they ordinarily let you through."

He didn't answer, seemed to be refusing to look at her.

"Why are you pissed at me?" she finally asked, irritated.

He looked at her then, his pointed stare sharp, angry. "Why? Because you had no idea what I was going to be like. You came over here, and you locked yourself in my house, and I could have still been in that fucked-up state of mind. I could have hurt you. I could have torn you apart. I could have destroyed you, Sophie," he said, raising his voice.

"But you didn't," she said.

He let out an angry growl, looked for the nearest thing to hit, ended up punching the wall next to his bedroom door. Chunks of plaster flew out into the room, and he punched again, giving the wall matching holes. She flinched back.

"Don't you get it?" he asked, turning to look at her again. "I don't even know how in control I'm going to be. And then you just wander in here What the hell ever possessed you to do that?"

"You were in pain. And it was my ancestor's fault. I had to make sure you were okay. I don't even know what I planned to do if you weren't," she said, throwing her hands up in the air. "I don't know. All I know is it hurt to see you that way, to listen to how much it hurt you. You were suffering, and there wasn't a thing I could do and that goes against everything I am, Calder. Okay?"

He was watching her. He took a deep breath, seeming to try to get his temper under control. This, too, was the curse. The Calder she'd known had always been even-tempered, almost laid back. The only times she'd ever seen him angry were when some of the dumber boys had said things to her, growing up. She was seeing, in bits and pieces, what it was doing to him, and she was even more determined to figure out a way to fix it.

"And you didn't hurt me," she added. "All you did was beg me to stay. And then you held me and we fell asleep. You didn't even come close to hurting me."

"But I could have," he said, crossing his arms over his chest and looking up at the ceiling, as if wishing for an answer to appear. Or his patience. One or the other. "You heard how crazed I was." He shook his head. "I should move."

"Don't be an idiot," she said before she could even think of what she was saying. His gaze swung to her, and she refused to look away.

"I'm not the one crawling into bed with men I barely know," he said.

"Fine. Screw yourself, Calder," she said, walking past him out of the room. He didn't answer, and he didn't try to stop her. She blinked back tears again, walked quickly out of the house and across the road.

When she got close to her house, the first thing she noticed was the yellow rose at the end of her driveway.

She picked it up, let out a frustrated, rage-filled scream, unlike any sound she'd ever made in her life. "And you, you sick bastard. Give me one reason, give me a chance, and I will gut you. You're not doing this to me again, Marshall!" she roared, her voice echoing in the cold morning, her breath steaming in front of her face. She tore the bloom off of the rose, threw it into the highway. As she did, she saw Calder standing on the shoulder of the road. She snarled at him, stalked to her house.

She was at her porch when she heard fast footsteps behind her. She spun, and Calder was there.

She didn't even think. She was full of hurt and anger, and she was exhausted emotionally and physically.

She held her hands up, and, coming almost unbidden, a weak but focused surge of power flew toward Calder, knocking him on his ass on her front walk. He stared at her in shock.

"Just stay away," she said, trying to disguise the hurt in her voice, the fear she was feeling, immediately, over what she'd just done. All she wanted was her home, safety. Quiet. And she felt weird. Twisted and messed up inside. Wrong. She looked out the peephole, watched as Calder picked himself up and stood, looking at her house for several long moments. And, just as she knew he would, he eventually turned and walked away.

CHAPTER THIRTEEN

What the ever-loving fuck had she been thinking? Calder fumed as he stormed back across the road. Following him, being anywhere near him when she'd just seen, all night long, what a walking disaster he was. He went around his house, grabbed the ax he'd swung into a log a few days ago. There was a pile of unsplit logs Jon had brought him the other day. He grabbed one with an irritated snarl, set it onto the tree stump, swung the ax, splitting the log in half in one blow.

He kept at it, methodically, mechanically, letting his body get exhausted, letting his arms, shoulders, and chest start burning with the ceaseless motion. He kept going.

The pile of split logs near the house grew. Jon would come and pick them up to warm the cabin he lived in. They'd learned the hard way not to bother giving their father a fire.

He kept chopping, her scent all over him, making him even crazier. He was raw, one giant angry nerve, hungry and tired and unable to rest, hating himself and everything he was, his heart pounding with fear every time he let himself remember that instant, that moment he'd woken up to find her there.

"Fuck," he roared, throwing the ax, where it stuck deep into the side of the garage. He could have killed her. He could have hurt her in ways she'd never recover from.

"Settle down, teddy bear," a smooth voice said behind him, and he swung, the scent of sulfur and smoke registering at the same moment he saw the asshole standing there in his dark suit, arms crossed, looking pleased with himself. "Does she know? Maybe she wouldn't have climbed into bed with you if she'd known."

Calder glared at him, fists flexing. The warlock smiled. "Does she know you haven't let yourself touch a woman in years? Does she know that the last time you were with someone, you came very near to losing control of your beast?"

Calder snarled, started walking toward the warlock.

"Ah ah ah," his prey cautioned. "That would be a bad idea. I could end you with a word, my friend. And you wouldn't care about that, because you want an escape. You live for the idea of freedom, someday. Death would be a reward." Then he laughed. Marshall. Calder remembered the name through the haze of rage in his mind. "But that wouldn't happen. I'd stand here, and I'd let you hurt me, and I'd make damn sure she saw it. What will it do to her, to her chances of fixing your pathetic ass? Lightwitches. Useless bitches," he said with a laugh. "She's weak, and you're even weaker."

Calder held himself still, knowing he wasn't lying, that she'd see and she'd know. And his biggest concern wasn't even Sophie's power anymore. It was that she'd see it and think less of him.

"There we go. You're not completely stupid," Marshall said. "She doesn't know, does she? That it's been so long that the chances are good your beast will lose control the second you touch her? Because she wants it. The whore wants it so bad it clings to her." He smiled then. "Should I tell her?"

Calder's beast was raging, wanting to be released, wanting to rip this smug bastard, who was daring to threaten his mate, into pieces.

Wait, what?

Calder shook his head. "What do you want?" he growled at Marshall.

"Oh, nothing. Just wanted to have a chat, check out the competition."

"There is no competition, dickhead," Calder said. "She's not a prize."

"Sure she is. Just ask your beast if it doesn't want to own her completely. We're not all that different in that way."

Even his beast had to snort in disbelief at that. "I'm going to end your ass," Calder said, feeling a weird calm settle over him. "I'm going to find a way to make it happen. If I don't do anything else with my life, I'm going to do that much."

Marshall smirked. "Better not let her hear you say that. And I'd watch your tone, animal. Your father and brother are very much isolated and unprotected where they are."

"What are you doing here?" Sophie's voice came from behind Calder, and he turned to see her stalking up the driveway, staring at Marshall, murder in her features. He took a step toward her, wanting her as far away from Marshall as she could be.

"He's being an asshole. Go home," Calder said, hating how he sounded like a demanding asshole.

"Butt out, Calder," she said, not even looking at him. She was pure adrenaline again, rage. His beast could smell it, and it was practically salivating over her. "What are you doing here?"

"Just having a chat," Marshall said, smiling.

Sophie didn't respond to him. She said a few words Calder didn't understand, and he watched as Marshall's expression went from smug satisfaction to sheer anger. Calder had to blink. It looked as if something, somehow, was moving Marshall. Even crazier, it looked as if the warlock was helpless against it, and Calder could feel what could only be described as energy around him. It swirled, and his ears popped. Even his beast was silent in its presence. Sophie was still saying words, her attention completely on Marshall, who was now shouting profanities at her, threats, trying to make her lose her focus.

All at once, it snapped, and Calder's ears popped again. Marshall had been pushed back to the road, off of Calder's property, and though he tried to ram his way forward, it was as if an invisible wall was keeping him back.

The same kind of invisible wall that had kept Calder away from Sophie the night before. He swung his gaze to Sophie.

Damn.

Her face was like marble, set into a determined, peaceful expression he didn't expect to see there. She practically glowed, the effects of her magic evident, the warm feel of it still surrounding him, though she'd finished speaking. She was watching Marshall, who was stalking away, then disappeared as if he'd never been there at all.

"Whoa," Calder said, then felt like an inarticulate asshole. There were no words to express what he was feeling, watching what she'd done. Her gaze flicked to him, and he swore he caught a glimmer of warm golden light in her eyes, but when he blinked, she just looked like Sophie. She rolled her eyes in typical Sophie fashion and stalked away, back across the road.

"Thanks," he managed to call after her. She answered him with a middle finger raised into the air as she walked up her front steps.

Sophie stalked into her house, full of adrenaline after using her magic that way, full of anger and irritation at

Calder, full of rage toward Marshall, for daring even to look at Calder, let alone talk to him. She smiled in satisfaction. He wouldn't get near his house again.

When she'd gone to the mailbox and heard his voice from across the road, she'd felt a cold fury roar through her. All she could think of was the fact that he'd murdered David, that one man who cared for her had already died at Marshall's hands. And while Calder didn't care for her that way, clearly, he was still part of her life and she'd rather die than lose anyone else to Marshall's particular brand of evil. As she'd run across the road, images, nightmares, of the sights that might greet her flashed across her mind. Calder, bloody. Calder, broken. Calder, in pain.

He was a jerk, and she was more hurt than she'd been in a long time. She'd forgotten how much more those you loved could hurt you than those you hated, and she was pretty sure she didn't want to speak to him ever again. He messed her up inside, and the things he'd said to her that morning had cut deep.

But she sure as hell wasn't going to let Marshall hurt him. So when she'd seen him there, looking smug, she'd sent a silent plea to her magic to work. No preparation, no gems or herbs or candles, all of which she'd always used to create a ward.

Her magic came unbidden, almost as if it could sense that she really, really needed it, that she was protecting someone who needed it, that she was working directly against the Shadow. When she'd felt her ward begin to take form, when she'd seen Marshall getting repelled, bodily removed from Calder's property, she could have cried with gratitude.

She stood in her house, trembling, sending a prayer of thanks to her ancestors. She was focusing on her breath, on keeping herself calm. As heady as it had been to use her magic that way, the crash afterward, that sense of emptiness she'd felt since waking up that morning felt all the worse now.

She was leaning against the front door, eyes closed, trying to find some kind of sense of calm. Once she felt like she wouldn't just erupt into screams or ridiculous sobbing, she opened her eyes and pushed herself away from the door.

The journals from the attic sat where she'd left them on the kitchen table, and she went over to it, glanced down at the books. That would give her something to focus on, at least. She put on some water for tea, forced down a handful of late strawberries from the garden, then sat down with her cup of tea and a pencil and paper. She glanced at the notes she'd taken the other day, the spell to enable her to translate the journal.

She lit a white candle, then realized everything felt wrong, unbalanced. She lit one of her smudge sticks, walked through her cabin with it, letting it cleanse the negative energy from her home. When she was done, she felt calmer and more focused.

That done, she settled herself at the table, set her intentions, issued an honorific to her ancestors, appealing to them for assistance. She launched into the spell, murmuring the words she'd memorized until they became a chant, until they took her to a place where she almost felt as if she wasn't even in her own body anymore. She was apart from herself, her mind clear. When she opened Migisi's journal, the one she'd written in Ojibwa, the previously unreadable words made sense.

She smiled, let herself sit with her gratitude for a moment. And she began reading.

Spells, recipes for teas and potions. Every single thing Migisi had written about, even her most personal thoughts, indicated someone who truly lived in the Light. Even her thoughts about a man from her tribe whom she found attractive were imbued with Light. "I want to worship him in the best way. His mind does nothing for me, but he is gentle and beautiful to look at. For a night or two, I know we would find joy in one another. Once upon a time, that kind of behavior on my part would have earned gossip, shock. I have, apparently, reached a certain status at which such behavior is attributed to my 'eccentricity.'" Later, she'd written about a French missionary who had also caught her eye, and her descriptions of making love to him read almost like a prayer.

Sophie felt the spell starting to waver, but was determined to keep reading. She was nearly through the smallest of the journals. Clearly this was pre-Luc, but she was reading it hoping to find out about the woman, trying to see if there was any indication she'd turn so horribly later.

Sophie found nothing like that. Late in the journal, Migisi noted that she felt she'd lost interest in physical relationships, that even those men who once had looked at her with interest now saw her only as a healer, a witch, as *Nimaamaa*. She felt they'd stopped seeing her as a woman. "I am conflicted," she'd written. "For is this not what I've worked for my entire life? To be seen as a dedicated woman of the Light? And now I am, and I find myself missing the days when men and women alike would look at me and just see a woman. We are never happy with things as they are. Or, perhaps some people are. I am not. I have not learned how to be content. Perhaps I never will."

Her magic snapped on her as she turned the last page, and Sophie shook her head, shaking off the effects of using her magic for so long. Her head was pounding, and her eyes were blurry. Her body even ached, as if every muscle had been held taut as she focused on keeping her magic steady enough to translate the book.

She looked with some trepidation at the thicker book. The one written in French. The one with Luc's name in it.

She almost didn't want to read it. She was finding she liked Migisi. She was thoughtful, intelligent, observant, clearly dedicated to the Light. She also had a dry wit that was enjoyable to read. In that way, she reminded Sophie of Layla.

She didn't want to read about her losing control.

"You're getting morose," she told herself, standing up from her seat at the table with a grimace.

She headed out the back door. Fresh air would help. She needed to do something that had nothing to do with curses or Calder.

And she was not, absolutely not, going to think about him, she told herself.

CHAPTER FOURTEEN

August 18, 1852

Migisi walked along the river beside Luc, his huge form casting a shadow over her, like walking with her own personal sun-shield. The air was humid, too warm, too quiet. It seemed to Migisi that everything around her had a sad, wistful feel to it. Late summer was the worst, she'd long ago decided. It spoke of loss yet to come, of shortening days and the trees around her looked tired, as if they, too, languished.

"So deep in thought, little ghost," Luc said, glancing at her, his usual mischievous gaze serious. She was warmed by the nickname. Little ghost, he'd begun calling her almost immediately, referring to the way she'd haunted his steps, ruined his traps, like an angry spirit. "What troubles you, that you haven't said a word to me in over an hour?"

Migisi shook her head. He was leaving, and she felt empty.

"Are you angry with me?" he asked, pressing the matter.

She shook her head again, not trusting her voice. If she spoke, she feared what would come out, that she would beg him to stay with her. She'd never begged anyone for anything, and it frightened her that this brawny trapper had come to mean so much to her in such a little time. That just a look from him was enough to bring her to her knees.

"Migisi," Luc said, stopping and taking her hand in his. She looked down at their joined hands, her small tan one in his large, strong, calloused one. "I will be back."

"I know you will," she said, willing her voice to stay steady, willing herself to keep the desperation out of her voice. "This area is a profitable one for you."

"Do you really believe that's the reason I'll be coming back?" he asked quietly.

She didn't answer for a moment. "Of course. You are a businessman. And now that we have worked out where it's appropriate for you to trap, you would be foolish not to return here."

"Why are you so silent with me lately?" he asked her, not releasing her hand. It became almost difficult to breathe, standing that close to him. They'd seen each other almost every day since the night they'd met, had walked the woods and talked about his work and her work, places he'd been. As the weeks had gone by, the initial attraction she felt toward him only grew, until he was almost everything she thought about.

It was a foreign state for her and she was not fond of it.

"Maybe you are just talking too much, and I cannot manage to get a word in," she said, trying to make light of the matter.

He usually appreciated her humor, but this time, he just continued watching her, looking down at her with those eyes, so reminiscent of the nearby lake, a deep blue storm that threatened to drag her under. "Migisi," he said again.

She didn't answer, and, instead of letting her go as he usually did when this moodiness came upon her, which seemed to happen more and more often, it seemed, he held her hand tighter. And then he pulled her toward him.

"I need to know, before I leave. I need to know, my little ghost, if you feel even a tiny bit of what I feel for you. I have been patient, I have waited for some sign that what we are goes beyond friendship. But you are mysterious and silent and I wish I knew your mind."

"And what is it you feel for me?" she asked quietly, "because I cannot tell you whether I feel the same until I know what your feelings are. And you are just as much of a mystery to me."

His face softened, and he brought his other hand to her face, traced her jawline gently with such tenderness it became impossible for Migisi to breathe. "I thought it was plain. I can't look at you enough, can't touch you enough. You're my reason for breathing, you're every dream I've ever had. But I think you are far too good for me. I have nothing to offer you—"

"That is not true," Migisi said. "You are everything."

He leaned in, slowly, carefully, and the first touch of his lips was like a breath of air, like fresh water quenching a thirst she thought she'd never be rid of. She trembled as he kissed her, as his mouth made love to hers, cherishing her, making her feel beautiful and desirable. Pleading, worshiping.

"Migisi," he whispered against her lips, and it went straight to her heart, the need in those three quiet syllables. "I am coming back," he repeated, kissing her between his words. "And when I do, I am going to make damn sure you never question how much I need you."

CHAPTER FIFTEEN

Sophie was repairing Merlin's fence again, trying to shore up the spots he was slowly but surely trying to work his way through. She heard gravel crunching on her driveway and looked up to see Calder coming around the side of the house.

"Go away," she said, looking away from him.

"I need to talk to you."

"That is not my problem."

He approached the pen, and Merlin went insane, butting the fences, trying to get to him, trying to protect Sophie. Sophie glared at Calder, shoved at Merlin, who bleated angrily at her. She went through the gate, closing it quickly behind her as the goat tried to run out, determined to cause some pain to Calder.

"Can you leave now?" Sophie asked, still trying not to look at him. "You made it clear this morning what you think of me. This isn't a game, Calder, and I'm already sick of playing."

"Can you let me say what I wanted to say?"

She went to walk past him, and he reached out and took her arm in his hand, pulling her back, not letting her go. She finally glared up at him. "I want you to leave."

"Sophie," he said, his tone gentle, his hand warm on her arm. "Come on, kitten. I'm sorry. Put the claws away for a while, all right?"

"Stop calling me that," she said, coming back to herself, forcing her breath into a more normal pace. The second he'd touched her, her heart had started pounding, a pleasurable shiver working its way through her body.

"I can't help it. You do that, get all bristling and skittish around me. Like the feral kittens I used to see in our barn when I was a kid." He smiled. "If you really want me to stop, I will. I'll still think it, though."

"What's with the attitude change?" she asked, yanking her arm out of his grip and heading toward the back door. She opened it and went inside, and he followed. She sighed in irritation, noting numbly that the wards had let him though this time. She walked into the kitchen.

"I acted like a jerk," he said.

"You think?" she asked incredulously, turning and looking at him.

"My point still stands. I could have hurt you, and you put yourself in a really, really bad position by doing what you did. I don't want to hurt you, Sophie. You get that, right?"

"Then don't," Sophie said, meeting his eyes.

"I won't. When I'm like this, when I'm myself, there's not a chance in hell I'd ever hurt you. Ever, in any way. Okay? But when I'm like that... You saw me, Sophie. You heard me. You know damn well I wasn't in control."

"I know," she said softly.

"And even after. I don't remember walking into my house. I don't remember getting into bed. I don't even remember shifting back. The last thing I remember is standing in your woods, raging that I couldn't get to you. And then the next thing I knew, you were lying in my bed.

And the first thing I thought was to panic that somehow I'd overpowered you..." He trailed off, shook his head. His jaw was tense again, his hands fisted at his sides.

The fight went out of her, just as quickly as it had come on. She rested her hands on the kitchen island, which was between her and Calder. "I'm sorry. I didn't think of that, that you wouldn't remember. I didn't want that. I just wanted to make you feel better. You were so out of it, Calder."

His gaze softened. "And you don't know what it means to me that after all that, after everything I put you through last night, you cared enough to check on me. I don't know what to think of that, Sophie. I didn't expect it." He shook his head. "Thank you, kitten. That's what I should have said first thing."

She blushed a little, looked him in the eye. "I think I'm insane," she said. "You're right. I should have been running. There's not a doubt in my mind that if you'd gotten in last night, if you'd gotten anywhere near me, that there's any way I'd still be alive and well right now."

He looked away, rubbed the back of his neck. "I hate that you had to go through that last night. I hate that I'm that way for you. I hate that things are the way they are between us in so many ways."

"Yeah?"

He looked at her again. "Yeah."

"Curses suck."

He let out a short laugh. "They do. Especially when, if I were a normal guy, I'd be trying to charm you. I'd be trying to impress you. And look at us. I'm holding your house over your head so you'll break a curse, and, lucky you, the same curse makes it so I'm the biggest danger to you."

"Well... nobody's perfect," Sophie said with a wry smile, and after a moment of silence, he laughed. "After seeing what you went through, I'm even more determined to break this thing. You were in so much pain. I mean, you were enraged and scary as hell, too, but mostly you sounded like it hurt."

He didn't answer, and the way that he looked at her nearly took her breath away.

"I'm going to find a way to break it. I promise."

"Soph—"

"Oh, wait. I wanted to show you. Look what I found in the attic." She walked past him to the kitchen table and picked up the journals. She set them gently on the counter in front of him and opened the one written in French. He leaned down to look at it, his arm brushing hers as he leaned in, and her stomach twisted. God, he smelled good.

"If there's an answer, it has to be in here somewhere," she said, pointing to the page with their names, Luc and Migisi. "Or at least this can push me in the right direction. Something," she said.

"Your magic," he reminded her gently.

"Well, maybe it won't have anything to do with magic. We don't know yet."

She was looking up at him, and he was standing beside her, looking down at her. The look on his face was pure longing, and it echoed the way everything in her wanted him.

Before she could think, she stood on tiptoe, leaned in, and pressed her lips to his, gently, just the barest of sweeps of her lips over his. And then again, giving both of them the chance to back away if they wanted to.

After a second of hesitation, Calder leaned closer, capturing her lips with his. He turned her toward him, rested his hands at her waist, gently running his fingertips over the curve of her hips.

"I remember, Sophie," he murmured against her lips, kissing her again. "I remember. I remember kissing you. I remember everything." He kissed her again, and rumbled in pleasure at the sound of her low whimper. She kissed him back, and when he deepened their kiss, she felt like she would drown in the torrent of emotion she was swept up in. "I remember. Your lips tasted so good. And your hair was like silk, and when I made myself pull away, your hair got tangled in that watch I used to wear."

She laughed a little, and kissed him again. "You remember that?" she whispered.

"I never forgot," he said, rubbing his face against hers, holding her tighter to his body. She reveled in the feel of his skin pressed to hers, his lips warm and needy, his heart beating fast against her chest.

A few seconds of gentle caresses of his lips to hers, so warm and careful she nearly wept, and he pulled back, though he kept his hands on her.

"I don't want to hurt you," he said, and she could hear the wistfulness in his voice. She knew then that he'd walk away.

"Then don't," she repeated.

He gave her waist a gentle squeeze, fluttered his lips over hers once more, then stepped back.

"The other day, you were pissed off at me because I'm tearing your life apart," he reminded her. "Last night my beast raged for you, and this morning you saw me lose it again."

She stepped forward and put her arms around his waist, unable to stop touching him now that she'd been in his arms. Without any hesitation, he put his arms around her. "I know what you are, Calder. I know what I am. It doesn't change the fact that I want you."

She felt him still. His arms tightened around her for a moment, and then he gently pushed her away.

"I have to go."

"Will you be back?"

He gave her what looked like a pained smile. "I couldn't stay away even if I wanted to. There's just something I need to do."

It took everything in him to walk away.

Calder cursed himself as he crossed the road to his house, his beast screaming, raging at him to get back in there and take what she was offering. His hands on her body, her lips pressed to his. It had been delicious, perfect, addictive torture. He'd been this close to burying his hands in those masses of dark curls and pulling her closer, giving in to the need he'd had for her since the moment he'd laid eyes on her again.

What the hell had she been thinking kissing him like that? Holding him like that?

Looking at him with understanding and care in her eyes instead of disgust?

He gritted his teeth as his beast raged, as it struggled against him for control.

Keep her safe. He had to keep her safe. Especially from himself.

As soon as he was in his woods, he shucked his clothing, shifted. And he raised his face to the sky, and released a roar that shook the forest. Part victory, part frustration, full of possessiveness. A warning: do not mess with what is mine.

And she was his. He and his beast were in agreement over that. He knew that would drive him insane even before his beast did, because there wasn't a chance in hell he'd risk losing control with her, not a chance in hell he'd lose it and come to, see her looking at him in fear. He'd been there once. It wouldn't happen again. And with her, it would be a constant battle. Before, it had been about slaking a need, scratching an itch, and he'd still nearly lost it.

But this? This was Sophie. This was his, and he and his beast both wanted her.

He ran.

So much energy and hunger. As he ran, he caught a familiar, unwelcome scent. Sulfur and smoke. The warlock. He focused, followed the trail of scent, which led through his woods and to a dirt road further down. The dickhead was clearly becoming familiar with Sophie's new neighborhood.

That wouldn't do.

His property was warded now. He knew that. He didn't know for how long, but it was for now, which meant that, most likely, Marshall would go back to hanging around near Sophie's, bothering her. He preferred Marshall bothering him. At least he knew then, that Sophie was safe and had some peace.

He thought as he loped back through the woods toward his house. It could easily just be an obsessive thing. From what Sophie had said, she'd been keeping him away for years. That seemed like a really, really long time for someone to harass a woman over a slight. But he knew, too, that some guys were just psychotic assholes, and they didn't need an actual reason to do shit like that.

His power, though. Her magic. Calder wondered if there was an extra motivation for the way the guy was about Sophie. The one thing he knew for sure was that this interference was distracting her from him, and that wouldn't do.

He shook his head. Stupid beast. No. It was making her scared and angry, and he wanted her the opposite. He wanted her safe, happy. Cared for. By him. Naked.

He growled and shook his head again.

That body pressed up against his, not once but twice in one day. He practically salivated at the memory. It would be best not to think about that too much. And definitely not about the way she'd kissed him, as if she was giving herself to him. And it appealed to everything he was. His beast had been in ecstasy. The man, impossibly enough, even more so.

When he got back near his house, he could smell wolf. He sniffed again, glanced at Sophie's house. That little convertible. Layla and Cara were there.

Good. She wasn't alone. And they were a good buffer between them. Because all he wanted just then was to set her on that counter in her kitchen and feast on her.

This was getting complicated, he thought for about the thousandth time as he shifted back. He grabbed his clothing and headed into his house, directly upstairs and into the bathroom. Standing under the jets of ice-cold water didn't help as much as he'd like, but it was something.

This was going to be the end of him.

CHAPTER SIXTEEN

"I wonder what happened to her," Layla said, lying back on Sophie's small, lumpy couch, her legs thrown over the arm. She'd come over to check on Sophie and hear how things had happened with the full moon. Sophie stood at the nearby kitchen counter, cutting a large block of soap into smaller bars as she filled Layla and Cara in on what had happened while sharing a bare minimum about the morning after. She also shared what she'd learned from Thea.

"I know. She's this hero, this selfless, amazing healer, and then she just loses it?" Sophie said. "Becomes 'Migisi the Mad?' And to be honest, I'm not even sure I want to hear why they started calling her that, because Thea didn't know anything about the curse, I don't think. So there are other things there and I swear I don't want to know."

"Luc must have messed up big time," Cara said from her spot on the daybed.

"Or she was nuts already," Sophie said.

"So she was in love, we're assuming, because we don't actually know that. She could have just been attracted to him."

"Maybe," Sophie agreed. "Everyone seems to agree that she loved him."

"But you haven't seen her actually say that anywhere yet," Layla pointed out. "Thea didn't have any evidence of that. And we definitely don't know how devoted he was to her. This could have been a friendship, or a fling, or any number of things that have nothing to do with love."

"Why are you so determined to believe they didn't love one another?" Sophie asked, setting her knife down and crossing her arms.

"Because I wonder if maybe you're romanticizing what they were to one another and maybe it's carrying over into the way you deal with Calder."

"That is such crap," Sophie said, and Layla cut her off.

"No. No, it's not, and you need to smarten up. You understand that this goes against everything I know about you, right? You spent years running from that warlock asshole. In the time you've been here, you've shied away from every guy I've ever tried to introduce you to, citing your fear of men because of what Marshall put you through with his stalking, and I don't think you've even told me everything. And then this guy, and granted you knew him when he was a kid, but people change. This guy, who's openly blackmailing you, and who, oh yeah, also turns into a beast that kinda gets stalkery... This guy makes his way into your life, and you're all about opening up and giving him chances and saving him. I'm just wondering where the hell my careful, level-headed friend went, because this definitely isn't her." Layla was sitting up now, watching Sophie. Cara watched silently, clearly wanting to stay out of it.

Sophie had no answer for her, because she'd wondered the same thing herself.

"You don't even know, do you?" Layla said, practically seeming to read her thoughts. "Do you see why I worry about this shit?"

"I know. I can't explain it. I want him. When he's near me, I feel safe."

"He's blackmailing you," Layla said, enunciating every syllable very clearly.

"He feels really bad about it," she said, and the words sounded lame even to her. Layla raised an eyebrow as if to say "Are you kidding me?" and even Cara shook her head. "It's not just him," she reminded them.

"If he cared for you, he'd be protecting you and trying to make your life easier. Not complicating it. I have no doubt at all that he's horny for you. You're gorgeous and amazing and he'd be stupid not to see that. And if you're horny for him, then okay. I can see it. The man is hot. But this isn't sounding like that. This is sounding like you're getting really, really emotionally involved. I don't want to see you hurt," she finished more gently. "Cara keeps telling me to keep my mouth shut. Screw that. I love you. And you've been through enough."

"I love you too. And I love you for caring," Sophie said.

"But you're going forward with him anyway," Layla said. Then she nodded. "I hope it works out, Soph. If he breaks your heart, I'm going to break his face. If he hurts you, he will see exactly what a wolf can do to a bear."

Sophie laughed then, because she didn't doubt Layla for a minute. She went and sat beside her, and Cara joined them, sitting on her other side. Layla rested her head on Sophie's shoulder.

"Just be careful, okay?"

"I will."

They spent the rest of the afternoon binge-watching a show they were all trying to catch up on before the new season started, and when the twins left around dinnertime,

Sophie felt better, though at the same time, she was relieved to have some time alone.

Sophie did her evening chores, then headed out front to see if there was any mail in her mailbox. She saw another of Marshall's roses resting on the mailbox, and she stalked toward it, grabbed the rose, bit the blossom off and spit it out, hoping he was watching.

Sophie woke to her phone ringing. She opened one eye, saw that the sun was fully up. The goats were going to be completely irritated with her for sleeping in like that yet again.

She fumbled around on the small table next to the daybed, saw Thea's number on the screen.

She answered with a groggy "Hello?"

"Sophie! Sorry if I woke you, kiddo," Thea's cheery voice greeted her, sounding very much like the middle school teacher she'd once known. Sophie had to smile to herself.

"You didn't," she lied. "What's up?"

"I spent some time searching the archives yesterday. It was quiet around here, so I had time. I found a few things that will likely interest you. I found some things about Luc, too. You said his last name was Turcotte, yes?"

Sophie's heart sped up, and she sat up, tossing the quilt she'd been wrapped up in aside. "Yes."

"Okay. Well.... Do you know where the Copper Falls cemetery is?"

"That old one with the iron fence?"

"That's the one. Can you meet me there in a half hour or so? I have some meetings this morning, but I really want you to see this."

Sophie got up. "Yes. I can be there in about twenty minutes."

"See you then." With that, Thea hung up. Sophie went into the bathroom, cleaned up and got dressed. Her hair seemed even more insistent on looking insane than usual, and she pulled it into an unruly ponytail, hid the rest of it with a scarf. She quickly let the animals out of their shelters and fed them, then jumped into her car and sped down the highway.

The tiny Copper Falls cemetery hadn't been in use since the early 1900s. There had been talk when she lived in town as a kid, of exhuming and moving the bodies to make space for a campground, but the whole idea had been scrapped after protests had disrupted village council meetings. So it remained, growing mossy and mostly unvisited except by tourists and grave hunters. Halloween was the busiest time of year for the mostly-forgotten site, idiots trying to play practical jokes, ghost hunters hoping to catch sight of something. For the most part, those buried there were men who had worked in the copper mines, fishermen, townspeople, and their families. There was a larger graveyard near the reservation, and it was still in use to this day, the final resting place for Ojibwa since the late 1700s.

Sophie saw the wooden signs announcing that the cemetery was ahead and she slowed and pulled into the small gravel parking lot.

She got out of her car, stuffed her keys in her pocket. The day was overcast, dreary. It felt like rain, smelled like the nearby lake. The wind blew steadily, carrying a chill with it that had Sophie trying to shrink further into the wool sweater she'd tossed on.

She put her hands in her pockets. She'd noticed Thea's silver truck already in the lot, the only other car. She made her way into the cemetery. Small headstones lined both sides of the central cobblestone path, like eternal soldiers. Some were broken and crumbled into the grass. Some had sunk into the sandy soil, and now sat crooked, looking drunk and dilapidated. Green moss covered most of the stones, and wildflowers grew thick around the edges, near the wrought iron fence.

Thea stood to the left, near the southern corner of the cemetery. She raised her hand in a wave to Sophie, and Sophie waved back, picked up her pace. She picked her way between the headstones, making her way to Thea.

"Morning," Thea said.

"Morning," Sophie said.

"This is for you," Thea said, handing Sophie a thick manila folder. "This is all from that book of articles, and the one of correspondence. There are a few things in there that make no sense to me. Like this," she said, opening the folder and taking out the photocopied article on top. "She was arrested near Mackinac for disorderly conduct. A woman claimed Migisi tried to kill her." Sophie glanced at the date. 1864.

"That's not exactly nearby," Sophie said.

"Right."

"'Migisi the Mad.' When did that nickname start?" Sophie asked her.

"Not long after this. The first references I have found to it is 1866. That's in there, too." She paused, watching Sophie. "Can I say something?"

"Of course."

"I think you should take all of this," she said, shaking the folder, "with a grain of salt. These were people who didn't understand Migisi, who didn't know her. I included writings from our own people as well. They note a change in her, primarily in her magic."

"Yet they still also ended up calling her Migisi the Mad," Sophie reminded her gently. "Maybe she tried to hold it together as well as she could, but she couldn't hide it forever."

Thea shook her head. "I hate this. This is wrong, and we shouldn't remember her that way."

"You are a historian," Sophie pointed out. "History isn't always pretty, as you know. I think we do her an injustice by not knowing her whole story. And I need to know it all. It matters."

Thea didn't answer.

"You said you found Luc as well," Sophie prompted.

Thea pointed at one of the gravestones in front of them. Sophie crouched down. The stone was maybe two feet tall, a bear carved above the name "Luc Henri Turcotte." Below, the dates April 2, 1831 - November 22, 1889.

"Is the rest of his family here?" Sophie asked, still looking at the stone.

"Well. That depends on how you define 'family'," Thea said. She crouched next to the stone to the left, gingerly pulled the vines of a wild white rose that grew around it.

Sophie stared. "Migisi," she finally said.

"Migisi," Thea agreed. Migisi's stone was even more plain than Luc's had been: a rectangle of granite,with the name "Migisi" and, below. *"Nimaamaa."* At the bottom were the dates July 1, 1827 - November 22, 1889.

"Oh, what the hell?" Sophie breathed when she registered the dates of death.

"I know," Thea said softly.

"Why wasn't his wife buried near him? He had one. Children, even. The story is that he committed suicide in front of his own son."

"I don't know the story. We'll see what else we can find." She was studying Sophie. "This is significant to you."

Sophie nodded, eyes still on the stones. "I don't know what it means, though." After a few moments, she transferred her gaze to Thea. "Thank you for this. How did you know about it?"

Thea shrugged, crouched beside her. "I didn't. I knew her grave was here, because it was somewhat of a scandal that she wasn't buried in our own burial site."

Sophie nodded.

"I would not even have thought twice about who was next to her if you hadn't told me the name. I came to see her grave, to see if there were any answers here. And our talk made me feel like I needed to come and honor her. It has been a while. So I was visiting, and then I glanced over there and there was Luc."

Sophie ran her hand over her face, studied the gravestones again. "Why, though? This makes no sense. By all accounts, she cursed him horribly, and he suffered, and they went their separate ways, started their own lives. So why this?"

Thea shook her head. "I do not believe it's a coincidence," she finally said.

"Neither do I," Sophie said, standing. She held her hand out, helped Thea stand straight.

"Is it possible she fixed it and they got back together? Maybe the story you know is wrong," Thea said.

Sophie shook her head. "The curse still lives. If she'd fixed it, that wouldn't be the case."

"You know this, how? How do you know the curse still lives?"

Sophie looked away. "I know one of Luc's descendants."

She watched Thea, saw the gears turning. "Wait. Turcotte. That boy who was always beating up anyone who looked at you funny?"

Sophie didn't answer.

"What does the curse do?"

"It's not my story to tell. But this," she said, gesturing to the headstones. "I wasn't expecting this."

"Be careful," Thea warned. "I have a very unsettled feeling about all of this."

"Well. That makes two of us," Sophie said. She gestured toward the cemetery exit, and Thea nodded. They walked out together.

"Is he a danger to you?"

Sophie shook her head.

"To anyone else?"

"He suffers. And he does it alone," Sophie said quietly. "I'm trying to see if it can be broken. I don't think I have enough power to do it, but I need to try."

"I'll pay extra attention to any mentions of curses or spells," Thea said, and Sophie nodded her thanks. "Be careful," Thea urged again as she climbed into her truck. Sophie held the manila folder of articles and journal entries to her chest, watched Thea drive away.

The rain started, a soaking, steady drizzle starting all at once, and Sophie got into her car, set the folder on the seat beside her. She sat there, gripping the steering wheel, the heat cranked up. It wasn't just the rain. She was cold to her core. There was hope, too. Impossible though it seemed, had Migisi and Luc worked it out? Had the stories Calder's family uncovered been wrong?

She knew the curse hadn't been reversed. And it seemed that if Migisi had made up with Luc Turcotte, she would have lifted his curse.

And she wondered, when all was said and done, if they hadn't ended up being each other's end. The thought sent a chill up her spine as her thoughts went to Calder, to waking up beside him, full of emptiness, facing his anger.

And later, reveling in the way his touch made her feel, more alive than she'd ever felt in her life.

If she were smart at all, she'd stay away from him, shut him out of her life now, before things went bad.

She might as well ask the sun to stop rising.

CHAPTER SEVENTEEN

Determined to keep her hands and mind busy, Sophie went home and got to work. She had soaps to slice into bars, another batch to package, and a few orders to fill. She put on the stereo, unable to stand the silence.

She'd glanced over at Calder's house as she got out of her car. He hadn't been in the driveway; the rain apparently could keep even Calder from tinkering. His motorcycle was gone, though, which meant he wasn't home.

And she wanted to see him. Stupid, imbecilic, clueless as it was, she wanted to see him. Seeing Luc's and Migisi's graves that way had thrown her, had made her feel raw, and on top of the weird emptiness she was already feeling, it was almost too much to take. He'd always, when they were kids, been the one to comfort her. Brash jerk though he'd often been to everyone else, he'd been the one she'd turned to when she needed to be soothed.

How ridiculous that, knowing damn well what he was, he was still the one she wanted to turn to.

Sophie finished putting the last couple bars of soap on the rack, glanced out the side window to see the rain still coming down in sheets. She jumped a little when she heard a knock at the door. She headed through the house, peeked out the peephole. Calder.

She opened the door, her stomach twisting, her body warming at the memory of his kisses, the look in his eyes the last time she'd seen him, in her kitchen.

He held up a bag, and whatever was in it smelled really, really good. "Have you eaten anything yet?"

She gave the bag another look, raised her eyebrow at him.

"Is Chinese food an appropriate peace offering when someone spent an entire night terrorizing someone else, and then acts like an idiot the morning after?" he asked. And though his tone was light, the serious look on his face, the intensity in his eyes, nearly made her breathless. The fact that he still felt like he had things to apologize for, when they both knew how hopeless and insane it all was, made her ache for him.

"I'm a vegetarian," she said quietly, at a loss for anything else.

He smiled, just the barest lift of the corners of his mouth. "I know."

"How do you know?" she asked, tilting her head.

"I can smell it. Meat eaters smell different."

"Okay. I'm sorry I asked," she said, and he laughed. "So what did you get?" she asked, crossing her arms.

"General Tso's tofu, sesame tofu, vegetable chow mein—"

"You had me at General Tso," Sophie said, pulling the door open all the way. He nodded, then walked past her, carrying the delicious-smelling bags. He walked into the kitchen and set them on the small table, and she grabbed a couple of plates.

"You're not a vegetarian," she said.

"Nope. That's why I got pepper steak."

She nodded and carried their dishes to the table. "Drink?"

"What are you having?" he asked

"Green tea."

He made a face at that, and she couldn't help laughing.

"I have water. Or goat's milk. Herbal tea?"

"Water, thanks," he said. "There's this thing called beer...." he said, and she rolled her eyes.

She grabbed their drinks, and he went to work unpacking the bags.

"You can start. I need to light a fire. It's getting cold in here," she said. He stood up.

"I've got it. Sit," he said. She watched him start loading logs into the fireplace, start the fire like someone who knew what he was doing. It had taken her a couple of weeks to be able to get a fire going easily. City girls didn't usually have a whole lot of experience with that kind of thing. She finished unpacking the food, and by the time she was done, he had a nice fire roaring.

"Chopsticks or fork?" she asked.

"Fork," was his answer. "Chopsticks take too long," he added, walking back into the kitchen and sitting in the chair opposite hers. She smiled and shook her head, then joined him at the table.

"I was starting to get worried," he said, digging into his container of pepper steak.

"About?" she asked.

"You. You were gone for a long time. If I hadn't seen that freak wandering around out there, I would have been more concerned that he'd gotten to you."

"You saw Marshall?"

"He was getting into his truck. Gone before I could have a chat with him. Hopefully next time," he said.

"Calder..." she warned.

"I know. No hurting the dipshit. I know. You did say I could scare him, though."

She smiled. "Yeah. You can scare him, but I really just wish you'd stay away from him."

They ate in silence for several minutes.

"Where were you today?" he asked.

"Meeting with Thea... Mrs. Redleaf, about something she found." She stopped.

"What, Sophie?" he asked, his fork stopping in midair as he studied her. "What's wrong?"

"They were buried side by side. They died on the same goddamn day. Did you know that?"

Calder stared at her. "Who?"

"Luc and Migisi. I was at their graves today."

Calder set his fork down. "I never heard that."

"They're buried in the little cemetery outside of town. The one with the wrought iron fence. His wife isn't there. His kids aren't there. But he is, right next to Migisi."

"Well. I think that gives us more questions than answers. Don't you?"

Sophie nodded, her appetite failing her.

"I wonder if he killed her," Calder said quietly, and she knew what he was thinking.

"I actually wonder the opposite," she told him. "She wasn't right. There are articles about her beating up some woman in Mackinac City, another near Iron Mountain. There are questions about missing children that she was suspected of kidnapping but a connection could never be made. She was messed up, and violent, and I don't doubt for a second that she could have killed him if she decided to."

"Doesn't change what the curse does," Calder argued. "He could have come across her, attacked her, ended her, realized what he did and killed himself after."

"But why would he do that? She cursed him. She kinda had it coming."

"Unless he still loved her, after all of it. And the beast went nuts and killed her, and he got control and saw what happened and couldn't live with it."

Sophie didn't answer. "You're just projecting because that's what you're worried about doing to me."

"Look who's talking. You want to believe my line isn't actually capable of killing those they love. Believe me, we are. My great-grandfather killed my great-grandmother. My dad tried hunting my mother down, and she took off on us the next day. It happens, and we are more than capable of it because our beasts are completely out of control and we're not strong enough to keep fighting back.."

"And yet here you are," Sophie said.

"Here I am," he murmured. "I shouldn't be."

"Why are you here? And what exactly is this an apology for?" she asked after a while, gesturing at the containers of food spread over the table. "We've already been over what happened."

"I still feel like a jerk. You deserved better than that bullshit. I meant what I said before. If things were different..." He trailed off, looking at her. "But they're not. And I'm sorry I was a jerk before, and I'm sorry I'm holding your land ransom." He blew out a breath. "If it was just me, I'd give it back now, Sophie."

"Your dad," she said.

"My dad, and my brother, and anyone else in my family who has to deal with this once I'm gone if we don't solve this. I felt, the other night, what my dad's been going through all these years. You saw what I was like. This has to end."

For many reasons, she thought to herself. First among them being there was no way she was walking away from him, or letting him walk away from her. She nodded. "I know. I still can't get your howls out of my head." She closed her eyes for a moment, his howls still echoing in her mind. "Does it hurt? Because it sounded like it did."

He ate in silence for a few moments. She started to feel like she'd asked him something too personal. "It doesn't hurt, exactly. I mean, it kind of does." He shook his head. "It's like I'm trapped. I can see everything my beast is doing, feel what it's feeling. It feels like I'm suffocating." He stopped, nodded. "I never really put my finger on it before. That's it. Suffocating, trapped, bound. And there's not a damn thing I can do but wait it out."

"You can't control it at all?"

"On an ordinary day, I can. I can still do that. For the most part, I just focus on fighting him down. I try to limit how often I shift, because it feels like he gets stronger when I do that. Sometimes I can't avoid it." He shook his head. "But he's way stronger during the full moon, apparently. That was the first time it's been so bad, where I was at its mercy all night. Before, I could usually wrestle control back after a while. It's been getting harder to do all the time, though."

"And what's that like?"

He set his fork down, crossed his arms over his chest. "It's like playing tug of war. It always has been. My beast is wild. It has no interest in being tamed. So it was always something I needed to fight, and I tried really hard to get good at it, because I knew what was coming." He blew out a breath. "Now, it's like the beast starts out with more of the rope on its side, you know? And he just gets more and more of it all the time, until the day comes when I start out with pretty much nothing, and all it takes from him is one good tug to make me lose it."

She took another small bite of her food, forced herself to focus on the spicy bite on her tongue rather than Calder and his damn eyes. The way he'd said that last. He'd sounded so defeated.

"I'll find a way," she said. "I found the spell to help me translate the journal, and like I mentioned before, I tracked down Mrs. Redleaf. She's like a walking Ojibwa history book, and she's helping me learn more about Migisi. And two of those journals are full of writing. There has to be something of use in there."

He seemed to perk up a little at that. He pushed his empty food container aside and rested his elbows on the table, leaning forward, closer to her. "Yeah? So you're pretty sure they're Migisi's?" He gestured to her half-full container of food, and she pushed it across the table toward him, watched him finish it off. The man had eaten four and a half containers of Chinese food, all of the rice, and bread. She wondered what his grocery bills were like.

"Remember when I showed you the carving on the cover of that one?" He nodded. "That's Migisi's rune. So right now, I'm going with the theory that they're her books. And if not her, then maybe a close descendant."

He nodded, and she could tell he was trying not to get his hopes up.

"And there were things in her correspondence that Thea translated for me. Mostly spells."

"What were they for?"

"One was a ward, and another was a healing spell. They both looked kind of out of my league, but I still want to try them, because that's my thing, you know?"

He nodded, watching her.

"There was a love potion recipe, which I don't think I'll ever use, because that just seems kind of wrong. And then there was another spell in there that was just kind of weird."

"Weird, how?"

She shook her head. "The stuff in it, the items used in the spell. I've never seen those items used in a Lightwitch spell. And it wasn't named and there was no description of what it did."

He didn't say anything at first, seeming to think. "If it is Migisi's book, I think it's pretty clear that she went dark at some point, right? So maybe she wrote the letter or whatever it was after she cursed Luc."

"It just makes no sense. The dates were wrong. It was from after she met him, based on what we know, but before she supposedly cursed him. I mean, Thea was going on about what a hero, what a legend she was. So she's this hero, and Luc does something stupid and all of a sudden she throws it all away? She becomes what she worked her whole life against?" She paused. "Thea also said that Migisi was later known as 'Megisi the Mad.'"

"Mad like pissed, or mad like crazy?"

"I'm guessing the last one," she said, getting up and carrying their empty food containers to the trash. "Though she might have been pissed, too. She cursed Luc for whatever reason, and I have no doubt it diminished her powers, because we aren't supposed to do things like that. And maybe being pissed and less powerful, having her magic corrupted, drove her mad."

"Or whatever Luc did to her drove her mad, and everything else happened after," he pointed out. She turned and looked at him.

"I hadn't considered that."

"It makes more sense to me. I mean, I don't know anything about this witchy stuff other than what I've heard from my family. You all are a secretive group," he said. He stood up and took his glass to the sink, washed it, put it in the drying rack. "But a Lightwitch wouldn't mess up her power if she was in her right mind, right?"

"She could have been really, extremely angry," Sophie said.

"Maybe. But think about it. You've been running from dipshit for years rather than hurt him. You have every reason to, and I'd cheer you on if you did it. But you won't, no matter how bad it gets. Evie was pretty much powerless, but she was also the type who wouldn't even swat a fly. Literally. I was over here asking for information once, and she gently captured one and freed it outside."

Sophie smiled. "I've done that with spiders."

"Weirdo."

She laughed then. They exchanged a glance, then both looked away quickly.

"Well, as much as I want to believe one of my people wouldn't go evil on purpose, it still doesn't solve the curse."

"But it might. We need to keep stuff like that in mind. Maybe it'll make a difference."

She nodded. "Um. Maybe you can come with me sometimes, if you want to."

"It's really your family business. I don't want to intrude."

"No, you wouldn't be. I just mean, maybe you'll see something I overlook."

"What do you want, Sophie?" he asked quietly. "Do you want me there, or are you just being nice by inviting me?"

She watched him. "I want you there, if you want to be there. And maybe it matters to me that you don't think my entire family is crap. Though it's completely deserved."

"I don't think your entire family is crap. Especially not you," he said quietly. "And you shouldn't care what I think of you."

"Because you still think this is going nowhere," she said, feeling a flush rise to her cheeks in her embarrassment.

He was silent. "That's not what I meant, and at any rate it's not true," he said after a while. "I meant you shouldn't care what I think of you, because I'm a jackass. I'm bribing you to help me."

"I'd help you anyway. Even if you weren't holding my house over my head," she said.

He groaned, and she could tell that it was shame, irritation with himself. "I know. I should have not been an asshole and talked to you first."

"Well, then someone else would have gotten it. At least with you, I have a chance of getting it back."

He crossed his arms over his chest, leaned back against the countertop. "As far as this not going anywhere," he said. "We both know that would be for the best. No one wants to be stuck with a monster."

"Which one of us is the monster?" she asked with a smile. "Because apparently, I have it in me somewhere to utterly destroy someone."

"I don't think there was any doubt the other night which of us is the actual monster. And it's only gonna get worse, kitten. Can you honestly say you'd be okay being involved with someone who gets like that? Who would destroy you in a heartbeat if you slipped up? Because it's going to happen more and more often until that's all that's left." He watched her, and she couldn't answer. "And I know what you're doing. You're separating my beast from me in your mind to make it okay. There is no separate. I am him, he is me. All of the rage, all of the hunger, that's me. I'm just holding on to control better than he does. Barely," he added, looking away.

She cocked her head, studied him. "We're already involved, Calder. There's no going back, as far as I'm concerned." She paused. "Is it hard for you, being around me?"

Nothing, and then he gave a terse nod, not looking at her. His jaw was clenched, his hands formed into fists.

"What was it like yesterday?" she asked, not wanting to put into words what she was referring to.

"Kissing you was the most amazing and most painful thing I've done in my entire life," he said in a low voice, a hint of a growl to his words, and it sent a shiver through Sophie's body.

"I'm sorry it hurt you, Calder," she said. "I didn't think."

"You forgot the amazing part," he said, giving her a small smile. He was sexy when he was serious. But he was irresistible when he smiled.

She was completely, totally gone, and she knew it.

"It was pretty amazing," she said, blushing again. "It was that first time, too."

"It was," he said, eyes on her. "The best thing would be to walk away from you."

"But you can't," Sophie said. "And I can't stay away from you either. And I don't want to. I'll tell you right now that I believe in you, Calder."

He crossed the room in three long strides, took her chin gently in his hand. His touch, just that slight brush of his fingers against her flesh, made her breath catch. "You believe in me?" he asked quietly, his eyes seeking hers, voice low, almost desperate. "Really?"

"I do," she whispered. "I do," she repeated, voice shaking as he lowered his lips to hers, claimed her mouth in a way that was both tender and demanding at the same time. She whimpered quietly, and he deepened his kiss, the hair of his short beard gently abrading her skin as he tilted her head back so he could taste her better. Sophie put her arms around his waist, relishing the feel of his hard, warm body against hers. No sooner had she wrapped him in her arms than he removed his hands from her face and buried his fingers in her hair, tangling the curls in his hands, pulling her head back just a little more as he traced her lips with his tongue, gently nipped at her lower lip. He feathered a few more kisses across her mouth, gave her full lower lip one final tug with his teeth, then slowly, gently pulled away.

"You're mine," he murmured, voice low, eyes locked onto hers.

She trembled beneath his touch. "I'm yours," she whispered.

"Kiss me again, Sophie," he murmured and she did, raising her face to his. He kissed her slowly, deliberately, as if he was determined to learn and remember her flavor, as if she was something precious. It nearly made her weep, how much she felt when he kissed her.

"You're so gorgeous," he whispered when he pulled away. "So soft, so sweet. Strong. You've always had that. I think it's part of what made me so nuts over you, even back then, that quiet strength."

"I was shy and awkward," she said with a smile.

"Only with most people. With our group, you opened up. And most of the idiots we went to school with didn't give you much reason to open up."

She smiled. It was true. At the time, the tiny elementary and middle school they'd gone to just outside of Copper Falls had been all white. While there were many Native American kids around, they tended to go to the school near the reservation. She'd heard that that had closed down since, and everyone went to the public school, for the most part. But back then, it had been different. She'd been the only obviously "other" kid in their school, and there were plenty of jerk kids who liked to point it out.

"I never did ask you, but I always wondered what else you were. We know Ojibwa now. What else?"

She laughed a little. "I'm all mixed up. Ojibwa, black, Mexican, German, Irish. Those are the ones I know, anyway."

"It's a really beautiful combination, Sophie," he said, and she swallowed, touched by the tenderness in his voice, the plain, straightforward way he said it.

She kissed him again, and when he kissed her back, she knew, that instant, that she would do whatever it took to save him. Because no one had ever kissed her the way he did, with that aching tenderness and care. Because despite what he was, she'd never felt safer than she felt in his arms. Because when she looked at him, she was looking at forever. And she wasn't giving that up. Nothing, not curses or Shadow warlocks or anything else, was going to stand in her way.

She found her body trapped between his body and the counter in her kitchen, his hands on her waist, her hips, gently tracing the curve at the sides of her breasts, which made her gasp in need.

"So goddamn beautiful," he growled, and it sent shivers down her spine. He was kissing her again, holding her tight to his body, his desire evident in the hardness pressing into her abdomen. He pulled back, breathless, nibbling at her lips before backing up completely.

"Was that too much?" he asked her.

She shook her head. "I just don't want you to be uncomfortable or..."

Calder grimaced. "Well. I'm uncomfortable. And if my stupid beast wasn't raging, I'd be trying really, really hard to convince you to make me more comfortable, kitten," he said, and she laughed.

"You wouldn't have to try all that hard, Calder."

He leaned forward and kissed her. "Good to know."

He led her into the living room, and kisses sitting on the sofa somehow turned into Calder's body on top of hers, his hips settled between her thighs, his lips at her throat, biting gently.

He pulled back with a groan, got off of her, slid behind her on the couch so they were lying side by side.

"You're tired," he said.

"I'm fine."

"I'm not," he said wryly, and she laughed and snuggled back against him.

A while later, after a couple of hours of talking and kissing, he dozed off, and she turned in his arms, watched him sleep. And she was on edge. She shouldn't have been. It was comforting, if a little frustrating, having him with her this way. And yet, the longer they'd been together, she'd felt more on edge, more empty, somehow. It made no sense, and she wondered if maybe she was just confused over getting what she'd wanted for so long. Screwed up over what she'd learned about Luc's and Migisi's ends. She tried convincing herself that that was it, and that the added issue of his curse, his still holding her house as collateral, was what was bothering her.

But that wasn't it. None of that was good, and she was enough of a realist to know that what they had was far from perfect. Whatever it was she had, she thought to herself. But it wasn't that.

She just felt weirdly wrong, somehow. And it irritated her that she couldn't put her finger on why that was. She usually managed to figure out what her problems were. Years and years of being alone had made her good at introspection, if nothing else. But she couldn't place it.

She forced it away, closed her eyes, and snuggled into Calder's body. It would pass.

Calder ended up sleeping beside her all night, and she woke feeling both as if she was in heaven and as if she was walking through the gates of hell. How many times had she dreamed of this, of him finding her again someday, of waking up next to him after a night in his arms? And now, the emptiness, the undercurrent of anger and anxiety that had been gnawing at her the night before only felt worse in the morning light. He woke, and his lips were on the back of her neck, her shoulders, his hands holding her hips firmly against his body. The low growl he gave when she turned her head so he could claim her lips sent a surge of need through her.

His kisses became harder, his hands less soft on her body, and then his body was on top of hers, his thigh pressed between her legs, urging them open. He squeezed her breasts firmly, and she whimpered, gave in to his insistence to open her legs.

"Should mark you right now," he growled. "Make you mine."

"Calder," she whispered.

He was tense, almost bristling on top of her. "Shit," he groaned. He leapt from the bed, and before she could even say another word to him, he was gone. A few moments later, she heard pained, angry growls from the woods west of her house, and she shivered.

"This is the worst idea ever," she muttered to herself. "I am an idiot. He's an idiot." She got up, locked the front door behind him. She headed into the bathroom to shower, knowing enough about Calder and his beast to know that the beast got a special kick out of smelling Calder on her. That whole ownership thing. She muttered to herself the whole time, not only irritated over how stupid she was being (and knowing that the second she saw him again, she'd fall right back into his arms) but also because she still felt weird. Wrong.

She got out of the shower, dressed, pulled her hair up, stepped into her rubber boots. She went out and milked the goats, fed the chickens, had her daily battle with Merlin over whichever spot he was currently trying to weaken so he could escape.

She went back inside, and, just as she'd finished pouring her tea, there was a knock at her door.

She closed her eyes, trying to calm the tumult of emotions running through her. It was Calder. She knew it was. And she was giddy that he'd come back so soon, and irritated with herself for being that way. She went to the door, pulled it open, waved him in.

Calder walked in, a sheepish, guilty look on his face. "I'm sorry" were the first words out of his mouth.

"I think we're complete morons," she said in response. "I am crazy about you, Calder. I am nuts about you. There is nothing I won't do for you, and that's completely stupid. Seeing you is enough to make my whole day better. You're gorgeous and you make me feel better than I've ever felt in my life, ever. But this is goddamned stupid and we are going to end up hating one another," she said, stomping through the living room back toward the kitchen.

She turned, and he was smiling at her, a half-grin that made her heart pound. "Finished?" he asked.

"Maybe," she said, crossing her arms over her chest. He walked toward her, lowered his head, kissed her gently, warmly. "We are being stupid, maybe. We've been over this," he said. "But I will never, ever hate you, Sophie." He kissed her again, and she felt her irritation fading, just a little. "I'm sorry," he said against her lips. "You deserve so much better. I'm not a very good man."

"That is complete nonsense, right there," she said. She put her arms around him. "I wonder if Luc was anything like you," she said after standing in his arms for a while.

"What do you mean?"

"If he was, I can see how Migisi fell so hard for him. And if he was, I can also see why it destroyed her to lose him."

He lowered his forehead to hers. "I think if he was anything like me, and if she was anything like you, he felt the same way. It's always been this between us, Soph. Do you remember the first day of fifth grade?"

She smiled a little. "Maybe."

"I remember. I was sitting in Mrs. Redleaf's class, acting like a typical eleven-year-old asshole with the other guys in the back corner of the room, and you walked in with Layla. I couldn't stop staring at you, and you stopped short, as if something froze you on the spot. Neither one of us understood it. You only moved when Layla pulled you toward your seat, but you kept glancing back at me. Even dumbass Bobby Hardley noticed."

"And you punched him," she said with a laugh.

He let out a short laugh. "And from that moment on, it was you and me, kitten." Absolute truth. How many boys, including high schoolers, had Calder beat up for saying the wrong thing to her or about her in middle school? Layla had been her best friend, but who had usually been the one she'd turned to with her worries and problems?

"I wish you would have told me some of what was going on back then. Your dad must have been bad already," she said softly, still resting her forehead against his. Her heart hurt, remembering how often he'd sat quietly and listened to her going on and on about some annoying thing her dad had done or some insult one of the other girls had thrown at her. And he'd been going through so much worse, and never said a word.

"I wasn't allowed to talk about it. I wanted to. I knew you'd listen. So many times, I almost did. But then I was already crazy about you and thought telling you I was destined to become a raging monster who'd eventually lose my humanity was probably not the best way to impress you."

She smiled, put her hands in his hair. She ran her fingers through it, and he sighed, closed his eyes. "I would have listened. And I still would have been crazy about you," she said softly. "When we left, I was a mess. It was like they were tearing me away from the only one who understood me at all. I cried for weeks. I tried to run away four times to come back here, hoping I could stay with Evie. I never got very far," she finished. She'd only stopped trying to run because it seemed like, eventually, her steps were haunted by the dark, brooding man who'd begun showing up everywhere. The idea of being too far away from anyone who knew her with him around was terrifying enough that it got her to stop running. "I dreamed for years that we'd find one another again someday."

She was still running her fingers lazily through his hair, and his eyes were still closed, relishing her touch.

"Me too," he said. "I was miserable after you left. My dad got notes and calls a few times a week because of fights I got into. Started failing classes. It felt like part of my heart was gone."

"My mom said it was a teenage crush and I'd get over it," Sophie said. "I very clearly didn't."

He laughed a little. "Me neither." He opened his eyes then. "I'm going to keep you safe. From me, from anyone who tries to mess with you. I swear it."

She felt tears come to her eyes. "I know you will, Calder. And I'm going to save you. Don't try to tell me I can't."

He smiled. "Okay."

"I'm not kidding. You've been mine since I was eleven years old. I'm not losing you again."

Calder kissed her again, and then they cooked together, Calder scrambling a couple of eggs, Sophie brewing coffee and putting bread in the chrome-plated toaster on the counter. Sophie watched him as he ate. It was one of those moments, those seemingly unimportant, mundane moments that she knew she'd remember for the rest of her life. The way the sun slanted in the window behind him, dust motes sparkling in its rays. The way he sat in her kitchen, forearms resting on the edge of the table. The way their eyes met over his coffee cup, the way the side of his foot was pressed to the side of her foot under the table, an unconscious move on both their parts, as if not touching when they were in the same room was a pointless hardship. She would remember it, she knew.

They finished eating, cleaned up, and he followed her into the living room. They settled on the couch, seeming to have come to an unspoken agreement that groping was, unfortunately, off limits for a while. He sat on the end of the couch, and she settled against his side, grabbing Migisi's journal as she did. She leaned against him, her back to his side, and he rested his arm around her, his forearm resting just below her collarbone. She opened the book, quickly cast the spell to allow her to translate it, and he sat silently behind her. She felt him move, glanced back to see him open the Ojibwa history book she'd checked out of the library.

They read together, sitting like that, for most of the morning and early afternoon. Every once in a while, she'd read a passage out loud to him. She had yet to learn anything all that useful about the curse, but she was learning a lot about Migisi; who her friends were, which spells she found difficult, her thoughts about the French *voyageurs* in the area. She did not have the world's highest opinion of them.

185

She was just about to call it quits for the day. The spell was starting to wear on her, and that weird emptiness that had seemed to have left her for a while was coming back, distracting her, making it harder for her to hold her magic in such a focused way.

She read faster, jumping ahead, then sat up with a jubilant shout.

"What?" Calder asked with a laugh, watching her. She scrambled onto his lap, straddled his thighs.

"Found him. Listen to this."

"I'll listen to anything you say as long as you're sitting on me like that," he said with a grin.

Sophie smacked his arm. "Behave and listen." She started reading.

"He finally caught me. The trapper I have been thwarting managed to trick me this time. He must have circled around after I'd sabotaged his traps. It is the only thing that makes sense, and I am irritated with myself for my carelessness.

Maybe I wanted to meet him. Perhaps, I would have been more careful otherwise. We have been playing this game for weeks now. When I am being honest, I admit to myself that I enjoy our game. This has gone beyond me protecting my territory from interlopers, though there is still that. I enjoy outsmarting him. I enjoy the way he tries to work around me, the way he growls in frustration.

Perhaps, I enjoyed the flash of his eyes a bit too much.

Perhaps. Perhaps I am lonely.

At any rate, he caught up with me. He confronted me, and I was impressed by the way he kept his irritation under control. He was respectful, if angry. And the way he looked at me— I would very much like someone to look at me like that regularly.

No. Not just someone. Him. I am embarrassed over how much I've thought about him. How I've dreamt about this brash, rough Frenchman.

To have someone see me not as a healer and wise woman first, but as a woman, period— to not have someone's hopes and dreams, someone's biggest fears laid bare at my feet — it is a relief. Under his gaze, I feel free.

And it is exhilarating.

We spoke. His voice is deep, so deep it reaches right into the depths of me. He is much more intelligent than I gave him credit for. He towers over me, pure strength. He wears a beard, as many of the white men do, and I find that I rather like it. It makes him look wild, which suits him. He is the most wild thing I've ever known. More wild, even, than me.

Look at me, writing about this man like a maiden with her first infatuation.

We will meet up again in the morning. And I will show him where it is acceptable for him to trap. Certainly nowhere in my forest...."

She looked up at Calder. "I mean, she doesn't name him, but it has to be him. It sounds like she was crazy about him from the beginning."

"It does," he said slowly. "I wonder how he felt about her. Like she says, she was messing with his trapping. I wonder if it went both ways, or whether she was the only one who felt it."

"I wonder," Sophie said quietly, running her fingers over the words. "If he didn't reciprocate, and she felt this strongly about him, you could see it hurting her over time. I mean, not that I can imagine that ever being a reason to curse someone, but still."

"Or maybe he was just as nuts about her. Maybe it started fast, and ended badly."

"Maybe," she admitted. "She doesn't write like someone who was evil."

"It's pretty much been established that she wasn't. I see that much now, at least." Calder leaned forward and kissed her, claiming her lips, and she leaned into him, and he pulled the journal out of her hands, set it aside. Her concentration was totally gone, anyway, and she was starting to get a headache from the strain of using her magic for such an extended period of time. When he pulled back, he did so with a sigh.

"I have to go," he said.

"Okay," she whispered.

"I promised Jon I'd stop by today," he explained. "Can I come see you again later?"

She nodded. "You can come to me whenever you want."

"Just like the old days," he said, smiling in a way that warmed her entire body.

"But with more kissing," she said, and he laughed.

"Thank god," he murmured, lowering his lips to hers again. He stood up, holding her body against his, and she wrapped her legs around his waist to keep herself up. He held her tight to him, and she held on to him just as tightly. When he finally broke their kiss, he did so reluctantly, slowly, as if trying to hold on to the taste of her lips.

"I'll be back in a while," he said, finally lowering her to the floor. She walked him to the door, and he took her hand, brought her wrist to her mouth. He inspected the lines across her wrist, the same scars he'd noticed before. His eyes met hers, and he pressed his lips to the sensitive flesh at her wrist. Something in his eyes blazed, and she knew, because she knew Calder, that he was angry on her behalf. "I wish I'd been there," he said as he gently released her hand.

"Me too," she said "But you're here now."

He nodded, gave her another quick kiss, told her he'd see her in a while. She watched him walk across the road and get on his motorcycle, felt something in her tighten at the sight of him riding away from her. She'd had the same feeling whenever they'd parted ways as kids. Some things just never seemed to change. Apparently, they were one of them.

She looked down at her wrist. Three scars. Two attempts as a teenager, one after David had died. Guilt, loneliness. She looked down the road in the direction he'd headed. She wouldn't let him meet the same fate. He was stronger than David, and she was no longer a naive, terrified girl.

They'd make it work, and she'd keep him safe. There were no other options.

CHAPTER EIGHTEEN

June 22, 1856

Migisi lay on the bank of the stream near the waterfall on the other side of her woods, in a patch of warm summer sunlight. Dragonflies flitted over the water, iridescent flashes in the still air. Birds called nearby, and the breeze kissed her naked skin. She glanced sleepily to her left, where Luc lay on his back, hands folded under his head, eyes closed. They'd been practically inseparable other than those times, twice each year, when he went to visit with his business partners. They'd spent every day, every night together in the tiny wood cabin he'd helped her build. One room: four walls, and a roof. It was all they needed.

He knew her. He was familiar with her magic, and she was used to seeing him in both his human and bear forms. He was equally breathtaking either way.

Most of the time they spent together, they spent in silence, reveling in one another's presence. The way he looked at her was like nourishment for her soul; the way he smiled made her feel lighter than she could remember feeling in her entire life.

The years had passed as if they were days. He'd quickly become the center of her world, and that was something Migisi never would have thought possible. She loved letting her gaze travel the well-honed muscles of his arms and back, the straight line of his nose. She found that she could stare into his eyes for an eternity.

"Staring again, my little ghost?" he asked, his voice relaxed, droll.

"Thinking of how horribly ugly you are," she answered, and he grinned at her.

"You are hideous as well," he said, and she laughed. Then she sobered, and his gaze focused more as she quieted. "What's wrong, Migisi?"

She shook her head and looked away.

"We have never had any trouble being open with one another, not in these last few months, anyway." It was true. She'd told him anything he'd asked, and he did the same with her. They'd explored one another's bodies without shame, done things to one another Migisi couldn't have imagined. There was no shame between them, no discomfort. "What is it?" he asked, sitting up and resting his elbows on his knees, watching her.

"What are we doing, exactly?" she asked quietly.

"We're enjoying the first day of summer," he said, and she closed her eyes in irritation.

"You know what I mean, Luc."

He was silent.

"Is this forever?" she asked, feeling stupid. Needy. These were things she did not feel. There was never any time or any reason to feel them.

"As far as I am concerned, yes, it is," he answered without hesitation.

She couldn't look at him. She felt like she had just lost all dignity.

"Is it marriage you need? Because we can do that. I would marry you today if that would assure you that I mean to spend my life with you. I have never pushed for that. You are fiercely independent, and I don't want to scare you off. I know you, Migisi. You love your solitude, and you don't do a damn thing until you want to, and the idea that you'd accept marriage because you felt like you had to... But if you want that, we will do it."

She looked at him then. "It's not that. In my heart, my soul, I'm married to you already. There will be no other."

"Then what is it?"

She swallowed. She took his hand, a hand that had explored every inch of her body, and she placed his palm on her abdomen, watched his eyes.

Confusion, and then he understood what she was trying to tell him, trusting that he'd understand, because she was terrified to say the words. He rubbed his hand gently over her abdomen a few times, and she shivered.

Luc stood up, reached out his hand, and she took it. He pulled her up gently, though of course she didn't need any help. She found that she liked letting him help anyway. He pulled gently, and she glided into the refreshing water of the river with him. They entered the water together, becoming more immersed with each step until they couldn't even touch the bottom. At any other time, Migisi would have been scrambling in the water to reach a firmer footing. With him, she let herself lose contact with the lake bed.

Luc pulled her into his arms, his eyes searching hers.

"How do you say 'I love you' in your native tongue?" he asked her.

Migisi bit back the sob that inexplicably wanted to surface. "*Gi zah gin*," she whispered.

Luc lowered his lips to hers, and the second their lips met, she felt like she was home, as if he was the life she'd been missing all along. She kissed him, let out a low whimper when he ran his tongue along her lower lip.

"*Gi zah gin*," he said, his voice a low rumble, his eyes on hers again, his lips a breath away from hers. "*Je t'aime. Migisi*," he said, and the need in his voice went straight through her, and then she did sob, leaning forward and claiming his mouth again. She gave him everything he wanted, took everything she needed, and by the time they left the water, she felt as if she'd been reborn and nothing felt the same.

"Our child is going to be so beautiful, Migisi," Luc murmured as he helped her into her light dress, which she'd left, folded, beside where they'd been sunbathing. "Let's have this, forever."

"I can't imagine it ever being otherwise, my heart," she said, watching with tenderness as he fumbled, trying to tie the belt at her waist, his normally steady hands shaking.

His eyes met hers again. "Same," he said. "I am yours."

He said it, and he said he loved her, and Migisi believed every promise he made her, because he was her heart, and the heart never lies.

CHAPTER NINTEEN

Sophie vacuumed the room she was cleaning, well aware that she had a stupid grin on her face. Calder had tried to stay with her last night and had had to leave, which was for the best, considering she was pretty sure she would have done just about anything he asked if he'd stayed, and, while she was all for the idea of doing that, the weird feeling she had lately only seemed to get worse the longer she was with him.

Really, it was pretty much impossible. His beast started acting up when they were together, and she started getting that weird, empty, edgy feeling, as if, for whatever reason, she was very near to lashing out. And it made no sense, because when she was with Calder, it was everything she hoped it would be. Better than she'd dreamed it could be, with him. He was warm, and attentive, and sexy as hell, and he made her feel like the single most important thing in the universe.

He'd always done that, though, she thought with a smile as she turned off the vacuum and started making the bed, tearing the old sheets off.

The previous night, he'd come over and they'd baked a couple pot pies (chicken for him, vegetable for her) and sat watching *Game of Thrones*, which she hadn't yet watched, on his laptop. He'd held her, and there had been plenty of kissing and touching, and then he'd had to leave.

Cold showers, it was becoming clear, were going to be a normal part of her life with Calder.

He'd shown up this morning. She'd walked out the back door to take care of the animals to find him already out there, pounding more stakes into Merlin's fencing. Merlin was bleating at him in a bad-natured way, and Calder was calling him a "cranky old bastard." Once he'd seen her there, he'd helped her with the milking, then taken her inside, and, once they'd cleaned up, he grabbed a bag off of the back porch, where he'd left it. Inside was a chocolate cream pie from the bakery in town.

"I remembered you liked these," he'd said, and she'd sat and had breakfast with him.

It was so easy to love him. And so hard to love him at the same time. His curse, her weird issues with her magic, the fact that, like it or not, he was still holding her house over her head. The fact that, despite her brave words, she was more worried every day that she wouldn't be enough to save him, and the equinox was fast approaching.

During her lunch break, she went into the empty employee lounge and pulled out Migisi's journal. She leafed through it, waiting for more mentions of the French trapper. There were many entries about people she'd healed, spells she used to do so, as if she was trying to ensure she'd remember them. In one, she'd ended with the words, "The darkness rises, and some days, I fear it will swallow me whole."

Sophie stared at the words, chills running up her spine. "What caused it, Migisi?" she asked under her breath. She kept reading. The writing, for the most part, remained intelligent and straightforward, but the penmanship changed, getting bigger, messier. She wondered how much time had passed as she saw the writing degrade over the course of many pages. Her break was nearly up when she saw Luc's name on the next page she was supposed to read. She focused, determined to hold on to the spell for a while longer, pushed herself to hold it. And she read.

"Nothing is right. I am wrong in my own body, unable to do even the most basic spells. My healing elixirs fail. My garden withers.

Even the tiny life growing inside me has failed. Luc mourns."

Sophie blinked back tears, looked at the words again. She sent a prayer of mourning, hoping Migisi, wherever she was, would hear it and know. Sophie tried to pull herself together to read on.

"I am a failure in every way that has ever mattered to me. Darkness clouds everything, and I have no more power to fight it back. My only comfort is Luc, and he grows distant as the darkness becomes harder to fight. I am lost, and I do not know how to fight my way back. Some days, it is as if there is a glimmer of light, just off to the side, and if I could only turn my head quickly enough, I could see it fully. But I am never fast enough, and it slips away. Everything feels corrupted. Luc was the most beautiful thing in my life and even that feels wrong, because of me. He mentioned going south before the snows fall, to update his business partners on his whereabouts and bring them their share of the furs he's stockpiled. I encouraged him to go. Perhaps, alone with my thoughts, I can shake this darkness from my soul.

I fear I may have lost everything already."

"Damn it," Sophie murmured, closing the book and resting her face in her hands, trying hard to get her emotions under control so she could go back to work.

Her heart ached for Migisi. But more, she feared she knew exactly what Migisi had gone through. And she saw where that road ended.

She just had to save him before it all fell apart.

Sophie made it through the rest of her shift, even managing to be polite to the few guests who were staying at the resort. Migisi's words kept running through her mind.

It really didn't make sense. What was causing it? Why was she feeling this way? Why had Migisi turned to the Shadow, when, from what Thea said, she was among the best of the best?

She decided to stop by the reservation and see if Thea could tell her anything else. Thea had called the night before, but Sophie had missed the call, wrapped up, literally, in Calder.

She considered going home first to change, but she didn't really want to get stuck driving home in the dark, not with Marshall out there again. Instead, she did her best to clean up a little, pulling her hair up into a messy bun, swiping on some lip gloss and a little bit of concealer, not that it did much for the dark circles under her eyes.

She grabbed her bag, which contained the three journals of Migisi's, and headed out to her car. After she climbed in, she dialed Calder's number to tell him she'd be late. He'd be worried otherwise. She got his voice mail, told him she was stopping off to see Thea. She ended with a breathy "love you," almost afraid to say the words. But she wanted him to know. He needed to know.

She hung up and drove out of town, past the campgrounds and kitschy tourist shops, down the highway. Her mind wandered, and she was there before she knew it. She pulled up in front of the meeting house, got out, shouldering her bag. Thea was just coming out of the building as she was heading up the walk.

"Hey! I'm so glad you stopped by," she greeted Sophie.

"I meant to call but I was all —" she wiggled her fingers, illustrating how absent-minded she was feeling, "today."

Thea laughed. "Don't worry about it. Drop in any time. We're your people too. You're welcome here, kiddo."

Sophie smiled, warmed by her former teacher's words. "Thanks."

"I gathered up a bunch of things I found about Migisi, and I made copies of a few things I thought you might like to have."

"Oh my gosh. You're amazing," Sophie said, taking Thea's hand.

Thea laughed. "Oh, I know I am," she said, squeezing Sophie's hand. "Come on in."

They headed back inside the building, and Thea led her back to her cramped, cozy little office.

"Any luck on the journals?" she asked Sophie.

Sophie sat down. "She and Luc were together for a while, it looks like. She was pregnant, and she lost it."

Thea stilled, watched Sophie. "Really?"

Sophie nodded. "She also wrote about how her magic was failing, that she felt the darkness encroaching."

"Shadow?"

"I think so. Which points to the idea of her going dark before she cursed Luc. Maybe she was just too far gone by the time that happened."

"What caused it, though?"

"I really wish I knew," Sophie answered quietly.

Thea sat in the chair behind her desk, studying Sophie. "Is this happening to you, Sophie? Is the Shadow encroaching?"

"I feel wrong. I don't know why."

"Does your magic still work?"

Sophie nodded. "It's more difficult than usual at times, but it works."

Thea studied her for a few moments, then shook her head.

"Tell me about Migisi the Mad. Please," she added.

Thea set the file she'd been holding down on the desk. "Migisi the Mad. The story goes that there was a great healer among us, of our people. That she could heal anything. That she could keep us from starving even in the worst of times. That the only reason this particular community didn't succumb completely to the diseases brought by the white man was because of her care and protection. She saved us, when so many others perished." She paused. "I dislike speaking of this. She should be remembered as she was. And we don't know how much of the Migisi the Mad tale is actually true," she hastened to add.

Sophie nodded. "Please."

"The story goes that Migisi was our healer. Our strength. We depended on her. Maybe we depended on her too much. Maybe we helped break her." Thea paused, and her shame was plain on her face, as if she, generations removed, was personally to blame. She went on. "One day, she was our beloved. And then she was gone. No one saw her, and the tribe feared her dead. But she wasn't. When she reappeared, she was no longer the healer we loved. She was angry. Cold. She wanted nothing to do with the people who relied on her. She became a hermit, only occasionally coming to the villages, where, it was said, she'd look around and then leave. Children started disappearing," she said, glancing at Sophie. "Children who were a little different." Her expression closed down, as if she'd said too much.

"You know what I am," Sophie said quietly.

After a moment, Thea nodded.

"I know shapeshifters. Witches. Warlocks," Sophie said. "They were special like that?"

"Yes," Thea answered, nodding. "Shapeshifters. From our records, six of them disappeared over a three-year span. Keep in mind, we never did have many. All that we had, we lost. There are no shapeshifters among us now."

"And Migisi had something to do with it?" Sophie asked, not really wanting to hear the answer.

"We never knew for sure. Tribal history shows that there were debates. The tribe wanted to march on her land, demand our children back. But, ultimately, no one wanted to anger her. The tribe mourned. And we never did see those children the way they were again."

"That makes it sound like they *were* seen again."

Thea nodded. "I will find the documents for you for next time. When they were finally returned to us, they were wrong. They couldn't shift back. They were only recognized because their families knew their scents."

"Did they act different?" Sophie asked.

Thea looked at her quizzically. "Different, how?"

"More violent? Hungrier? Anything like that?"

"No. None of the records mention anything like that. At least, I don't remember it being part of the reports. I will double check. They just couldn't shift back to their human forms. They did not live much longer after they came back to us."

Sophie sat in silence, mourning for children she'd never known. "Migisi did it?"

"It was assumed she did something. It was months between the time they disappeared and when the tribe got them back."

"Did anyone search her land for them?"

Thea nodded. "Of course. She was powerful. I don't find it very hard to believe that she hid them well." She picked up the journal Sophie had set on the desk after removing it from her bag, the one with the paintings and drawings in it. She flipped back in the journal, to the painting of the bear. "This has something to do with this, doesn't it?" she asked Sophie, gesturing to the bear.

"Maybe. I kind of hope not."

"Me too. Because if this is the kind of magic we're dealing with, I really don't want to be any part of it."

"I'm not trying to replicate it. I'm trying to figure out what went wrong," Sophie said.

Thea studied her. "Do you hope to fix it?"

"If I can," Sophie replied softly. "I'm not very powerful. But I have to try."

"What does it matter to you?" Thea asked, though her voice was gentle. "You're a young woman. You should be living your life, not worrying about a history none of us can change."

"Not everything that's in the past remains there, I guess," Sophie said. "You know who Luc's descendant is. I am as much a fool for him as Migisi once was for Luc. But in our case, I need to save him. This is his family's last chance for salvation." She took a deep breath, focused on Thea. "Can you trust me? Can I trust you?"

Thea sighed, then took Sophie's hand in hers. "Until you give me reason not to, I trust you. Know that I will be watching you. And if I even see you so much as looking at one of our children in a funny way, I will do whatever it takes to protect them."

"I would never hurt anyone!" Sophie said in shock.

"Neither would Migisi. And yet..." she said, shrugging. "We need to understand one another. Do we?"

After a moment, Sophie nodded.

"Good." She picked up the folder again. "Here are those documents I found." She got up and sat next to Sophie, opened the folder. The first paper she took out was a photocopy of an old photograph of a Native American woman. She was stunning. The photo showed the woman in profile, and she was looking up slightly. She was dressed, it looked like, in leathers, and a beaded headband with traditional Ojibwa symbols. Her hair flowed down in two long braids over her shoulders. In it, Sophie recognized her own nose, slightly pointed, yet a little flat. The woman's narrow chin was also something Sophie saw in the mirror every day.

"Migisi?" she whispered, unable to take her eyes off of the photo.

"Yes. This is the only known photograph of her. It was taken in 1860."

"That was after she met Luc," Sophie murmured.

"When did they meet again?"

"1852, according to the journals."

"So eight years, at least, she was fine. She was not yet mad when this was taken. This next page is from a newspaper article that this photo accompanied, talking about her accomplishments."

Sophie glanced over the article, still holding the photograph in her other hand. "The French really seemed to respect her," she said.

"As they should have. She healed many of them as well, when they fell ill."

Sophie leafed through the rest of the folder, which contained mostly newspaper articles and narrated histories of people who'd known Migisi. She kept holding the photograph, but put the rest of the folder on the desk and slumped back in her chair.

"So she was fine for quite a while. If this was taken in 1860, she'd known him for at least eight years by this point," she said. "How old would she have been here again?"

"Born in 1827, so 33 or so," Thea said.

"She'd lost the baby by this point, and she was already beginning to feel the effects of the Shadow taking her over." She narrowed her eyes, looked at Thea. "Was it normal for someone to be that age and still single? And still that healthy? She looks so young."

Thea laughed. "Not at all. But who was going to argue with her? She was our tribe's healer, our protection. She was married to her magic, to her woods, and our people were understanding of that. Not that there weren't men who wanted her. She had many suitors, our own men and men from other tribes alike. She was described by one Iroquois as "'like a rabid dog, more likely to snap than anything else.' As far as her age, I've heard that your kind, and shapeshifters as well, can be quite long-lived."

Sophie laughed, looked at the photo again. "Damn it, Migisi. What went wrong?"

Thea had picked up the journal of paintings again. "This one is different," Thea said. Sophie forced her concentration back to the woman and Migisi's journal.

"What is?" she asked.

"This drawing. Did you see this one?" Thea asked, tilting the journal toward Sophie. Sophie recognized it immediately, having thought the same thing herself when she'd quickly flipped through the journal.

"I haven't looked through that one much. I do like the painting of the falls, though."

She tore her eyes away from it. The image had made her uncomfortable before, and it made her equally uncomfortable now. Where Migisi's earlier art had been full of color and life, this one was in shades of gray, black, and deep blue. A fall forest, it looked like, brown leaves on the forest floor, trees bare of life. The entire thing looked barren and dark, the branches of the forlorn-looking trees reaching up into a lifeless sky. It had Migisi's style, the line weights typical of her hand based on the other drawings and paintings. The mood was all wrong.

Thea was studying her, and Sophie looked down at her notes.

"Did you notice that this one has a title?" Thea finally asked. Sophie looked back at the book, to where Thea was pointing. There, at the base of the tree, what Sophie had mistaken as leaf litter, was writing. Not French.

"What does it say?" Sophie asked.

"*Niboowin*. It is our word for death."

"Lovely," Sophie said, looking away from the drawing again.

"It gets worse. Did you notice the writing on the back of it?" Thea asked.

"There was some scribbling back there. Those are actually words?"

Thea nodded. "Again, in our language. Hm," she said with a frown. "Well, that isn't good." She glanced up at Sophie. "The darkness rises," she said with a grimace.

Sophie sat, feeling numb.

"So it was Luc she destroyed," Thea said, trying to piece it all together. "What does that have to do with the painting? With this one?" She flipped back to the one of the bear on the rock.

"That's Luc," Sophie said.

"Oh," Thea said, as if she was beginning to understand it all. "Oh good god."

"Yeah."

"Sophie. What did she do to him? This is why you're here. What happened?" Thea asked. "What does that curse do?"

"She cursed him, and even now, his line suffers with it. His descendant tracked me down and we worked out a deal that I would try to break the curse."

"So, Calder is cursed as well?" Thea asked softly. Sophie nodded.

"What does it do?"

Sophie stood up and looked out the window. "The cursed feels insatiable hunger. Dissatisfaction. It eats away at them until it slowly but surely drives them insane, because no matter how much they eat, how much sex they have, how much water they drink... they're never all right. They're never satisfied. The insanity makes it so they forget how to shift back, and they are nothing but a mindless beast, a monster who has ceaseless hunger."

The room was silent other than the ticking of the clock over the door for several long moments. "Wendigo," Thea said.

Sophie turned to her. "What?"

"She based the curse on the wendigo. *Wiindigoo*, in our tongue," Thea said, grabbing a book off of the nearby bookshelf and flipping through it. "Of course, the tale of the wendigo is a warning against the evils of cannibalism. Er. They don't eat people, do they?" she asked, looking at Sophie.

Sophie shrugged. "Not that I've heard. I know they're violent once they become insane. I guess if they were hungry enough and a human was nearby, they would."

Thea gave a small shiver. "All right, well, Migisi would have known of *wiindigoo*. The thing with the *wiindigoo* is that once it gets that first taste of human flesh, it hungers endlessly for more. Its hunger is never, ever satisfied. There is no way for it to ever feel satisfied again. It just wants more and more. It was a cautionary tale."

Sophie thought. "What we have heard is that Luc cheated on Migisi and she caught him. In her rage, she cursed him and his entire line."

Thea nodded slowly. "As if she was saying 'oh, I wasn't enough for you? There'll never be such a thing as enough for you again.'"

"Right."

"Wow."

"Yeah."

Thea shook her head. "But a curse like that... I mean, I know nothing about witches, so you're going to have to fill me in, but Migisi wasn't that kind of witch, right? She was a healer."

Sophie flipped to the back of the drawing of the dark forest, to the words "the darkness rises," and Thea sighed, her entire body slumping in sadness.

On that happy note, Sophie gathered the journals, as well as the folder of papers Thea had found for her, and promised to meet up again in a few days' time.

More questions, and still no answers.

When she pulled into her driveway, she paid the barest of attention to the stupid rose sitting at the end of her driveway. Instead, she found her attention drawn to Calder, leaning over the engine of Bryce's ugly car.

She put her car into park, looked out her window toward him, irritated, as if there was something just out of reach, some thought that hadn't quite made its way through, as if there was something she needed to remember, wanted to remember, but couldn't.

She climbed out of the car and walked across the road, eyes on him. He'd been looking toward her already, and he stood up straight, wiped his hands on a nearby rag.

"What's wrong?" he asked as she stalked up to him.

"Nothing," she murmured, pulling his shirt a little, then standing on tiptoe so she could brush her lips across his. Instantly, his arms were around her, holding her tight to his body, his lips warm and insistent on hers. She let him turn her body, press her up against the side of the car. The sensation of being trapped between his big body and the steel of the car was exactly what she needed. So firm, so real. He buried his fingers in her hair again, and she let out a low moan. He kissed her, then trailed his lips down her chin, her jaw, her throat, and she held him close to her.

"What happened?" he asked, kissing the side of her neck. "You look spooked. You're all adrenaline right now."

She shook her head, held him tighter. He rubbed his cheek against hers, and she closed her eyes. She could feel his heart pounding against her. A tremor went through him.

"Okay?" she asked him.

"I think I have to back off a little," he said, and the regret in his voice made her want him even more. She nodded, and slowly let him go. He took a step back. His jaw was clenched, every muscle tense.

"I'm sorry," she said softly.

"Don't be. I'm going to be replaying you walking across the street and laying that kiss on me over and over in my mind for days." He gave a tight smile.

"Should I go?" she asked. He shook his head.

"I don't want you to. I'm okay. Just don't touch me for a while."

"A girl could get insulted by something like that," she said, trying to shake him out of the frustration she could read all over his face.

She was rewarded with a wry smile. "You know damn well if I had my way you'd be touching me all the time, kitten."

She smiled then, glancing at the car. "Does this help?" she asked, nodding toward it. "Working on stuff like this?"

He nodded. "It helps to have something concrete to focus on. And it's just kind of rewarding, saving one of those badasses from the scrap heap."

She ran her hand over roof of the car. She glanced inside, and the sight of the back seat made her mind go places it probably shouldn't have gone right then. She heard a low growl, and she looked back at Calder. He was staring at her, head lifted, just a bit, as if he was scenting the air.

"You're driving me insane," he said, his voice a low, rumbling growl.

"I have a proposition for you, big guy," she said, leaning back against the car.

He groaned. "Sophie...."

"Why don't you come over to my place? I'll change, light some candles...."

He was staring at her hungrily. She bit back a smile.

"And you can help me milk the goats."

He shook his head a little, and she burst out laughing. A few seconds later, he was laughing, too. "You are crazy," he said, shaking his head.

"Maybe," she agreed.

He stepped toward her again, leaned down and pressed a soft kiss to her lips, and a shiver went through her. He backed off again, eyes on hers. "Beautiful, too."

"Now you're just trying to get out of milking," she said, turning and heading toward her house, a smile on her face. "I see how it is."

"Tell you what. I'll try to help you milk if you'll tell me what has you so spooked that you came over here with that look in your eyes." He had caught up with her, and was walking across the road beside her.

She gave him a sideways glance. "Deal."

They walked up her driveway, and she grabbed the bucket for the milk. She greeted Merlin and the three females, then got to work milking. She did the milking, and he insisted on carrying the full buckets for her. She shut the henhouse, then they headed in, going in the back door of the cottage. He set the buckets of milk on the counter, and she poured them into large pitchers, then put them in the refrigerator. She put a pot of water on for tea, barely caught his grimace, and she laughed.

She nodded toward the grocery bag she'd grabbed from her car. There was rotisserie chicken, a container of red potatoes, and a six-pack of beer.

"Goddess," he murmured, and she laughed. She turned the oven on to preheat it, poured tea leaves into the small pot she liked to use. Calder came up behind her and wrapped his arms around her waist, nuzzled the side of her neck. Sophie closed her eyes and leaned back into him.

"You feel so good," he murmured. "You smell so good." He nipped the sensitive skin at the side of her neck gently. "You taste good," he continued. "I love the sound of your voice."

"Did you get my message earlier?" she asked, leaning into him.

"Do you have any idea what hearing your voice say the words 'love you' in my ear did to me?" He trailed more kisses down the side of her neck.

"I meant it, Calder," she said, and he held her tighter.

"I love you, Sophie," he said in her ear, his breath tickling her earlobe. "I always have. I will love you for the rest of my life."

She closed her eyes again, let herself feel his arms around her, his lips on her neck, his warm, solid body behind hers.

"So what happened?" he asked her.

"Thea had this photograph of Migisi. She looked like me, but without the crazy hair."

"I love your hair," he murmured, resting his chin on the top of her head, still holding her tight.

"I look like her. And the photo was taken several years after she met Luc, after she lost the baby."

"What baby?" he asked, straightening up.

She explained about the journal and what she'd read at work, including about how her magic had started going weird.

"Is yours going weird?" he asked, letting her go only to spin her around on her feet so she was looking at him. "Kitten?" he prompted when she didn't answer.

"I feel... weird," she said with a shrug. "It's probably just the stress over Marshall showing up and worrying about the curse and all that," she hurried to say, but he'd already given a deep growl. He crossed his arms over his chest, watching her, his gaze so intense she had to look away.

"And were you planning on telling me this?" he asked.

"It's not a big deal. I'm fine."

"You're not goddamned fine, if you're starting to feel like your magic is whacking out on you, especially given who your ancestor was."

Now it was her turn to cross her arms. "What? Worried I'll freak out on you the way Migisi did with Luc?" she demanded hotly.

He reached for her then, his hand around her biceps, and pulled her close to him, got his face right in hers. "You are not Migisi, and I sure the fuck am not Luc," he snarled. And then his mouth came crashing down on hers, and she fumbled, trying to get a hold of something, ended up fisting his flannel shirt in her hands. She met his kisses with equal intensity, hungry for him, for the taste of him, for his warmth.

The tea kettle stated whistling, and he reached around without letting her go, moved it onto another burner and flicked the flame off. He held her closer, kissed her, traced his tongue along her lips, and she opened for him.

He broke away from her, backing up, running his hand over his mouth.

Without another word, he ran out of the house with a howl, and she could have screamed in irritation and need. She shook her head and closed the door, noticing his clothing shed just outside.

"This is apparently the only way I'm ever going to get that man naked," she muttered to herself. "Another cold shower tonight, I guess." She headed toward the front door to lock up and saw Marshall standing at the end of her driveway, looking extraordinarily smug with himself.

She opened the door. "Get the hell away from my house. Do you want to die?" she said, not too loudly, not wanting to draw Calder's attention. "Not that I'd particularly mind, but..."

Marshall smiled and crossed his arms. Unconcerned. The light from the black post at the end of the driveway highlighted that dimple that seemed to charm so many, those light gray eyes, like powdered steel. "He'll be busy for a while. Poor guy," he said, not sounding at all like he had much empathy for Calder. "Must be difficult for you, caring for someone like that."

"Stay away from him, Marshall," Sophie said, stalking down the stairs before she even had a chance to think about it. "I swear to god, if you even look twice at him, I am going to rip your heart out and shove it up your ass."

An oily, overly-pleased smile spread across his face. "My, my, Sophie. Is that any way for a daughter of the Light to speak? Could it be that maybe, just maybe, you're starting to realize that being a goody-two-shoes isn't all it's cracked up to be?"

210

She crossed her arms, watched him. Mostly, she wanted to leap at him and claw his eyes out.

He laughed again. "You'll come to me, eventually. You'll beg for my help, for my power."

"I'd rather die," she told him.

"Oh, that wouldn't happen. But... if you don't, he just might," he said, nodding toward the woods.

"Was that a threat?"

Marshall smiled again. "I have no need for threats, Lightwitch. His time is limited and you and I both know it. How far are you willing to go to save him?"

She didn't answer, focused on keeping her face impassive.

"You'll keep trying. I will give you that. You are a determined woman. You always have been," he said, sounding gentle, understanding. She knew better. "But in time, even you have to see that you don't have a chance in hell of doing what he needs you to do. Not in your current state." He smiled then. "And when you come to your senses, you'll come to me. I am easy to find." And with that, he gave her a genial nod and sauntered away. A few moments later, she heard a car start up, and then a motor receding into the distance.

A roar sounded through the woods a few moments later, and Sophie shook her head and went inside, locking the door and checking her wards before slipping into her bed.

She woke to a soft knock at the front door, and she got up, let Calder in. He fell into bed beside her.

"I don't want to hurt you," he murmured. "I could smell you. You want me, and you have no idea what that does to me."

"I'm beginning to get an idea," she said, smiling despite her frustration.

He cupped her breast in his hand, and she gasped. "I am going to keep it together," he said, and she wasn't sure if he was promising her or himself. Possibly both. He squeezed her breasts, gently tweaked and pinched her nipples until they pebbled under his touch, and she whimpered. He let out a low growl at the sound, and pulled her shirt up, pulled it off of her, then he rolled her onto her back.

She lay there under his gaze as he took her in.

"You're perfect, Sophie," he murmured, his voice hoarse with need. "Do you have any idea how gorgeous you are?"

She couldn't answer, and when he leaned down to kiss her, she kissed him back hungrily, determined to let him know how perfect she thought he was, too. How much she wanted him. How much she loved him, despite whatever crap was hanging over them. He started tweaking, pulling at her breasts again, and she cried out already writhing with need as he kissed his way down her throat, her chest, then her cleavage, which he licked, then moaned, as if he was tasting the best thing in the universe.

"Calder," she gasped, and he turned his attention to her breasts, sucking, lapping at her as she pushed her body toward him, arching her back, needy for his touch. And he gave it to her. He touched her in a tender, yet hungry and demanding way that had her on edge instantly, and she clutched at his shoulders, at his head, urging him to keep up the toe-curling pleasure. He stopped, and she whined in need. He laughed, a low rough chuckle, and kissed and licked his way down her stomach, stopping to nibble the sensitive skin around her navel, which, to her surprise, had her crying out in need. He trailed his tongue down one of her hips, kissed her thigh. Realization hit her, just as he gently spread her thighs, what he was planning to do.

"Calder," she gasped.

He didn't answer, except for the touch of his lips to her body, and she bucked at the sensation.

It was torture. He kissed and licked her so slowly, so gently, as if he was savoring every bit of her, and when she tried pressing closer to his mouth, he let her, chuckling again against her, which only served to make her crazier. Her hands were in his hair, urging him on desperately, and he kept up his slow, maddening pace as she felt herself drawing closer and closer to the edge.

She was perfection. Complete and total perfection, and every gasp, every sigh, every time she cried his name, Calder became more determined to give her every bit of pleasure he could. His beast was going wild, but, to his surprise and relief, seemed grateful to have her like this. He couldn't let his guard down, because the instant he did, he'd risk losing control.

She tasted better than anything he'd ever had. Her fingers pulled his hair, and even that, he enjoyed. He could feel that she was on the edge, her lushness swollen from his lips, his tongue. He drew her pleasure out, teasing, going slower, lighter just as she drew close, and she wailed in frustration. He smiled against her.

And then he took her sensitive bud between his lips, and sucked, not exactly gently.

She went over the edge with a scream, clutching at the bed sheets, her hips bucking wildly in her ecstasy. He lifted his gaze, wanting to see what her face looked like. She was the most beautiful thing he'd ever seen, her face lifted, eyes closed in her ecstasy.

His beast delighted in the taste of her body, the screams it had drawn from her. Of course, what it really wanted to do was enter her body and take her, hard, over and over again, until he was sated.

To be honest, Calder wanted exactly the same thing.

He pressed his tongue to her body again, and she trembled, still feeling the after-effects of her orgasm.

"Please, Calder," she whispered. "You need this too."

"I don't want to hurt you."

"You want me. Your beast wants me. What? Does it want me hard and fast? Does it want me to submit to you?"

At the words his beast nearly howled. Fuck yes, that was exactly what it wanted.

She was watching him, her skin nearly glowing in the dim lamplight, her body glistening with a light sheen after what he'd done to her.

"That's what it wants," she said softly. As he knelt at the foot of the bed, she grasped the iron bars of her headboard, opened her thighs, which had him growling with need.

"I'm yours, Calder," she whispered. "Take me. Claim me if you want to. My life is yours."

He ripped his clothing off, rolled on a condom he'd had in his wallet (wishful thinking, but now he was glad he'd been foolish enough to hope) and positioned himself between her thighs.

"Yes," she murmured at the first touch of his body to hers. He was watching her face, his eyes on hers. She bit her lip, gasped as he entered her, filling her.

Fuck, she was perfect. His beast was out of his mind with lust.

He groaned, seated himself all the way inside her, feeling her body tremble beneath him, around him. When he started moving his hips, each thrust was met with a needy moan, or, even better, her pleading, moaning his name.

"Hold me," he said, aware of how rough his voice sounded. She did immediately, putting her arms round him, rubbing his shoulders, then clasping her hands behind his neck. As he took her harder, her hands found their way to his hair, grasping helplessly, and when he sent her over the edge again, she screamed his name over and over again as if it was a prayer, or one of her spells, and he followed her right over, focusing as hard as he could on staying aware of her, of making sure he wasn't hurting her. The blissful look on her face hit him hard.

He wasn't hurting her.

Once he was done, he replaced the condom with a new one, and she only welcomed him with a whispered "yes," when he entered her again. It pleased him, more than a little, how often he made her scream his name over the next few hours, as well as the fact that, despite the fact he'd gone for round three and still wasn't tiring, it seemed as if the thought of pushing him away never even entered her mind.

After their third time, he forced himself to lie beside her and gather her into his arms. She was trembling, and she snuggled into him as she tried to catch her breath.

He rested his lips against her forehead.

"Okay?" he murmured.

She giggled, and it was the single most adorable thing he'd ever heard. "I am more than okay. My god, I feel drunk on you," she said, holding him tighter. "Are you okay?"

"While my beast is ready to take you a few more times, I figured you needed a break. I'm fine," he said, grinning. "Actually, I'm amazing. I've never felt that good. Ever."

She laughed, and kissed his chest, and they settled in together.

"Did it help with the beast, letting you know that you could have me like that?" she asked softly.

"It did. How did you guess?"

She lifted her shoulder in a shrug. "What it definitely does not want is to be denied, right? It doesn't want to be told 'no' in regard to the things it's craving. You've already said that it hates when I walk away. So I was wondering if maybe I let you know that you can have me any way you want me, it would be happier."

He groaned when she'd said the words "any way you want me" and she laughed.

"It's still not satisfied though, right?" she asked after a few moments. "It wants more."

He nodded. "It's an insatiable asshole," he said.

She sat up then, and pushed him onto his back, and when she straddled him, took him inside her, he was pretty sure he was about to die of ecstasy.

They lay together later, and she slept, and all he could do was stare at her and hope they'd find a way to make it work.

Already, his beast was on edge, wanting to take her again, wanting to mark her.

That, he wouldn't do. Shifters did that when they claimed a mate. A mark on her flesh, at the side of her neck, would be a sign to other shifter males that she was taken. And he wanted that just as much as his beast did, if not more. But it did more. It intensified a shifter's senses when it came to its mate. He'd be able to smell her, track her, no matter how far she got from him.

Considering the way things were likely to end, being able to track her would be the worst thing imaginable. Because if he lost his mind, and his beast could track her... He didn't even want to think about it.

So he wouldn't mark her. But she was his. She'd said it, and it had to be enough.

CHAPTER TWENTY

When Sophie woke the next morning, she did so aware of Calder snoring softly behind her, his arm around her waist, his leg thrust between hers. She was aware, as well, of the way her body ached. She was sore in places she didn't know it was possible to be sore, in addition to the way her thighs protested when she tried to move.

She was also aware that she was in a really, really terrible mood for someone who'd just spent a night making love with the man of her dreams. It was like her worst-ever case of PMS, times about a thousand. She gritted her teeth in irritation and shoved his arm off of her.

Calder woke with a start. "What's wrong?" he asked.

"I need some space," she said, and she knew she sounded like a bitch. She yanked the blanket up over her shoulder, stayed turned away from him. He'd backed off onto his own side of the small bed.

She could hear him breathing, and after a few minutes of it, she got up, ready to lose her mind if she didn't have some time alone. "It's time for you to go," she said, pulling on the clothing he'd removed from her body the night before.

"Hey," he said softly. She looked at him as he sat up in bed. "What's wrong?" he asked again.

"I need some alone time," she said.

"Oh," he said, and he looked away, but not before she saw the hurt and irritation in his eyes. "I should get to work on Bryce's car anyway." He got up and started pulling his jeans on, and she headed to the bathroom without another word. When she got in there, she turned on the shower full blast, well aware that his scent was all over her. She smelled like sex and Calder, and she was elated about that, but she was so irritated she couldn't even experience the joy of having been with him. It was as if the edginess, the irritation and anger she'd woken with clouded everything else. She knew she should feel differently; she *wanted* to feel differently. Hell, she wanted to be out there kissing him and holding him and laughing with him the way a normal woman would, but she just couldn't do it.

She stepped into the shower and the punishing heat of the water made her clench her teeth. "I just need time," she whispered to herself, remembering the hurt in his eyes. She hated herself for that, for putting that there, when he'd done nothing to deserve it. She knew he'd be blaming himself, thinking he hurt her, that he'd taken it all too far, when nothing could be further from the truth. And she knew that if she told him what was going on with her, that she felt off, that her magic was starting to feel weird, that she could practically feel the Shadow clouding everything, it would only make him worry about her. It would make him even more sure she couldn't break the curse.

After standing in the shower for far too long, she forced herself to get out, hoping, and yet not hoping, that Calder would be gone. She wrapped up in the ugly terry robe she always used after a shower and peeked out into the living room.

It was silent, and she sighed. In relief or sadness, she wasn't even sure anymore.

Sophie quickly threw on some jeans and a t-shirt, pulled her hair into a low ponytail and headed out to do the milking, which she was late for. She saw that the chickens had already been let out, the goats watered, but clearly not milked, since she hadn't seen any fresh milk in the refrigerator when she'd grabbed a hard-boiled egg on her way out.

Damn him for continuing to be considerate and sweet even when she acted like a jerk, she thought to herself. And why that bothered her, she couldn't even say, because it shouldn't have bothered her at all. He loved her. He was taking care of her in a way that mattered to her more than she could ever say.

She took the bucket to the first female goat, May. May watched her warily, as she always did, but just went on standing there, chewing some of the hay she'd pulled from the feeder. Sophie set the galvanized pail under May, cleaned her, then started squeezing.

Nothing.

Sophie furrowed her brow, gave another squeeze, felt May's underside. There was none of the usual heavy, full feeling that indicated she needed to be milked.

She sat back on her heels and looked up at the goat. "What the heck, goat?" she asked. May just continued chewing. Sophie went to the next goat, Clarice. Same thing. And when the third of her females had nothing as well, all Sophie could do was stare at her in disbelief.

She rested her forehead against the goat's side, took deep breaths, dread settling into her gut. These same goats had given gallons of milk the day before. She'd been in a hurry to turn it into soaps as well as a few wheels of cheese to store for the coming winter.

Well. The garden, then. She'd harvest some of the greens and carrots.

The garden, when she got there, was a withered, pathetic mess. Plants that had been standing tall, if a little less than perfectly healthy looking the day before, were slumped over, withered, yellowed.

Sophie dropped the harvest basket, ran to the chicken coop. A search of their nesting boxes showed nothing. Nothing, when she could always count on a few eggs every day.

"No," she whispered.

She closed her eyes and opened her senses, hoping to be comforted by the spirits of her ancestors. And when she did it, she felt nothing.

"No, no, no, no," she whimpered, slumping to her knees. "Please, no. Not now."

Migisi's words from the journal came back to her: "Nothing is right. I am wrong in my own body, unable to do even the most basic spells. My healing elixirs fail. My garden withers."

"Why?" she screamed into the silence, and a group of sparrows flew from their perch atop the chicken coop.

It wasn't even her overwhelming need to protect herself anymore. Calder. If she didn't have her magic, she didn't stand a chance in hell of saving him.

"No," she said, standing up and wiping her eyes. "No, I'm just tired. I just need to do a few things, get back into the groove of things, and I'm fine."

Even she didn't believe the words she was mumbling.

She marched into the house, gathered her soap-making supplies together, and got to work. She went to work on a new batch of soap, combining the lye and beeswax, jojoba oil, goat's milk and essential oils. She whispered spells, though it felt like a child pretending, because when she reached for it, though she could easily see *how* her spells were supposed to work, there was no magic there.

She took several deep breaths, determined to keep herself together.

She watched the soap, continued stirring. And just at the point where it looked as if this batch would reach the soponification stage, when everything came together into a perfect, creamy, fragrant liquid, it separated, falling into what looked like globs of rice in the pot. A failure.

"Damn it," she shouted, grabbing the pot off of the woodstove and hurling it into the field beside her house. It hissed in the damp grasses when it fell, and she turned and stormed into the house.

She tried a simple calming spell. Failure.

She tried her spell to translate Migisi's journal. Failure.

She was about to start crying when she looked at her door. Her heart stilled. She walked slowly up to it, reached out tentatively, and ran her hand along the woodwork.

Her wards had failed. There wasn't even a single wisp of her own Light magic left. Nothing.

Her heart sped up, beating wildly as if it was about to beat out of her chest, as the realization hit her. She was sitting here, unprotected and powerless, and Marshall was somewhere out there, and Calder's beast was somewhere out there and all it took was one wrong stupid move, one wrong step, and she was completely doomed.

Calder's beast. How in the hell was she going to save him now?

"Aw. Poor little Lightwitch," a voice she knew all too well said, way too close to her. Sophie scrambled up, and Marshall laughed from the place he'd suddenly inhabited on her sofa. She grabbed the fireplace poker, and he laughed again. "Do you really think that's going to do anything against me? Powerless whelp."

"What did you do to me?" she asked him, hating how her voice was shaking.

All it earned her was a derisive laugh. "You give me too much credit. No, you did all this yourself."

"I didn't do anything. What did you do, Marshall?" she asked, close to shouting in her fear and panic.

"Hm. Maybe you should have been focusing more on do-gooding, and less on screwing. Are Lightwitches supposed to be such lustful, filthy creatures?" he asked with another slimy grin as he stood up. "I could hear the two of you last night. Such impurity, for a creature of the Light."

The thought of him standing out there, listening in as Calder had loved her. The thought of him invading a moment that was possibly one of the most beautiful, pure moments of her life, enraged her. Before she even realized what she was doing, she'd dropped the poker and raised her hands. With a snarl, she shot a concussive blast of energy at him, much like the one she'd used to knock Calder on his butt the previous week, but so much stronger. He went flying through the room, out the large window behind the sofa, landing over a dozen feet away outside, in her gravel driveway.

He picked himself up, laughing, and it took every ounce of willpower she had not to kill him.

Because she wanted to. She wanted to see, right then, exactly what it was she could do to him.

He tipped his hat at her. "You'll come to me. You have the beginnings of power, raw and unfocused. You come to me, you'll have power. Unlimited power." He stopped, crossed his arms, watching her through the broken pane of glass. He looked completely unruffled, as if he hadn't just been hurled twenty feet through a pane of glass. "What do you suppose you'd do with unlimited power, little girl? Anything your heart desires, you can have. All you have to do is come to me." And with that, he was gone, as if he'd never been there at all.

She stared out the window, at nothing.

Unlimited power. The words echoed in her conscience.

She shook her head. She stood there for several long minutes, just breathing, just trying to get herself back together again.

"Holy shit! What happened here?"

Sophie jumped, spun to see Layla standing just inside her front door.

"Soph?" she asked.

Sophie shook her head, and she felt her face crumple. Within an instant, Layla was there, arms around Sophie, holding her and murmuring comforting, useless words as she fell apart in huge, wracking sobs.

"What's wrong, Soph? Come on, girl, I can't kick anyone's ass until you tell me what happened. Did Calder do something to you?"

At Calder's name, Sophie backed away. "Don't you tell him you saw any of this," she said.

"Sophie. I come over here and you're goddamn pale as a sheet and your window's all busted out. What the hell happened, because if you don't convince me in about two seconds that he didn't do something to you, I'm gonna hunt Calder's ass down and make him hurt."

"Calder would never hurt me," she said, and Layla gave her a disbelieving look. "He wouldn't. I love him, and he loves me, and this wasn't him."

"The warlock?" Layla asked, and Sophie nodded. "What about your wards?"

"They failed," Sophie said quietly, hating the words.

Layla stared at her. "What?"

"They failed. I can't even do the simplest spell. Wards down, even my soap failed. My garden is dead, my animals are dried up..."

"Girl, you need to run, then. Run far, and run fast, and don't goddamn come back."

Sophie stared at her in shock. "What?"

"You have a warlock stalker who's been on your ass for years, just waiting for the first sign of weakness. You have Calder, who I totally believe loves you more than anything in the entire world, but who has less and less control over a beast that will do god-knows-what to you if it gets a chance. You need to go," she said, each of those last words delivered deliberately, slowly.

"No."

Layla gave her an incredulous look. "Have you lost your mind along with your powers?"

"Maybe," Sophie said, raising her voice. "Maybe I have. I'm not leaving. Not when he's still cursed. Not when I still need this house. Not—"

"You are completely fucked here, Soph," Layla said, shouting over Sophie. "You can't stay. You can't solve his curse. This place is a loss. You either come home with me, or you run. But you can't stay here."

"I'm not running anymore. And I'm not just bailing on Calder. I have another couple weeks until the equinox."

"And no power to help him with, sweetie," Layla said gently. "Soph, you know I love you. You know that. I know it's going to hurt you. I know you love him. I know that the second you two saw each other in fifth grade, something happened. Okay? I know, girl. But you can't save him."

I have to try, she thought, and her mind went to Marshall. Just as soon, she forced it away. "Maybe there's still something I can do."

Layla sighed, shook her head. "Didn't you just get done telling me the other day that Migisi's powers got messed up over time, too?"

Sophie nodded.

"And how'd that end for her? Because I'm pretty sure Calder could remind you how it ended."

"I'm not Migisi," she said, something, again, irritating her as if there was something she'd forgotten.

"No. You're not. But her blood runs through your veins, her magic lives in you, and if you're losing your magic, where do you think that's going to lead? She lost her mind, Soph."

"I'm not her," Sophie repeated. "And Calder is not Luc. I'm going to fix this, and I'm not running."

Layla growled in irritation. "Have you ever considered that no matter how much you love him, the boy's bad for you? Have you thought of that?"

Sophie stared at her, refusing to dignify it with a response.

"Think about it. He's all 'I love you baby' and I can smell him all over this place, so I'm guessing he's gotten lucky a few times."

Sophie glared at her.

"Okay. He definitely has. So all that's going on, and the bastard's still holding this house over your head? If he loved you, he'd fucking give it back, Soph. And even if that wasn't all, there's the fact that your magic was getting better. It was growing. You were gaining even more control over it since you moved back here. And then he comes into your life, and boom! You're powerless."

Sophie didn't answer. She didn't feel like correcting Layla. She wasn't powerless. She just didn't have the right kind of power anymore.

As Layla stood there staring at her, the gears started turning in Sophie's brain.

"I was fine until Calder," she said softly.

"Yeah. You were," Layla said, crossing her arms.

"Migisi was fine until Luc," Sophie said, thinking. She looked up at Layla. "Doesn't that seem like an awfully impossible coincidence to you?"

Layla didn't answer, and Sophie started pacing, thinking. "Migisi was a hero. Healer, everyone loved her. She was the most powerful Lightwitch of her time, right?" She kept pacing, not waiting for Layla's response. "She meets Luc, they fall in love, start spending time together, and she starts having problems with her magic." She looked at Layla, who was giving her a sad look. "I meet Calder again, after years of healing myself, of getting my magic to a point where it was useful. We start spending time together. And my magic gets messed up." She thought back. "When I'm with him, it happens. I can feel it. I'm fine, and then all of a sudden, I feel this... irritation creeping in. It's not me. It's him."

"Okay," Layla said, holding her hands out as if pleading with Sophie. "Okay. So that's one more reason to stay away from him then, right? One more, of about a million."

Sophie shook her head, still pacing. "But why? Why does his line do this to mine? I mean, Migisi and Luc meeting was a fluke. In her journal, she's just talking about how she didn't like him trapping in her woods, so she was following him, messing up his traps, and he caught up with her. Probably sniffed her out, right?"

Layla nodded slowly, still not looking all that pleased with Sophie.

"Okay. So why? Something in him messed up Migisi..." She stopped talking, stared at Layla.

"What?" Layla asked, looking alarmed.

"It was us. It was always us."

"What?" Layla repeated, looking helpless now, on top of looking alarmed.

"Someone knew. Someone saw. Someone noticed her paying attention to him." Her mind went back to Marshall, how he'd disappeared earlier that day, how he'd always seemed to appear, just out of nowhere. "They were a tool to get to us."

"That's kind of a leap..." Layla began.

"It makes sense, though. I mean, Migisi was dedicated. She was good, and she was powerful, and she was the best at what she did. The best. Unmoved by the Shadow. That amount of power would have been attractive." That, she knew. Even her meager amount of power had been attractive to Marshall.

"Attractive how?" Layla asked.

"I don't know," Sophie said, slumping a little. "To use? To try to take?"

"But she went dark and screwed your line, right? So the magic was gone."

"Or it's not. Not really." Not with the way she'd tossed Marshall across the room earlier. She'd never felt a burst of power like that in her life. Not even on her best days.

"Okay. Even so. Even if you're right: someone cursed Luc so he'd somehow make Migisi's powers go away, and that curse carried on down his line, and it just so happens that his descendant ends up with a descendant of Migisi's. Even if all that is true, what difference does it make?"

"I don't know. Maybe none. But it's something. Magic is always in a state of balance, right?"

"If you say so. We don't do much with magic," Layla said, plopping down on one of the chairs.

"Maybe Migisi figured it out. Maybe she tried to fix it later. Maybe she came to her senses somewhere along the line."

"Sweetie, have you found any evidence of that, anywhere?" Layla asked.

Sophie didn't answer.

"You're hoping for impossible things. You need to smarten up before you get hurt. Now come on, let's at least board up that window before it gets absolutely freezing in here."

Sophie didn't answer, walking out the back door toward the small barn, still thinking. She and Layla grabbed a sheet of plywood, a hammer, and a box of nails. They carried it back out and went to work, one of them holding the plywood while the other nailed, then switching roles until it was up.

"Glad it wasn't a huge window," Layla said.

Sophie nodded.

"What went through it, Soph?" she asked gently.

"A warlock," Sophie said.

Layla stared at her. "He crashed through the window to get to you?"

Sophie gave a humorless smile. "No. He crashed through the window when I showed him the way out."

Layla was studying her. "Please come stay with us," she finally said.

Sophie shook her head. "I love you. Thanks for worrying about me. But I'm not going anywhere. Not now. Not when he still needs me and I need to figure this mess out."

Layla looked at her helplessly, then sighed and pulled her into a hug. "Call if you need me."

"I will," Sophie said, hugging her back. She watched as Layla shifted, picked up her clothing in her mouth, and ran through the woods, heading in the direction of town.

CHAPTER TWENTY-ONE

She went back inside and settled on the sofa with Migisi's journals. She was just grateful that she'd read her way through the ones with writing in them before losing her magic. While they hadn't revealed a whole lot, at least it was something. She opened the third journal, the one with the sketches and paintings in it. She flipped the pages, studying each one. The first few were drawings and small paintings of flowers and trees, birds that she'd often seen around. It was the painting of a bear that she kept going back to, knowing though there was no proof, that it was Luc. Its massive size, its shaggy fur. The almost knowing look it wore. But it was more than that. The way she'd rendered it in such exacting, careful detail, as if determined to capture all of it, spoke to a certain adoration. She'd loved whatever was in that painting. Whomever. And Sophie knew it had to be Luc, because she'd seen that form so often now in Calder. She still intended to show the painting to him, to show him that, no matter what else Migisi was, she'd been someone who had been deeply in love at one point in time. She didn't want him to forget that.

When she was being realistic, she knew she needed him to know that so he'd remember it when she acted like a jerk, as she had that morning.

She glanced toward the door. He hadn't been home all day. She wondered what he was feeling. Was he angry at her? Did he think they were over? Did he want them to be over, tired of dealing with her crap?

She shook her head, tearing her thoughts away. She flipped to the page with the painting of the falls, this one, once again, in lush, perfect detail. Sophie knew the scene well. There was the huge rock on which she and Calder had been sitting when they'd kissed so long ago; there was the deep pool right to the left of the falls where they'd enjoyed swimming on hot summer days. Whatever else this place had been, it seemed to have been a place that brought Migisi joy.

She flipped to the next page, the one of the bleak forest and its depressing moon. She still hated this one. It felt wrong. Her eyes went to the word Thea had pointed out, the Ojibwa word for "death" at the base of the tree.

She turned the page quickly, to the final painting, a barren meadow in what looked to be late summer, the grasses dry and dead looking, the sky hazy and gray. "Barren" was the only word she could think of, other than "menacing." Even the birds in the trees, mere splashes of dark paint, looked menacing. How a summer scene could look so frightening escaped Sophie, but it did.

She kept flipping. Something about the paintings bothered her, but she couldn't put her finger on it. When she flipped to the page with the falls on it, she sat looking at it for a long time.

And she had a feeling she knew where she'd find Calder.

She jumped up, pulled on a sweater, stepped into her boots. The falls were a short hike through her field, then through some forest. It was already dusk, but she hardly cared. She closed the animals in their pens as she headed out, thinking to herself that she might as well find someone who could use them. She was a lost cause.

She trudged through the tall grasses of the prairie behind her land, through the woods, which got thicker and darker as she walked. She could hear the rushing of the falls, the owls hooting in the trees nearby, already active and ready for their nightly hunt.

As she emerged from the woods to the mossy, log-strewn shoreline of the river, she saw him immediately. Calder sat on the huge rock, looking at the falls.

"What are you doing here, kitten?" he asked her softly.

"I missed you. Had a feeling you'd be here," she said, walking the rest of the way toward the rock. He held out his hand, and she took it, and he pulled while she scrambled up onto the rock.

"How'd you figure? I wasn't planning on coming this way," he asked. He let her hand go, crossed his arms over his chest.

She shrugged. "I was looking at that journal of Migisi's, and she had a painting of this place in it. I knew you weren't home, so... I just took a guess," she said.

He didn't answer.

"Honey, I'm sorry," she said softly. "This morning—"

He shook his head, took her hand in his. "You don't have anything to apologize for. You needed to be alone."

"I hurt your feelings, though," she said, bringing his hand to her lips and kissing his knuckles gently. "I'm sorry for that. I was just not feeling right."

He was watching her. "That's happening a lot lately," he said. "When we started this, I thought I'd always be the one running out on you. You do it as least as often to me."

"I know," she said, still holding his hand. "It wasn't you. I hope you know that. I love you, Calder. Every second of last night was perfect. I've never felt that loved in my life."

"I'm glad. I actually figured it wasn't me. I mean, at first I did, because I just wanted to spend all day in bed with you and I figured you were fed up with me."

"Never," she said, and he smiled a little.

"But then, once I had been out running for a while, I realized this isn't new. You keep having this reaction to me when we're together, where you just start getting pissed off out of nowhere. I want to know why."

"So do I," she said softly. "I'm working on it. I think maybe there's more to the story than just Migisi going dark out of nowhere."

He seemed to pick up her thoughts. "You think Luc had something to do with it?"

"Maybe. I don't think he meant to, probably. I wonder if someone did something." They sat in silence, hands clasped.

"Like someone messed with Luc to get to her?" he finally said, and she nodded. "And what? I still have whatever it is that they used to get to her, and it's messing with you?"

She didn't answer.

"That's it, though, isn't it?"

"We don't know that."

"But you think so."

After a while, she nodded. "And if you even suggest staying away from me as a solution, I will lose my mind." Sophie looked over at him to see him watching her intently. "I'm fine," she said.

"I couldn't stay away anyway," he said. "I have something for you." He reached into his coat pocket, pulled out a long envelope.

"What's this?"

"Open it."

She slid her thumbnail under the flap of the envelope, pulled out several sheets of white paper. She stared at them, her breath caught in her throat.

"This is the deed to my house," she whispered.

"Signed over to you. All it needs is to be notarized, and we can do that whenever you want."

She stared at him, the papers trembling in her hand. "Calder, why?"

"Because I love you. Because I'm not going to hold your land, which you need and I don't, ransom. Because I don't want this," he said, gesturing to the papers, "between us. It was wrong in the first place, and it's more wrong the longer it goes on."

"You've given up, too," she said.

He looked away from her, shaking his head.

"Calder."

"Sophie," he said, still not looking at her. "I know you want to fix it, kitten. I know you're going to try." He turned and looked at her, finally. "But you just said yourself your magic is messed up. I can tell it is. The way you act sometimes around me isn't right. And if I'm causing that, and us being together makes it worse, and we both seem determined to keep seeing one another...yeah. It's over. I'll take what time I have with you, and when it starts getting too bad—"

"Calder!"

"We'll figure it out when the time comes. It's coming on fast, sweetheart. It wasn't like this with my dad. He had years. I intended to come to you earlier. I couldn't remember how to shift back," he finished, and his tone sent shivers down her spine.

"No," she whispered, dread settling over her like ice.

He cleared his throat, seemed to be trying to keep his voice steady. "So we have what we have, and I'm going to do everything I can to give you something good to remember. And I know you are determined to fix this. I hope you can. But I need you to start preparing yourself to let me go. Because it's going to be sooner rather than later."

She shook her head, denying it, and he pulled her into his arms. Her tears spilled down her face as he kissed her, and when they broke apart, breathless, he rested his forehead against hers. "I love you. Promise me, kitten. Promise me you won't try to follow me when I take off. Promise me you'll know that I love you, and that walking away is the hardest thing I'm ever going to do."

She held him tighter, made a promise to herself right then and there.

It wouldn't come to that.

She didn't say a word, just jumped down off the rock and held her hand out. He followed her, back through the woods, through the meadow, and into her house. She loved him frantically, desperately, giving him everything he and his beast desired, until she fell asleep under his weight, his breath warming the side of her neck as he slept, having exhausted both of them.

When she woke up later, the room was pitch black, and Calder was beside her, arm thrown over her waist. She could feel the darkness swirling within her, agitated, fed by his nearness. There would be no more sleeping now.

She carefully, slowly slipped out of bed with a wince, her body sore from his frantic attentions. She knew that, if he woke, he'd want her again, and she'd want him just as much, and there would be no peace for the rest of the night.

She managed to get out of bed and creep to the living room, pulling on the t-shirt he'd discarded. She breathed it in, loving the clean, wild scent of him surrounding her. She clicked on the small electric space heater she used sometimes, not wanting to start a fire, and clicked on the reading lamp near the chair in the corner, bringing Migisi's journals with her. She turned the pages, drawn to the paintings. Something about them wasn't right. There were four watercolors all together: one of Luc on the rock, one of the falls, the gray and black death one, and, finally, that dry summer scene, hazy sun giving everything a harsh glare, a feeling of complete exhaustion and defeat, just as the gray and black moon one had.

It wasn't the subject matter of them. They were all essentially scenes from around Copper Falls, and Sophie recognized them. She flipped through them several times. There was something there. Something in the lines, something that she saw was different, but couldn't figure out why. It was always along the base, the ground. She looked closer at the one on which Thea had noticed the word "death." She let her eyes sweep over it. There, to the left, in what she'd also thought was leaf litter, tiny letters, three lines of writing, disguised as shading, as light and shadow.

Her heart sped up, and she quickly got up, wincing again, and grabbed her notebook and pen, as well as the magnifying glass from the drawer in the kitchen.

Sophie set the journal on the floor, craned the lamp to better illuminate it. Whereas "death" had been written in Ojibwa, and the journals themselves had been written in French and Ojibwa, she was shocked to see that the new bits of text, tiny though they were, were recognizable. English.

"What the hell, Migisi?" she whispered. She flipped her notebook open, inspected the painting, started copying what was there. When she'd completed the four lines, she had:

"Some years hence, a son of Luc's line
will swear everything he is to a daughter of mine.
He will love her fully and absolutely.
And she will destroy him."

She stared at it in horror. Shook her head, and flipped through, transcribing hidden bits of text from the other paintings in the book. In order, all four paintings' text read:

*"I have wronged
the one I loved above all others.
Corrupted by the Shadow,
distraught and alone,*

I became that which I disdain.
Some years hence, a son of Luc's line
will give everything he is to a daughter of mine.
He will love her fully and absolutely.
And she will destroy him.
On that day the curse will be lifted
And Luc's line will be free
And my soul will rest in peace.
She who reads this is chosen by Migisi."

She read over it again and again, hating the words more every single time, wondering if there was some way to rearrange the lines to make them mean something else. Her heart was pounding, and it took everything in her not to start crying again.

She shut the book, stuffed the notebook under the chair. She turned off the light and sat in the chair, hugging her knees.

She didn't want to believe it. It had to mean something else. The words were burned into her mind. She'd been right when she'd suggested that maybe the way to break the spell had nothing to do with spells.

Destroy him.

She looked toward the bed, where Calder was still sleeping, snoring quietly.

She got up, peeled her clothing off, and climbed back into bed with him. There had to be another way, she thought as she snuggled closer to him, as he sleepily pulled her against his body.

Killing Calder was something she could not do.

She was awakened a while later by the feeling of Calder moving, and she missed his warmth as he stood up. She heard a phone ringing.

She watched his shadowy form in the dark room as he bent to where he'd tossed his jeans and dug his phone out of his pocket. The conversation on his side was minimal.

"Hello? Hey. Wait, what? Slow down.... Okay, I'm on my way. You have the gun, right?" He hung up and started pulling his clothes on. She climbed out of bed.

"What's going on?" she asked, pulling her panties on, then slipping into her top.

"My dad's raging. That was my brother. He's worried the fences we're using to keep him contained won't hold. I have to go help him reinforce them." He was pulling on a shirt. "What happened there?" he asked, gesturing to the boarded-over window. He'd been in such a frenzy to be with her the night before, he hadn't even noticed it.

"Oh. I was clumsy," she said, waving it off.

Calder gave her a look that said he didn't completely believe her and was about to press her on it.

"I'll come," she said, pulling on her jeans.

"No."

"Calder—"

"I don't want you anywhere near him. Especially not when he's like this," he said. "If he got out..."

"He won't. Besides, I can help. I could try warding the fences."

He stopped moving for a moment, watched her. "Would that work?"

She knew better. It wouldn't. Her wards had already failed her. But she had to try. "I can try. I'm not sure how well it will work, considering how messed up my magic is. But I want to try."

He was studying her. "Yeah. Maybe you should come along."

"So I can help."

"Sure. And so you can see what's in our future. See how smart this all looks when you see what I'll become."

She glared at him. "Stop it, Calder," she said, her heart twisting inside her.

"I should have left you alone," he said, turning away from her.

She didn't answer, didn't trust herself not to start bawling. Instead, she stayed silent, stalking past him. "Your car or mine?" she managed to mutter.

"Mine," he answered after a moment. She waited until he stepped out of her house, then locked the door and followed him across the street to his driveway, to the truck he drove sometimes when he wasn't riding the motorcycle. He opened her door for her and she climbed in. She put her seatbelt on and crossed her arms over her chest, looking straight ahead out the windshield.

He got in and started the truck. They drove wordlessly, the only sound the truck's engine as they wound their way along a dark two-lane highway, the trees at either side of the road getting thicker the longer they drove. She started seeing signs for Copper County State Forest, and she knew they were getting closer.

"I love you. All I meant was that I regret that this is going to make everything harder for you. For my own selfish ass, I don't regret a second that I spent in your arms. You're going to see what I'm gonna become. If you love me, how hard do you think it's going to be for you to end it with me? Because you're going to need to. I fucking hate that I'm going to put you through that, okay? That's what I regret. I regret that I can't give you the life you deserve, that I can't love you the way you deserve."

She didn't answer.

He let out an irritated breath. "I become a complete idiot around you," he said.

"You know what I'm tired of?" Sophie said, still looking straight ahead. "I'm tired of everyone underestimating me. I'm tired of everyone seeming to think I'm this weak, stupid little thing who can't handle what life throws at her. I've made it through years of having a goddamned Shadow warlock stalking me. I've made it through the death of my parents, the death of a husband, and all of their deaths were on my hands, to get to me. I made it through wanting to take my own life so badly that it was all I thought about for days on end. But no, Sophie's so fucking weak we need to protect her from every stupid little thing."

"I never said you were weak," he said.

"Right," she said, not looking at him. Part of her felt like an absolute jerk for fighting with him at a time like this, when he was already stressed out about his father. And part of her understood and believed what he was saying. But part of her, a pretty big part, if she was being honest, was sick and tired of being underestimated. She could have all the power she wanted...

She shook her head a little, bile rising in her throat. And she understood what that page in Migisi's journal had meant.

"The darkness rises."

He was doomed.

As she had the thought, he turned up a long gravel driveway, then put the truck in park. She gathered the small sack of stones, herbs, and candles, she'd brought with her and got out of the truck before he could say a word to her. She could hear insane, pained roars coming from behind the house, and she winced. She knew those roars. She'd heard them, the night of the full moon. She could hear the sounds of metal slamming, crashing. Calder took her hand and they ran down a path that led around the house and toward the sounds of the roars.

Jon stood there with a rifle in his hands, aiming it at the raging bear behind the huge iron fence. At that moment, the bear roared again and slammed his body into the fence.

Metal squealed.

"Let's get this done," Calder said.

Jon glanced at him, then at Sophie. "Are you sure this is a good idea?"

"She's going to try to ward the fences to keep him in."

"Her line did this. How in the hell could you think this was a good idea?" Jon asked, gesturing at their father, who was raging.

"Watch it," Calder warned, looking at his brother. "I'm already on edge, and you really, really don't want to piss me off right now."

"It's making him worse," Jon said as the three of them watched the beast behind the tall fences rage, its roars becoming louder, its leaps toward the fence getting more desperate. "Don't threaten me, man," Jon muttered to Calder.

"Shut it," Calder warned, that growl she knew all too well entering his voice. Jon clearly recognized it too. He shot Sophie a concerned glance and set the gun down, leaning it against the garage wall. Without another word, he grabbed a tall iron bar, and he held it while Calder climbed up onto a ladder just outside of the fence where their father was penned in. Calder hammered the steel into the ground, strengthening the existing fence. They did it again a few feet down, and though their father continued bashing against the fence, it started shaking less.

Calder and Jon continued to the other side of the pen, and Sophie approached where they'd been working, taking stones out of her bag. She laid them on the ground, black tourmaline, one of the stones she used often around her home to anchor her protective wards. She set one on each side of the square pen, focusing on what she was doing rather than Calder and his brother, who continued to pound steel into the ground. She reached the first stone she'd set, and she knelt near it, a few feet outside of the pen. Calder's father stood there, growling, snapping at her, foamy saliva dripping from his mouth. The smell of him was terrible. He stunk of decay and lack of care. She met his eyes as he raged. "I am sorry," she whispered to him. "I am going to fix this."

She focused, envisioning a protective net over the pen. With the one she created for her home, the net was there to keep things out. In this case, she focused on creating one that would keep Calder's dad in. She closed her eyes, tried to build the ward bit by bit in her mind.

She tried, time and time again, and the wards crumbled, fell apart just before completion, like her magic was just out of touch. There, but not. Shadow was there, though, swirling within her, excited by her trying to access the magic within her.

As she worked, she tried not to freak out. Mr. Turcotte continued to snarl at her, and she focused, instead, on Calder and Jon. Jon was talking. "I'm sorry. I know I acted like an asshole," he was saying.

"Forget it," Calder said. "Sorry I threatened beast mode on you. That was a shitty thing to do."

Sophie heard it all, felt it all, and yet, felt separate from it. Numb. Calder's father, looking so much like Calder, stood there growling at her, fur on his shoulders bristling, teeth snapping at her.

There was no man there. No sense. Only rage and the need to destroy. The way he looked, the smell of him... everything about it was wrong. He was skinny, his flesh seeming to flow off of bone. His teeth were yellow, his claws bloody, broken from trying to dig at the fences through the concrete that reinforced them on the inside of the pen.

This thing. This was what Calder would become, because of Migisi. Because of her line.

Every spell she'd known, every spell she'd learned from Migisi's journal, none of them had worked to lift the taint from Calder's family.

Could she do this, when the time came? Could she keep the man she loved in a cage, listen to him roaring in rage and agony? Could she end his life?

She couldn't do it. She couldn't see Calder look at her with that expression in his eyes.

She felt Calder's hand on her arm, pulling her gently away from the pen, and she went, unable to take her eyes away from Mr. Turcotte.

Mr. Turcotte was growling, roaring, ramming the fences, trying to get to her. She guessed, maybe, that he knew a little of what was going on. Knew who and what she was.

"Sophie, you need to leave. You're making him worse," Calder said quietly, gently. He pressed his car keys into her hand. "Just go, okay?"

She nodded numbly, gave his father one more look, then walked down the driveway, Mr. Turcotte's insane, anguished roars even more frenzied behind her.

CHAPTER TWENTY-TWO

December 9, 1860

"What I need, is for you to get away from me for a while. Go trap some helpless animal so you can profit off of it," Migisi said, rolling, turning away from Luc in their cozy bed of furs and woolen blankets.

She looked at the wall, waiting for him to leave. The cabin had expanded in the past few years. Luc had gone to work, gathering large stones and setting them, building a large stone fireplace in the main room of the cabin. That had been his project after they'd lost their first child.

The small cooking area off to the side, he'd added after they lost their second. That one, she'd carried for months, and they'd thought the family they'd started to want so badly would finally happen. When she'd delivered it, the tiny girl had already been gone for some time.

She didn't allow Luc to touch her for nearly a year after, her nights full of nightmares about children she'd lost, looking at her mournfully. Blaming her.

She blamed herself too. She was weak. Not weak of body; child-bearing should not have been a problem. Weak of spirit, of mind, maybe. She blamed Shadow. She felt it oozing into every part of her being, and she'd stopped trying to fight it back. She'd tried. She'd tried for years, and failed, and she was tired of fighting.

Her once-great magic was failing her. She could still work simple healing spells. Not like those she used to, though.

"Aren't you gone yet?" she huffed as Luc put a hand on her waist.

"I miss you, little ghost," he said, and she closed her eyes, his pet name for her like a stab to the heart. The fact that he could still say it so tenderly confused her. She abhorred herself; how could he still look at her, with everything she'd put him through, with love in his eyes? "I will go. A run might be a good idea," he said. "But I need you to know something."

She turned. That serious tone. Here it comes, she thought. He will tell me he's heading south, to his partners, and that he won't be back. She'd been preparing herself for this moment for years.

"What is it?" she asked.

His eyes searched hers. "I love you. I love you in the Light, and I love you in the Shadow. I know you can barely stand yourself. I know you feel wrong in your skin."

Migisi stared at him. She'd been so sure she'd been hiding it well. The damnable man saw everything.

"I need you to know that I love the woman, not her magic."

"We are one and the same," she said, and he pulled her closer. She usually stiffened and refused his attentions, but he was not the only one who missed the closeness they'd once shared. This wall she'd built between them, preparing herself for his eventual desertion... she hated it. So she let him pull her close, and, after a moment, she pressed her face into his broad chest.

"You say that, but I have been here through it all. I was here when you were at your most powerful in the Light. I've been here as you've sunk, slowly but surely, into Shadow. I love you as much as always, Migisi. You hate yourself. You struggle. My love for you has never faltered."

Tears came to her eyes, and she held him tighter. She let him love her, and when he left to check his traps a few hours later, he looked happier than she'd seen him in months.

She washed herself, sending a prayer that no child would take. She couldn't handle another loss. She dressed, added a few more logs to the fireplace, then went outside.

The woods she'd loved no longer gave her the solace they once did. She walked them every day nonetheless, hoping, waiting to feel something of the Light again. She still held it together. Other than Luc, everyone believed she was fine. They attributed any oddness to mourning over the child they'd lost. It was probably for the best that they thought that.

As she made her way back to the cabin, she stopped, pulled out the small knife she kept on her belt, and carved her rune into another of the trees nearby. She didn't know, anymore, if they worked to keep her land safe, but she wanted to believe they did.

"Still superstitious," a smooth voice said behind her, in her own language. She knew what she'd see. The gray-eyed man with his cold, hard gaze. He who stalked her steps. She had yet to exchange a word with him, for, while he often talked to her now, she refused to give him her attention.

He felt wrong. He was Shadow, and even as far gone as she was, he felt wrong.

"You have fought so long, so hard. Stubborn witch," he said, following her as she continued walking. "Foolish. Don't you know you will ultimately fail? You and your piety, your devotion to Light. What good has it done you? Light has forsaken you, deserted you."

She walked faster. He laughed. "Fine. Have it your way, then."

She glanced back, and he was gone. Migisi closed her eyes, tried to pull herself together. He did this sometimes, as if he was checking to see just how far gone she was, as if he was waiting for the day she'd denounce the Light.

She cursed the day she'd met him. He'd been traveling with the missionaries and had taken an immediate interest in her. It was years before she'd met Luc, and, since he wasn't asking her for blessings or healing or trying to turn her into a Christian, she'd found him refreshing. She only realized later that he was everything she hated. He was vile. He was Shadow. He found her ways amusing. She told him she didn't want to see him again, once she realized what he was. He hadn't taken it well. He'd followed her, showed up in the places she usually visited. But she was more powerful than he was, and his pathetic attempts to hurt her were met with her own derisive laughter. For a few years, it seemed as if he'd finally given up, though she'd occasionally see him among the Europeans.

It seemed he'd decided he wasn't finished with her. Why now, she didn't even want to wonder. She hoped that ignoring him would be enough.

Arriving at the cabin, she saw a group of people from her tribe, as well as a couple of white men. One had a contraption she recognized as a camera from a newspaper article she'd read. She held out her hand, and the white man holding the camera handed it to her, looking confused. Migisi inspected it.

"Such a beautiful machine, really," she remarked in French to her visitors, repeating it in Ojibwa for her people. "Thank you for letting me look at it. I hadn't yet seen one in person," she said to the man, handing his camera back.

"We were hoping to take a few photos of you, Healer," the man with the camera said. The white men often called her that, simply "Healer," as if that was the entirety of what she was. She forced a smile onto her face.

"And why is that?"

"Because you are a woman of some renown and mystery. Because one can't walk among your people without hearing tales of your greatness. And because you healed one of the priests who lived here for a while, and he still sings your praises. People are interested in you. And pictures sell newspapers," he added with a grin.

She looked at the camera doubtfully.

"Please," the other white man said. "It will only take a few minutes."

She sighed, knowing it would only prolong their visit if she refused, and her small confrontation with the one who stalked her steps had left her feeling unsettled. She nodded, and someone grabbed a stool from near the cabin, set it near her.

"There, there. Sit there," the photographer said, and she did. "All right, look over here. Smile now."

"Maybe a profile shot," the other man said, and they argued over that for a while. Her patience was already wearing thin.

She heard icy ground crunching beneath heavy footsteps to her left, and she looked that way, watched Luc as he approached, so much larger, so much more pleasing to the eye than anything else she could imagine. He studied the scene, met her eyes, and smiled at her, clearly being able to read her annoyance at the situation.

She raised her face a little, a small smile lighting her face, sharing, for just a moment, in his mirth. She heard the camera click, smelled the scent of the flash, and looked toward the photographer.

"That was perfect. Thank you," he said, bowing to her a little. She nodded in response, and watched as they all trooped away from her land. Luc reached her, pulled her into his arms.

"You looked like you were considering trying to turn them into toads or something," he remarked, and she shook her head, a slight smile on her lips.

"Maggots, actually," she said, and Luc laughed and followed her into the house. These were the moments that held them together, those moments when he reminded her, just by being himself, that he understood her. It was enough.

CHAPTER TWENTY-THREE

She'd had every intention of just going home and waiting for Calder, waiting to hear what had happened with his father. Sophie got home, and parked Calder's truck in his driveway and tucked his keys between the storm door and heavy front door at the front of his house. She wandered back across the road toward her house, numbly noted yet another yellow rose on her mailbox. She made a gesture with her hand, and the rose burst into flames, which died out just a quickly, leaving nothing.

She looked down at her hands, remembered Mr. Turcotte's crazed howls.

Instead of going into her house, she got into her car and drove down the highway, her mind racing. She nearly missed the wrought iron fence, she was so deep in thought. She pulled into the gravel parking lot, walked quickly between the graves until she got to Luc's grave. Migisi's grave.

She stood there for a while, then knelt on the damp ground. Another gray fall day, and the ground was littered with leaves. Red maple leaves, yellow birch covered Luc and Migisi's graves.

"I wish I knew what I was supposed to do," Sophie said quietly, feeling stupid. She pushed the rose vines away from Migisi's headstone again, looked at her name, those dates. "I wish I knew how you ended." There had been a message on her voice mail from Thea. There were obituaries for both of them. Migisi had died of "a sudden illness" and Luc had died of "a fall."

Sophie had the feeling there was so much more to the story. And she'd never know, most likely.

"The only thing I know is, I'm not you. I won't let it take me completely. I won't give up the way you did. I won't be used."

She sat there a while longer, Migisi's writings, Mr. Turcotte's snarls, Calder's words "I forgot how to shift back," running through her mind.

She came to a decision, because of her two options, it was the only choice that made any sense.

When Sophie entered the small, dark bar near the interstate, it took a moment for her eyes to adjust. The place smelled of stale beer and whiskey, and a tired old Randy Travis song played. The place was small, and mostly empty. A corpulent bartender stood behind the scarred bar, and a few men sat on stools, either staring at their drinks or at the television mounted behind the bar, which was showing some sports thing. In the corner, she spotted Marshall sitting at a small table. She took a breath and headed to him. He stood up, grinning widely, and sat only after she'd sat down.

"I told you you'd come to me," he said.

"Don't gloat. I'm not doing it for you."

"It doesn't matter why. All that matters is that you're doing it."

"I am still me," Sophie said, and he laughed.

"Your magic has failed you. You know it, and I know it. And look, here I am, not hurting you. All of that needless running, little girl." He took a sip of the dark-colored drink in front of him.

"Will it break the curse?" she asked.

"Will the paltry bit of magic you have now break it?" he asked in response.

"That's not an answer," she said, raising her voice, aware that she was losing her temper and, for once, not caring.

He smiled, a slow, knowing smile that would have been attractive if she didn't know what he actually was. "It is all the answer you need. You have zero chance to save him as you are. Come to me, and you have the unlimited power that comes with the Shadow."

"And what do you get?" she asked quietly.

"A goal met. A feeling of accomplishment. You."

She studied him.

"Not your body, though I'd take it. You're a little fat for my tastes, but all that really matters is what's between your thighs in that regard."

She felt like vomiting.

"No, my little weakling. I'd get to turn a Lightwitch. That is a reward all its own."

"Why?"

He smiled again. "Someone hasn't studied up on witchy history as much as she should have."

"Tell me why. Why is this happening? You know why, damn it."

"You have it figured out. I heard you talking to that delectable shifter woman."

"You stay away from her," she warned.

"I would not touch one of yours, if you are of the Shadow," he said, smiling. "At any rate, you had it right. Some smart chap ensured that the object of Migisi's desires would end up being her downfall."

"Who?"

He just smiled smugly.

"Not you. You're not that old," she said, rolling her eyes.

"Ah, little girl. Looks are deceiving. Power is all that matters."

"How old are you?"

"You wouldn't believe me if I told you."

"So you've what? Spent the last two hundred years messing with my line? Why?"

He laughed, and it was cold and heartless and sent shivers down her spine. "Oh, it's cute how you think you understand. Two hundred years is nothing, and your line has been my plaything for centuries."

Sophie stared at him, and he grinned. "Feeling less significant now, aren't you? It's not all about you. Hurts, doesn't it?" He watched her for a few moments. "This is checkmate. This is the part where you surrender, because every option has been taken from you." His voice was low, serious. "Wait, and he's lost. Wait, and you're just as lost. Do you want to know what happened after she cursed him?"

Sophie didn't answer.

He shook his head. "It didn't end there. She cursed him, and came to her senses shortly after and tried to fix it. Her methods of trying to repair the damage were... unconventional. It helped pull her deeper into the Shadow. It was a beautiful thing to watch."

"I don't believe you. You are a liar and a murderer."

"Have I ever lied to you yet? Think about it. Every word I've ever said to you has been the truth, and you know it."

"You said you can help me save him."

He nodded.

"How?"

"Our powers are great. Limitless," he added, his steely eyes searching hers. "Anything we desire, anything at all, becomes ours."

"Yet it took you almost twenty years to succeed with me," she said, raising her eyebrow.

He smiled. "But I succeeded. That is all that matters. And as we've established, it felt like nothing to me."

"But not because of anything you did. I don't have a choice."

"There is always a choice. You want added power, this gives it to you." A twinkle came to his eyes. Amusement. "And you are desperate. Poor little witch," he murmured.

"As if you care."

"I care about you."

"This doesn't mean you are anything to me," she said, staring him straight in the eye.

"My darling, if I welcome you into the Shadow, if I help you gain control over the darkness, I am the center of your world. I will always know where you are, and I can order you to do whatever I please." He paused, smiled. "Despite what you think of me, I am not a liar. I am telling you flat out what I get in return. Nothing more and nothing less than your soul." He took a sip of the drink in front of him. "So you need to decide right now: is he worth it?"

"It's not just him. It's his entire family. His father. Any descendants down the line. They would be free."

"Which is all sweet and noble, and exactly what a Lightwitch would be expected to say. But when it comes right down to it, you're doing it for him. Because you want him, and the thought of losing him that way enrages you."

She tilted her head. "You're not just a warlock, are you?"

He smiled, a sharp, toothy grin that made her skin crawl. "I am a Shadow lord."

Sophie remembered mentions of those. Stories, tales of warning from the books on witchcraft she'd read. Shadow lords were rare, and attained their power through causing chaos. They were the essence of everything wrong with the Shadow. They were an antithesis to Light. And she was about to give herself to one of them. "Aren't the Shadow lords just supposed to be spirits?"

"I can take whichever form I like. And this form is capable of sex, which I quite enjoy."

She chose to ignore that. "Power is a tool. I still believe in the Light."

He gave a derisive snort. "As if that matters to me. Are we here to talk about you and your worthless faith, or do you want the power you crave so badly?"

"I don't crave power," she argued, and he laughed.

"If you say so." He snapped his fingers, and her own voice came back to her:

"I'm tired of everyone underestimating me. I'm tired of everyone seeming to think I'm this weak, stupid little thing who can't handle what life throws at her... But no, Sophie's so fucking weak we need to protect her from every stupid little thing."

He gave her a derisive look. "You are just as power hungry, lustful, and self-absorbed as any of my children. You want the power? Give your loyalty to me, and you have it."

"Why don't you just take it, if you're so powerful?" she shot back.

"It doesn't work that way. I get so much more out of the deal if you beg for it. If you want it. So, I'll ask again: is lover boy worth it?"

"He's worth it," she said, telling herself that she was doing it for all the right reasons, no matter what Marshall said. That she was saving Calder and his line, and if she had to sacrifice herself to do it, she would.

She was a Lightwitch, no matter what else she became.

Marshall smiled. "Give me your wrist."

She hesitated for a moment, then laid her arm on the table, wrist up, close to him.

"This will hurt. You'll like it, though," he said, giving her a slimy smile.

Though his hands had looked normal just moments ago, Sophie watched as he used a black claw to draw a ragged line down her arm, from about midway up her lower arm and down to her wrist, over the scars she'd created so long ago. It burned, and the pain was so intense Sophie could barely breathe. Her stomach turned, and she shed silent tears as she told herself over and over again that it was worth it. Blood pooled, looking like a strand of dark rubies reflecting the dim light of the pendant over the table. Marshall raised her arm to his mouth, and she tried not to yank her hand away in disgust when he licked the blood from her. She looked around. No one was paying any attention, as if they were invisible or something.

It burned, and a pained whimper escaped her. She felt dizzy, foggy, nauseous. He groaned in pleasure as he drank from her opened vein. As he did, she began to feel the twisted, cold tendrils of darkness seeping into her soul. As he took from her, he claimed her as his, and she felt the power of Shadow infusing her.

She felt the last tiny glimmers of Light fading inside her, and she closed her eyes, apologized and wept as she felt Shadow eradicating the Light. A deep mourning stuck deep in her soul, alongside the power granted to her by Shadow.

Marshall released her hand, and she opened her eyes, tears spilling down her face.

"You'll want to wrap that up," Shadow said to her. She glanced down at her arm, which was still pooling blood. She put a napkin over it, held it tight.

"You won't bleed out. You'll likely have a scar, though. It'll match the others," Shadow said.

"How do I remove his curse?" she asked flatly.

"It is made of Shadow. You are Shadow now. Shadow will always be drawn to Shadow. Draw it out of him." Shadow looked very pleased with himself, and a wide grin spread across his face. "You're mine now."

"Never."

"If you say so, 'kitten,'" Shadow said, getting up. "I hope it was worth it." He laughed and strolled away, disappearing before he'd even reached the door.

Sophie sat at the table in the stinking, depressing bar for a while after Marshall had strolled away. She sopped her blood up with napkins, gave up and ended up tying the scarf she'd been wearing around her arm to staunch the bleeding.

She could feel it. Slimy, slithering, and vile, deep in her soul. Wrong. Wrong in every single way, and she hated it.

But she could save him from what she'd just seen in his father.

She was doing it for the right reasons. That had to count for something, she hoped.

She finally pulled herself up. She watched as the men at the bar finally seemed to notice her, shrinking away from her as she passed, looking uncomfortable.

Sophie took a deep breath. It would be worth it.

She had one more stop to make before she went home. She checked her messages as she sat in the car, trying to get herself together again. Calder had called, saying he and Jon were going hunting and he'd be home the next morning. "He needs to blow off some steam," he said, and she listened to his deep, warm voice, closed her eyes. "The old man's getting worse. It's hard on Jon. Anyway. I'll be home tomorrow morning. I love you, kitten."

She focused herself. He was worth it. And she was worth it. Her soul was her own, no matter what Marshall thought he'd just accomplished.

She nodded, started her car, and turned back onto the highway. She drove through town, then veered toward the woods. Layla had a cute little house close to town, but with enough space around it that she could run as her wolf easily. Sophie glanced at the clock on the dashboard. It was late afternoon. She hoped she was home. She'd lose her nerve if she had to try to talk to her later.

She pulled up in front of Layla's house, got out of the car. She walked up the wooden front steps and knocked on the door. Within moments, Layla was there, hair tousled as if she'd been napping.

"Hey," Layla said, looking surprised. Her gaze flicked over Sophie, and she held the door open. Sophie walked in, stopped short when she saw Bryce, shirtless, standing up from the couch in Layla's cozy, cluttered living room.

"Oh, hey, Bryce," Sophie said in surprise. She glanced at Layla, who was looking a little red in the face, but had a goofy smile on her face. "Um. I can come back," she said.

"No, no. You never drop by like this. Stay," Layla said.

"I'm going to head to the bakery. Donuts," Bryce said, looking a little flustered. He shared a glance with Layla, pulled on his shirt, and headed out.

"I am so sorry," Sophie said as Layla closed the door.

"He'll be back," Layla said with a smile. "You were right, by the way. I asked him out last night and he's been by my side ever since."

Sophie laughed. "Still. Crappy timing, huh?"

Layla was studying her. "What's going on, Soph?"

Sophie took a deep breath. "You know how you're always getting on me for never asking for help?"

Layla nodded.

"Okay. Well, I need your help."

Layla took her hand, led her to the sofa. They both sat, Sophie's hand still in Layla's.

"You're Shadow now, aren't you?" Layla asked before Sophie could say a word. Sophie nodded. "You smell wrong."

"Calder will be able to tell, then," Sophie said.

"He'll be able to smell it," Layla confirmed. "It's kind of a sulfurous, smoky smell."

Sophie nodded, remembering Calder describing Marshall's scent the same way.

"Did he force you to?"

Sophie shook her head. "I did it willingly. This is my only chance to save him. It's my only chance to keep myself from falling helplessly into the Shadow." She met Layla's eyes. "This is a choice I made, rather than have it made for me. It was happening. At least I have some control over it now."

"Soph, this is exactly what he wanted," Layla argued.

Sophie shook her head. "My most immediate problem is Calder. I can help him now. Once that's done, I can focus on dealing with whatever's next."

They sat in silence for a while.

"What do you need, Soph?" Layla finally asked.

Sophie told her what she had in mind, what she was planning to do, and what it would mean. "So I need you to keep an eye on me. If it starts to look like I'm too far gone, I need you to end me."

Sophie hadn't known what to expect. She expected anger, or arguments. Instead, Layla sat there, watching her. "You think it will come to that?" she asked.

"I hope not. I believe I can manage it. But it would be careless and stupid to leave that to chance, and you're the only one I trust enough to do what needs to be done if the time ever comes."

Layla squeezed her hand. "I love you, you know that," she said to Sophie, and tears came to Sophie's eyes.

"I know. I love you too. I'm sorry I have to ask this of you."

"It means a lot to me that you did. How messed up is that?" she said with a roll of her eyes, tears rolling down her cheeks. "You can count on me, Soph. Don't make it come to that, though."

"I'm going to try not to," Sophie promised.

After a few more minutes, she hugged Layla and left, after making Layla promise to keep their conversation to herself. She did, and hugged Sophie again, and watched

Sophie as she got into her car. Sophie gave her a wave and drove off.

When she got home, she slept the sleep of the dead.

She went in to work early the next morning, but ended up leaving when, right before lunchtime, the high winds blowing outside knocked the power out. When it didn't come back up in the next hour, her boss sent everyone home. They didn't have any guests anyway, it being midweek in the off season. Sophie was grateful.

She drove home, hoping she'd see Calder at some point that day. She didn't know how long the two of them would hunt. Sometimes, she knew, he and Bryce would hunt for an entire weekend, but she guessed Jon and Calder's hunt wouldn't go on that long, considering that someone needed to be there to watch over their father.

She got home. There were no yellow roses. She shook her head. Clearly, Marshall considered it done, considered himself the victor. And maybe he was for now, but he wouldn't be forever.

As she unlocked her door, she realized that her power was out, too, the generator having kicked on. She could hear it running at the back of the house. When she stepped inside, her phone rang. She glanced at it. Calder's number.

"Hey, Sophie," he said, and his voice was tense.

"Hey," she said. "Are you home?"

"No."

His voice was wrong. Tight.

"What's wrong?"

"Do you have power?"

"No. The wind knocked the power out at work, and I just got home. Luckily the generator's going."

He didn't answer.

"Calder?"

"We lost power at my dad's house, too. We have solar at the main house, but we ran wires to the fences around my dad's pen. A fallen tree branch crashed into the wire we had running, and the power went out."

"Are you there fixing it now, then?" Sophie asked, rifling through her mail.

"He got out. We weren't there at the time. We felt the wind kicking up, and we headed back. He was already out."

Sophie froze, didn't respond right away. "Oh, no," she finally managed. "Any idea where he would have gone?"

"We're hoping deeper into the woods. We're looking for him now. If you hear anything from around town, call me, okay? Christ, if he heads toward town..." he said, the worry in his voice making her ache for him.

"It'll be okay. I'll call if I hear anything. I promise."

"Thanks," he said.

"Be careful, Calder," she said softly.

"I will. I love you."

"I love you," she said. He hung up, and she set the phone on the mantel.

This wouldn't end well. How many times had he said he should have put his father out of his misery long ago? Her heart ached for what Calder was likely to have to face when they finally found their father.

Of course, it would be so much worse if they didn't find him. She'd seen him now. It was obvious he was a danger to anyone he came across.

She went outside, gave the animals food and water. It would be her last time doing this. One of the other maids at the resort was starting her own little homestead in the country, and she'd been thrilled to hear Sophie was looking to re-home her animals. Keeping them around now was pointless. They weren't producing anymore, though she had no doubt they'd start producing again away from her.

Of course, Merlin would still be there. She still seemed to be the only one who wanted the bad-tempered jerk of a goat.

She finished with the animals, then headed to the garden, started pulling out the dead plants. She tossed them into a wheelbarrow, then, once it was all clean, she wheeled all of it to the large compost pile she'd started behind the barn.

As she turned the corner, she heard a growl.

Mr. Turcotte stood there, growling, mouth foaming, his fur standing up in disheveled clumps.

"Tracked me here, did you?" she asked softly. He snarled again, and a movement in the nearby woods caught his attention. He lunged in that direction, on the hunt, and Sophie ran for the house.

The animals, it seemed, had more sense than she'd given them credit for. The chickens and goats had all retreated into their structures, and Sophie quickly locked them in before running for the back door. She could hear crazed growls, howls from the woods.

Her phone was ringing, and she grabbed it off the mantel.

"Sophie. Bryce said he thought he saw my dad not too far from you," Calder's voice came over the phone, tense.

"Calder. He's here. He was behind my barn a minute ago. I just ran for the house. He's hunting in my woods, I think."

"Sophie, stay in the house. Promise me," Calder said.

"Okay," she said.

"We're coming. Just hold tight."

She hung up, looked toward her front window. Mr. Turcotte was standing out there, looking in at her, growling, snapping in his insane rage.

He carried the curse, too, Sophie thought to herself, and just as the realization hit her, he sprang, came crashing through the glass and into her living room.

Sophie ran out the front door, knowing it would be a really, really bad idea to let him back her into a corner. At least outside, she could run.

Right. Because she was so likely to be able to outrun a crazed bear beast.

Mr. Turcotte came charging out of her house, back to where he'd been standing in her front yard.

CHAPTER TWENTY-FOUR

He stood there, fur bristling, blood on his snout. He'd clearly hunted, eaten. At his feet was the carcass of some small animal. Sophie's stomach threatened to empty itself, and she gulped, looked away from him. He snarled.

"I am trying to lift the curse, Mr. Turcotte. I swear it."

She readied herself. He lunged at her, and she acted on instinct, focusing on pushing out energy the way she had with Calder, and later with Marshall. It struck the raging bear, and he fell back, jumped up again, and sprang at her with a spine-chilling roar. She threw out another energy blast, knocking him away.

"I do not want to hurt you," she said, trying to keep her voice calm. He lunged again, and she knocked him back.

She understood then, more than she would have expected, exactly how it was that the magic generated by the Shadow became so addictive to those who wielded it. The first time she'd used it against Mr. Turcotte, it had come to her easily, and every time thereafter, she'd felt a euphoria, as if using it triggered something inside her. It was wrong. Causing pain, especially against someone who had no clue what he was doing, was wrong. In her heart, she felt wrong. But the magic was powerful, and it was all too natural to go with what felt good.

"Stop," she said, and he lunged again. With a cry, she sent out another blast. He was just picking himself up, snarling, when she saw two headlights approaching, heard the distinct rumble of Calder's bike. Two motorcycles turned into the driveway, and Calder and his brother each got off of a bike.

"I'll do it," Calder said in a low voice to Jon. "Protect her."

Jon patted Calder on the shoulder, and the brothers exchanged a look. Sophie watched as Jon gave Calder's shoulder a squeeze, then walked toward her, keeping an eye on his father. Mr. Turcotte got ready to spring at Sophie again, and before she even got off the blast of energy she was holding at the ready, Calder, in full bear form, was leaping in front of his father. The two bears crashed into each other, and the night was filled with snarls, growls. Jon had shifted as well, and stood in front of Sophie. He was not as big a bear as Calder, or even what Mr. Turcotte must have been once up on a time, but he had that same shaggy black fur, same powerful form.

Sophie closed her eyes, trying, working feverishly, seeing if there was some way she could stop the curse before Calder did something he'd hate himself for for the rest of his life. She focused on the tangle of magic, of Shadow, in Calder's soul. She could barely concentrate with all of the roaring and growling, the occasional pained howl. She continued working, but her eyes snapped open when she heard Calder give a pained yelp, and she lost any headway she'd made. Calder sported a deep gash across his chest. She put her hands to her face, trying not to cry out. He was limping a little. Mr. Turcotte, however, was in much worse shape. Bloodied, limping. She watched Calder. Everyone knew he had the advantage. He knew it. All he had to do was leap forward and end it. His injuries, he'd taken since gaining the advantage. She knew what it was. He didn't want to do it.

And she hated herself for not solving this before he had to do this.

"If he weakens him enough, can we just put him back in the pen? He doesn't have to do this," Sophie said. Jon gave her a long look, shifted back.

"This is the end. It should have been done years ago, but neither of us had the heart. The injuries he already has... He'd die a slow, painful death from them anyway." He watched his brother, remorse in his eyes. "He doesn't want to do it."

"I know," she said softly.

Mr. Turcotte made a final lunge at Calder, limping, bleeding, and Calder gave a loud, rage-filled roar. Tears came to Sophie's eyes. He'd made a decision. He jumped at his father, clamped his huge jaw around Mr. Turcotte's throat, and bit down. Sophie wanted to look away, but she felt like she owed Mr. Turcotte and Calder this at least, to bear witness to the end, to watch Calder so she'd understand the coming grief he'd feel as well as she possibly could. Tears were flowing from her eyes, and she watched as Mr. Turcotte's movements weakened, then ceased. When he'd been still for a few moments, she could see his eyes flatten, as if the life had left them. Calder stepped back, and his father's body started changing, fur disappearing, bones popping, until all that was left was a much older, emaciated-looking version of Calder. She covered her eyes and cried. Jon turned, roared, and punched the wood pillar of the porch.

Sophie looked back at Calder, who had shifted back. He ran for the bushes and started retching. She ran off the porch, stood behind him, tentatively putting a hand on his back. He was trembling, retching, taking deep gulps of breath as if he couldn't breathe. Eventually, he fell to his knees, and Sophie did as well, gathering him into her arms. He rested his face against her, and she could feel hot tears on her neck. She held him as tightly as she could, rode out the fist tide of his grief with him.

A few minutes later, he gently pushed her away, stood up, helping her up as he did. He pulled on the jeans he'd discarded before shifting and went to his brother, who was standing over his father's body. Sophie stayed where she was, hating herself for not being able to end the curse before it came to this point.

"You should have her heal that, man," Jon said in a flat voice, referring to the slice across Calder's chest.

"It's mostly healed. Just bloody. She can't heal it anyway."

She watched as Jon shot Calder a look, then looked back at her.

"That's what Lightwitches do," Jon said.

"Drop it," Calder said, his voice a low growl. A warning. He hadn't taken his eyes off his father.

Jon tore his gaze from Sophie, looked at his brother.

"This isn't your fate. She's here. She's going to fix it," Jon said. Calder waved it off. "You did what you had to do," Jon said more quietly. "I would have done it."

"You shouldn't have to. You shouldn't have had to do any of the shit you've been doing."

Jon gave his father's body a last glance. As sad as he was, as angry, Sophie also got the sense that there was relief there. She couldn't blame him for that. From what Calder had said, he'd given up his life, for the most part, to be his father's caretaker and guard.

"I'm going to go dig."

"It's mostly dug. I did it after the other day," Calder said, referring to the day they'd had to go and shore up the fences around their father's pen.

Jon clapped him on the shoulder again. "I'll go check on it, do anything else that needs to be done." He shot another look at Sophie, then walked around to the back of Calder's house. Sophie slowly walked toward Calder, tentatively put a hand on his back. He didn't respond. She took his hand, and after a moment he twined his fingers with hers.

"I'm sorry, Calder," she said softly.

He didn't respond. She stood there with him, feeling at a loss, wanting to comfort him in his grief, and not knowing how, getting the distinct sense that he didn't really want her comfort.

"You lost your magic. Whatever you had, it's gone. The wards failed."

She nodded. "They never took in the first place. I'm sorry," she repeated.

"I don't care about the wards, Sophie," he said, eyes hard, watching her.

She didn't respond.

"And you smell wrong. Like him. So I need you to tell me, right now: did he do something to you to make you lose your powers? Did he hurt you? Did he force something on you?" She knew what he wanted. He wanted something to hurt, something to punish.

"I did it willingly," she said softly, and he stared at her. "I did what he's wanted me to do all these years."

"Which is?"

"Turn from the Light."

Calder let go of her hand, not trusting himself to touch her just then. It was like she'd just knocked the air from his lungs, like she'd just gutted him. "Why the hell would you do that?" he asked, taking a step back from her.

"Because my power wasn't enough, Calder. It wasn't enough! Every spell that I learned from Migisi's book, that maybe, might have been something I could have used, I don't have the power to pull off."

"So you threw away what you are because....." He wanted to hit something so bad. He knew he was close to losing it completely. And she stood there, looking small and soft, her eyes bright with tears. Trembling, and it broke him, to see her that way.

"Because the Shadow offers me more power," she said, looking away. "It's the only chance I have to save you."

Rage roared through him. Because of him, she'd given up everything she believed in. What the hell had he ever done, in his entire life, to deserve someone who'd give up that much for him? He didn't deserve it, and he didn't want it. "Go inside, Sophie," he said, his voice rough. His chest hurt, thinking of what she'd done. "Just stay away from me for a while."

"I get it, Calder. This is my fault. My wards failed and now this. I don't blame you for hating me—"

He let out a frustrated, angry shout, grabbed her arms and pulled her to him, breathed her in. She was still there, below the sulfur and smoke. He gritted his teeth. "I don't hate you, Sophie. It's not even possible for me to hate you. I don't blame you for this. When are you going to get it through your head that I love you, that out of everything that's happening, keeping you whole is all that matters to me? That protecting you is the only thing that gives my life any meaning now? And you fucking threw away everything you stand for, and you never even asked me what I thought about that. Get. Away," he growled, releasing her and stalking away. He heard her door slam behind him, and he ran into the woods, roaring, letting his beast run free before he completely lost his mind.

Afterward, he and Jon buried their father, then he watched his brother shift and take to the woods, lumbering toward the cabin he'd now live in by himself.

He shook his head, went to Sophie's house. He let himself in with the key she'd given him, stripped, and got into the daybed in the living room beside her.

"I don't regret it," she said. "And if you love me as much as you say you do, you'll respect that maybe I'm not a complete idiot."

The room was dark, and all he could smell was her. Her warmth beside him soothed him in a way nothing else did. She was naked beneath the blankets, her soft skin pressing against his. Her voice was hoarse, and he knew she'd been crying.

"I know you're not an idiot. You're amazing, and I love you. And you're stubborn as hell. You would have done it anyway. Doesn't mean I'm not pissed off at you over it."

"It's likely you'll be even more pissed at me before it's all over," she said quietly. "Come on. You need me."

He took a deep breath, rolled her body under his, lost himself in her body, in the way she sighed his name. She had no idea, none at all, how true her words had been.

He needed her.

CHAPTER TWENTY-FIVE

October 29, 1861

It had been a mistake, Migisi thought to herself as she stalked through the woods. Letting Luc leave the way he had. Letting him believe she would be grateful to be without him for a while. She'd seen the hurt in his eyes. Not for the first time. She knew, when she was in her right mind, that she'd been progressively more terrible toward him the longer they'd been together. What kind of monster spent day after day hurting the one she loved? Yet, that was exactly what Migisi had been doing. As the Shadow had slowly and surely worked itself into her soul, she'd gotten worse, verging on abusive. Her mind flashed to the the previous morning, when, in an incoherent rage, she'd hurled a hot cast iron pan toward him. His reflexes had been the only thing to save him from injury.

She knew. She knew that she should let him go, that trying to keep him would only hurt him more as time went on. She also knew that he wouldn't leave.

She'd tried. She'd tried to tell him he should go, that he should move on. But he'd marked her. Claimed her. He refused to leave. Even getting him to meet with his business partners for a couple of days had been a challenge. No matter how terrible she was, he stayed. And for the life of her, she could not understand why.

But without him, she was lost. She missed his touch, his scent. She thought of him, away from her. If he had any sense, he'd decide to stay gone. But she had to let him know she loved him. She had to let him know how sorry she was for what their lives had become.

She'd been walking for two days, and knew from the way the river was narrowing that it would soon be meeting the other, smaller river. That was where his business partners had set up camp. That was where she'd find her love.

As she neared the camp in the waning daylight, she could hear the sounds of male voices, a harmonica playing.

And, so soft she could have missed it had she not always been hyper-attuned to her surroundings, a passionate sigh.

Followed by a muttered curse she knew well. How many times had she heard it in her own ear, his hot breath coming in hard pants, as he went over the edge with her?

She didn't want to see.

She needed to know.

She crept silently, like a ghost, in the direction of the sounds, her heart pounding, her nerves making her tremble.

"Stop. What in the hell?" she heard him say. And then, "Migisi?"

She took one more silent step, and they came into view. Her back was against a tree, the top of her dress pulled down revealing pale breasts, much fuller than her own. She had shining red curls, a painted face.

Luc's eyes were on Migisi. And then on the woman, and he shook his head, confusion on his features.

She felt cold. Empty, as if what she'd just seen had taken the very life from her. She felt the last shreds of Light leave her as her heart shattered.

"I see I am not missed," she said in French to Luc, who was holding out his hands, approaching her slowly.

"What? Migisi," Luc said. "I don't know what is happening. This is not what it looks like."

"No? I suppose it's not what it sounds like, either," she said, and she barely recognized her voice, so dead and cold.

"Migisi," he whispered, eyes unfocused, widened in fear, hands held out to her.

The words came to her, unbidden, words in a language older than anything she knew, words she never, in her entire life, would have imagined herself saying.

They came easily, naturally, as if they'd been waiting for her, a stream of syllables that condemned and sentenced the man she'd loved, her heart and soul, to a life of suffering. He, and his children, his children's children, would live with the emptiness she was feeling just then.

When the words stopped, the twilight was silent around them. The woman had long since disappeared, to who, or where, Migisi did not care.

"What did you do to me, my little ghost?" Luc asked, pressing his hand to his stomach. She could hear it rumbling, could see the discomfort in his face.

"Suffer. And then die, my love. I will haunt your every remaining moment," she said coldly. She turned her back on him, and walked through the forest, and creatures great and small trembled in her wake, and she was too far gone to hear the faint laugh that echoed on the breeze.

CHAPTER TWENTY-SIX

Sophie lay next to Calder in the daybed in her living room. She held him, and his arms were wrapped tightly around her waist, as if he was afraid to let her go. His face rested on her chest, his warm breath raising goose bumps over her flesh. He was sleeping now, though it had been a long time coming. She'd given him everything she could, had held him when he'd sunk into grief over his father. She'd watched as he ate every bit of food she offered him as if he hadn't eaten in days. He'd drunk gallons of milk, cartons of cider.

It was getting worse.

With his father dead, and no descendants to help bear the burden of the curse, Calder seemed to be bearing the full brunt of it. And while she could and would give him everything she had to help him feel better, she knew there was a limit to how much she could give, and that his hunger was never-ending.

Destroying him was not an option. Maybe she was selfish, but life without him, a life in which she ended *his* life, was an impossibility.

She watched him sleep, and she gently, lazily ran her fingertips through his tousled hair.

She had the ability to help him now. And it terrified her. She could see, every time she looked at him, what it looked like. She could feel, every time he loved her, what desperation was.

She would take it. For him. For herself.

She closed her eyes, matched her breathing to his, almost without thinking. She went by instinct, completely opened herself up to the Shadow, to the power granted to her by giving herself up to Marshall.

It came, without hesitation, as if all it had been waiting for was her summons. She focused on Calder, on seeing the fine, yet unbreakable threads of her ancestor's curse in his soul. So much clearer now than she'd ever seen them before, because, unlike before, they were part of her.

They were Shadow, and so was she. It was just a matter of opening herself, of drawing them inside.

Nearly effortless. Marshall had been right. Shadow would always flow to Shadow, just as Light had always flowed into Light. As she lay there, and held him, and breathed with him, she felt his curse twining its way into her soul, and every bit of it that filled her made her feel empty, until it was finally done and she felt the curse solidify in her own soul.

The emptiness was terrifying.

Painful.

Overwhelming.

It was as if every scent, every sight, every touch ignited hunger. Calder beside her was enough to make her mad, and the things she wanted to do to him, the things she wanted to do to his body, had her aching with need. Her stomach growled, feeling emptier than it ever had, cramping so completely she thought she'd pass out from pain if she didn't have something soon. Her mouth was dry, her throat barely able to work when she tried to swallow.

And she understood, now better than ever, why Calder had snapped so easily at times. The car parts flying out of his garage, tree trunks hurled away from him, walls punched. And she marveled that, enduring it, he'd been endlessly gentle with her.

She opened her eyes and looked down at him, still asleep, but looking more relaxed than she'd ever seen him.

It was worth it. She would survive, and he was free.

Hands on her wrists, lips at her throat.

"What did you do, kitten?" Calder's deep voice, his chest rumbling against hers as he held himself above her.

She whimpered.

"It's gone. All of a sudden, like that, it's gone. What did you do?"

She opened her legs, urging him to fill her, take her.

"Not until you tell me," he said, raising his face, eyes searching hers. "Tell me."

"I took it," she whispered. "Please."

"You took it."

"Shadow goes to Shadow. I took it."

He growled. "You didn't even think of running this little idea past me?"

"Like you would have said. 'yes, dear, go ahead and take my curse. Great idea', if I had," she said.

"Sophie, you can't—"

"It's already done. I have it, and you're here with me and alive and I'm not going to lose you and there is no taking it back now."

He looked at her, seeming at a loss. "It hurts, doesn't it?" he said, voice low.

She nodded, tears coming to her eyes, and she fought them back. It was agony.

"I didn't want this for you," he growled, gripping her wrists tighter, eyes still boring into hers.

"I'm better able to take it than you are."

"When I go mad, someone can kill me. If you go mad? You're a Shadow witch now. Do you think you're going to remember to be good when you're in the throes of hunger, when you're desperate for relief, when you're so full of rage, so sick of being empty that you just want to make someone hurt as much as you're hurting? Do you think you're going to remember then, with that dark power slithering through you, that you don't believe in violence?" He delivered all of it in a low, urgent tone, not taking his eyes from hers. "What did you do to yourself?"

"I did what I had to do. Just as I always have," she whispered.

"I hate this."

"I don't. Believe in me, Calder."

"You know I do. I always have. You're going to be in so much pain, kitten." His eyes searched hers.

"You were nearing the end. We both know it. With your father gone it was worse."

He didn't answer.

"I'm stronger than you in that way, Calder," she said. "I can contain it until I can figure out how to get rid of it. Because that's still the goal. I'm still going to break it. But I couldn't watch you lose it. I couldn't watch you become like your father," she whispered, tears leaking from the corners of her eyes as she looked up at him, begging him to understand. "This was my line's fault. I refuse to let you feel this anymore."

His face softened, and he lowered his face to her neck, breathing her in, his shoulders slumping.

"Have faith in me," she whispered. "I need you to."

He raised his eyes to hers again. "I do. I promise you right now, Sophie... I promise I'll feed you when you're hungry, I promise I'll walk to the ends of the earth to get you enough water to drink if that's what it takes to relieve your thirst. I promise I'll love you as often as you want me. I'll hold you every second you want it, and when you need me to back off, I'll do that, too. I can't believe you did this for me," he finished, and he swallowed hard, as if trying to get his emotions in check. "I love you," he whispered, eyes locked onto hers. "I will love you until the day I die. I always have, and I always will."

"I love you," she whispered. "Always."

He did as he promised, loving her until she dozed back off, exhausted. When she woke, it was to find a warm apple pie, milk, and tea waiting for her on the table. She got up, not even taking time to dress, and began devouring it all as Calder looked on. He got up and stood behind her, pulling her hair up and clipping it behind her head so it would stop hanging down over her food. She tried her best not to be out of control. She even stopped at two slices of pie, though she could have devoured the whole thing with no problem. She wouldn't let him see her out of control. He'd protected her from the worst of what he'd gone through, and she promised herself that she'd do the same for him.

"You're still hungry."

"It's enough. I'm going to get so huge if I keep eating like that."

He knelt in front of her, took her hands in his. "You'd still be gorgeous, too. But that won't happen. You feel all of that insane energy running through your system, like if you don't move, you'll go nuts? Your skin practically crawls with it."

She nodded.

He nodded back. "You'll run it off. It's impossible not to. And when you want to run, if you want company, I'll run with you."

"I'm not a shifter, though," she said.

"Doesn't matter. You'll still need to run. That amount of emptiness, you can only distract by doing stuff. Which was why I stated tinkering with cars. You'll need to find things to keep your mind and body occupied, keep your hands busy."

She nodded. Then she forced herself to smile at him despite the emptiness threatening to drive her mad. She ran her fingers through his beard. "Have you run yet as a bear, now that you can do it without being worried about what your beast will do?"

He shook his head. She smiled again, stood up, pulled on her jeans and his t-shirt. She held her hand out. "Come on, Calder. I want to see you run."

"I should stay here with you," he argued.

"It would make me feel better. And you know you need it, too."

A hint of a smile curved his lips, and he took her hand and let her lead him out the back door and toward the woods.

"Go on. Run," she said, laughing a little as he rushed to get out of his clothes, so full of anticipation he reminded her of a kid on Christmas morning.

He kissed her, pulling her toward him, and she backed away before she pulled him down to the ground to take care of her again. "Go," she murmured against his lips, laughing a little through the hunger.

He grinned, turned, and blurred, shifting from magnificent man to equally magnificent bear, and she watched him run, bounding toward the woods, a lightness in his gait she hadn't seen before.

As she watched him walk into the woods, Layla came up to her, stood at her side.

"It's done, then," Layla said, watching Calder with her.

"It is."

"I think this was a huge mistake."

Sophie glanced at her. "If I get bad, you're going to end me."

Layla crossed her arms, an angry look on her features. "I already said I would." She put her arm around Sophie's waist, rested her head against Sophie's. "I can't believe you did all this to save him. God, I hope he's worth it."

"He is. And I didn't just do it to save him. I mean, that's great, but I did it to save myself," Sophie said, turning and meeting Layla's eyes.

"How so? You're suffering now."

"I'm stronger than I was. His curse makes me dangerous, strong. I would have lost everything if I'd let things go on as they were. Marshall will regret ever finding me again. He gave me all the tools I need to destroy him and free myself. All I need is the time to figure out how it all works."

"Can you work your way back to the Light?"

Sophie stood silently, feeling the cool, clean autumn air on her face, smelling Calder on her skin. "I'll find my way back, if it's the last thing I do. This is far from over, and I am just getting started."

Layla sighed. "Some of my mom's macaroni and cheese, then? I grabbed a few pans of it."

"Excellent idea," Sophie said, and they headed back into the cottage, arm-in-arm.

The End

Sophie will return in *Shadow Sworn*,
the second book in the *Copper Falls* series.

Never Miss an Update!

Sign Up for Colleen's Newsletter.
http://bit.ly/colleensnewsletter

For backstory material, news, and upcoming events be sure to check out http://www.colleenvanderlinden.com

LETTER FROM THE AUTHOR

I hope you enjoyed this beginning to the *Copper Falls* series! Sophie has solved one major problem, but she's managed to make her life more complicated.

This is, after all, one of my books, right? My heroines never have it easy.

Shadow Witch Rising was a scary book to write. As you've seen, it's fairly different from the *Hidden* series. I absolutely loved writing it, though, and I hope you loved reading it.

So many people offered their help during the writing and publishing process for this book, and I want to take a moment to thank them.

First and always, thanks and love to my husband Roger, who is my tech guy, my designer, my therapist, and my biggest fan. I love you.

Thank you to my awesome kids. You guys make every day an adventure, in the best of ways.

Many thanks to the phenomenally talented Elizabeth Hunter for reading through the book and giving me her (often hilarious) feedback, as well as for bearing with me through all of those moments of "oh my god I completely suck at this." You are amazing.

Thanks to the lovely, ridiculously talented Grace Draven, for reading through *Shadow Witch Rising* and assuring me that I had something good here. That is huge praise from an author I admire so much. Thank you.

Once again, I had a great group of beta readers, and this book is much stronger thanks to their feedback. Thanks and chocolate to Susan Cambra, Shawna Cerda, Jo Dawson, Jennifer G., Ginger Garff, Amber Hegarty, Brenda Hopkins, Sarah Leenart, Jayna Longstreet, Kathie Littlemore, Katherine Peters, Rachel Scott, and Sarah Wicks.

Finally, a huge, huge thank you to my readers. Thank you for giving this book a chance. Thank you for the amazing enthusiasm you showed for the *Hidden* series. I could not do what I do without you, and I appreciate every single one of you. Thank you, from the very bottom of my heart. Your emails, tweets, Facebook posts, and reviews are always appreciated. You are the absolute best.

Colleen Vanderlinden
Detroit
February 23, 2015

ABOUT THE AUTHOR

Colleen Vanderlinden is the author and publisher of the *Hidden* series, which currently includes *Lost Girl*, *Broken*, *Home*, *Strife*, and *Nether*. She lives in the Detroit area with her husband, children, and two lazy cats. She enjoys reading, obsessing over comic book characters, gardening, and playing *World of Warcraft*.

Learn more about Colleen at her website, colleenvanderlinden.com, contact her via email at email@colleenvanderlinden.com, or follow her on Twitter and Facebook.

The Hidden Series
Book One: Lost Girl
Book Two: Broken
Book Three: Home
Book Four: Strife
Book Five: Nether
Hidden Series Novellas
Forever Night
Earth Bound

The Copper Falls Series
Shadow Witch Rising

Never Miss an Update!
Sign Up for Colleen's Newsletter
http://bit.ly/colleensnewsletter